Checked Out
for
Murder

Also available by Allison Brook

Buried in the Stacks
Read and Gone
Death Overdue

Checked Out
for
Murder

A HAUNTED LIBRARY
MYSTERY

Allison Brook

NEW YORK

Copyright © 2020 by Marilyn Levinson

Published in the United States by Crooked Lane Books, an imprint of The Quick Brown Fox & Company LLC.

Crooked Lane Books and its logo are trademarks of The Quick Brown Fox & Company LLC.

Library of Congress Catalog-in-Publication data available upon request.

ISBN (hardcover): 978-1-64385-447-2
ISBN (ebook): 978-1-64385-448-9

Cover illustration by Griesbach/Martucci

Printed in the United States.

www.crookedlanebooks.com

Crooked Lane Books
34 West 27th St., 10th Floor
New York, NY 10001

First Edition: August 2020

10 9 8 7 6 5 4 3 2 1

For my darling granddaughter
Olivia Brooke Levinson, who loves
to read and write.
From her Meema Marilyn

Chapter One

"More coffee?" I asked Dylan as I got up from the table to pour us both a refill.

"I'd love some, babe, but I'd better leave now if I'm going to squeeze in a few important phone calls before my ten-thirty appointment." He stood and planted a kiss on my lips. "Traffic's bumper-to-bumper this time of the day."

I wrapped my arms around his waist. "All the larceny out there sure is keeping you busy. I'm glad you had time to stop by for breakfast."

"My pleasure. The eggs were prefect, Carrie. Just the way I love 'em."

Dylan shrugged into his leather jacket and I walked him out to his car, making sure that Smoky Joe didn't follow me. It was the first week of April, and the balmy weather and budding trees and bushes were sure signs that spring was on its way. My gray feline had a bad case of spring fever and was doing his best to escape the confines of my cottage to explore the great outdoors. But I couldn't allow that, not if Smoky Joe and I were going to get to work at the library on time. As the head of programs and events, I needed to be punctual, and the library patrons would be wanting a friendly visit from their library cat.

Dylan slid into the driver's seat of his BMW. "Have fun. I'll call or text when I have a free moment."

I smiled as I watched him drive off. Dylan was an investigator—a new partner in the company where he'd been working for years recovering stolen art and jewelry. A few months ago he'd opened his own office in New Haven, where he was investigating all sorts of situations. His first client had been a member of a family of restaurateurs who suspected that one of his cousins was skimming money off the top. Dylan had proved his client's suspicions correct, and now the thief was cooling his heels in jail. Dylan Avery was clever and handsome, and I considered myself lucky that he'd fallen in love with me.

I was lucky in many ways, I thought as I reentered my cottage, which stood at the end of the Avery property and faced the river. I had my wonderful job at the library, and good friends and loving relatives nearby. Of course, there were some less-than-wonderful aspects of my life—like my mother and her young husband, who were about to descend on Clover Ridge because Tom was going to be in a movie they were filming here in town. But I had a week until they arrived, so there was no point in dwelling on how Brianna, as my mother now called herself, was going to drive me crazy.

I stacked our breakfast dishes in the dishwasher, glad that Dylan and I had been able to have this hour together. We both had busy work schedules that rarely left us time for each other outside of weekends. Still, it was better having him living in the manor house a quarter mile up the private road than in Atlanta, Georgia, where his company headquarters were located.

Twenty minutes later, I put Smoky Joe in his carrier and brought it out to my car. I talked to him as I drove to the library.

"The trees have sprouted their light-green leaves and the forsythia is out. But maybe I shouldn't be telling you this. You'll want to go frolicking in the woods, where you can pick up ticks and fleas."

I made a mental note to stop at the vet to buy medicine to ward off ticks and fleas. Just in case Smoky Joe managed to get outside. Thank goodness he had been altered the month before, so there was no chance of his racing into the street chasing after female cats in heat.

Ten minutes later I pulled into the parking lot behind the library. Like the other centuries-old buildings bordering the Clover Ridge Green, the library had once been a large private residence. And like the other edifices, many of which had been converted into restaurants, shops, and art galleries, the library retained its white, wood-framed exterior. Across the Green, which was squarish in shape and roughly two small blocks wide in every direction, my Great-Uncle Bosco and Great-Aunt Harriet lived in one of the eight original homes still used as private residences.

As soon as we entered the library, I set Smoky Joe's carrier on the floor and slid open the metal door. He took off like a bullet.

"Someone's feeling his oats," Max, our senior custodian, commented as he halted the dolly cart he was using to move three large cartons.

"I'm afraid Smoky Joe has spring fever," I said. "I have to watch him at home and make sure he doesn't sneak out to explore the countryside."

"We wouldn't want him to run out of the library and into traffic. I'll keep an eye on him when I can. I'll mention it to Pete as well."

"Thanks, Max. I think I'll put up signs so patrons will know to watch out for him near the exit doors—at least for the next few weeks."

"Good idea, Carrie. We'd all be heartbroken if anything happened to our little friend."

I continued to my office, reflecting on how Smoky Joe had become a fixture in the library in just a matter of months. Last fall he'd ventured through the woods to my cottage from a nearby farm. He'd jumped into my car, and I'd ended up carrying him into the library for safekeeping. Smoky Joe had proved to be a very social creature. Patrons loved to make a fuss over him, and he enjoyed the attention of young and old alike. I loved him fiercely, and I knew that the many people who frequented the library would be distraught if anything were to happen to their little mascot.

I sat down at my desk and turned on the computer to find several emails waiting for me. I was responsible for making sure our many activities ran smoothly. Given the variety of programs we offered, with new ones being added each month, my job kept me on my toes. My goal was to entertain and educate our patrons, and so far I'd been pretty successful. Sally, my boss, gave me a good degree of freedom and flexibility—as long as I didn't go crazy moneywise.

I pulled out three sheets of printing paper. With a blue magic marker, I wrote on each of them:

When exiting the library, please make sure that Smoky Joe, the library cat, isn't leaving with you.
Thank you,
Carrie Singleton, Head of Programs and Events

I drew the outline of a cat with a bushy tail on each note. Scotch tape in hand, I set out to post them—one in the coffee shop, another in the reading room, and the third beside the circulation desk.

At the circulation desk, my best friend, Angela Vecchio, glanced up from the book she was checking out for a patron and waved to me. "See you at noon!"

I gave her a thumbs-up. Whenever Angela and I had the same lunch hour, we ate together, usually at the Cozy Corner Café a few blocks away. I'd just stepped back inside my office when a ping sounded from my cell phone. I read the message. *Thinking of u. XOXO.*

Me 2. I smiled as I texted back.

I glanced at the schedule of the day's activities. An exercise class, a current-events discussion, and a writers' workshop. Then in the afternoon, a book discussion, a lecture on "How to Remain Beautiful as You Age," and a food presentation of spring desserts.

I heard a knock on my door and looked up, expecting to see Sally or Angela or Marion, the children's librarian.

"Come in," I called.

A woman who looked a few years older than me—maybe midthirties—stepped into my office. Her jacket, pants, and boots nicely set off her shapely figure. Well-styled wavy brown hair framed her pretty face. Her smile was tentative, as though she was expecting a rejection of some kind.

"Hello. I hope I'm not interrupting. I'm interested in giving a library program, and the girl at the circulation desk told me to speak to the head of programs and events and directed me to your office. Am I in the right place?"

"You are—in the right place, that is." I stood and held out my hand. "Hi. I'm Carrie Singleton."

She shook my hand briefly. "My name is Daphne Marriott." She gave a little laugh. "No relation to the hotel chain. But I know the name Singleton."

"My family once owned what was the Singleton Farm outside of town. My uncle's on the library board." I rolled out the only other chair in my office from behind the desk my part-time assistants shared. "Please have a seat and tell me about the program you'd like to present."

"Of course." Daphne cleared her throat. "I recently moved to the area. I'm starting over, so to speak. New location, new career, new life."

I laughed. "I can relate to that."

"Really?" Her eyes lit up. When she realized I wasn't going to elaborate, she cleared her throat again. "Before I moved here, I had a near-death experience."

"Oh. I'm so sorry to hear that."

"I'm all right. I'm only mentioning it because, after I kind of blinked out for a short time, I discovered I had psychic powers."

I nodded, wondering where this was going. Did I have a nutcase on my hands?

Daphne must have realized my discomfort, because she continued, "I know this must sound weird to someone who's never had an experience like this, but after I recovered from my injuries, I discovered I knew things about people and situations—things that no one told me.

"I started giving readings. My clients found the information I shared with them to be authentic and helpful. I'd like to do that here, and I figured the best way to introduce myself to the people in the area would be to offer programs in the local libraries." She smiled. "And the Clover Ridge Library is the prettiest library around."

"You mean like a séance?" I asked. "I don't think—"

"No." Daphne laughed, all signs of her nervousness banished. "I don't communicate with the dead."

I do, I thought.

Daphne's eyes widened with surprise, as if she'd read my thought. Thank goodness she didn't pursue that. Instead she said, "I'd like to talk about the many different types of psychic abilities there are. Some psychics have the gift of divination and can foresee the future; others can heal; still others are mediums and are able to speak to the dead."

"And what type of psychic ability do you have?" I asked.

"Telepathy. Clairvoyance. They put me in touch with a person's innermost thoughts, fears, and occasionally his or her future. Honestly, it varies and depends on the person and the situation."

"So it depends on various factors?" *How convenient.*

"I know." Daphne smiled. "It sounds self-serving to say it depends on the person and the situation. Gives me an easy out if I'm unable to read someone who asked for my help with a problem. Did you ever watch the TV show *Medium* with Patricia Arquette?"

"I've seen a few episodes," I said.

"Then you probably know the show is based on the real Allison DuBois, who claimed she helped law enforcement agencies solve crimes."

I nodded. "She got her information about killers through dreams."

"That's right," Daphne said. "But if you'll remember, the dreams were never straightforward. They never revealed the entire picture or situation. They presented themselves as puzzles that Allison had to figure out in order to help her boss, the DA, ID the killer and go after him."

"I get it. It works sometimes."

"A good deal of the time," Daphne said. "For example, I've gotten a pretty clear picture of you in the few minutes we've been talking. You've had your position here in the library a short time, and you thoroughly enjoy what you do. You're in a loving relationship with a man you knew briefly as a child. Your parents are divorced, and your older brother died in a car accident."

My mouth fell open. "Everything you say is true, but it's also common knowledge. Clover Ridge is a small town. We all know quite a lot about our neighbors."

Daphne pursed her lips. "That may be so, but I swear no one ever told me anything about you or your background."

Is she telling the truth? Before I could decide how to answer, Evelyn Havers, the library ghost, began to manifest a few feet from where Daphne and I were sitting. Weird! Though my little cousin Tacey and I were the only people who could see and communicate with Evelyn, she never showed up when I had someone in the office. But here she was, with a Cheshire cat grin on her face, looking extremely pleased with herself.

"Oh!"

I turned to Daphne. Her hand was pressed to her chest, her body still as a statue.

"What's wrong?" I asked.

"I sense the presence of an entity from another plane."

"Really? You mean a ghost?" I had no intention of explaining Evelyn to someone I'd just met.

"Yes. An older woman, I believe, who died close by."

Bingo! Right on target! I pursed my lips together so I wouldn't burst out laughing at the sight of Evelyn thrusting her fist in the air. So unlike her!

Daphne must have thought I was frowning at her, because she said, "You don't have to believe me. Many people can't accept what I know to be true." She stood. "Well, thank you for hearing me out."

"Wait!" I called as she opened the door, eager to make a quick getaway. "I think our patrons would enjoy hearing you talk about the different psychic abilities."

Daphne turned. "Really?"

I nodded. "You're in luck! A presenter had to cancel his program a week from next Tuesday evening. Are you interested?"

"You bet!" She grinned. "If time permits, I'll be happy to go around the room and give what I call minute readings."

9

"The patrons will love that." I handed her a form. "Please fill this out ASAP. You can return it via email or bring it back here."

"Thank you! Thank you, Carrie."

For a moment, I was afraid she was going to hug me, but instead she held out her hand. As we shook, a small shock ran up my arm and I had a divination of my own—that Daphne Marriott had a troubled past, which was about to spill over into my life.

Chapter Two

I glared at Evelyn. "Why did you come here when you knew I had someone in the office? You nearly scared the poor woman to death."

"Daphne Harper! As I live and breathe! Well, I neither live nor breathe, but I like the expression. And I must say, I'm pleased that she sensed my presence!"

My mouth fell open. "You know her?"

"Indeed I do. I happened to be floating around the library when Daphne showed up. I recognized her though she left Clover Ridge many years ago. I decided to follow her to find out why she came back after that terrible business. And to my surprise, she ended up here in your office."

I couldn't make much sense of what Evelyn was saying. "Daphne came to see me because she wants to give a program about different psychic abilities. She claims to have acquired some psychic abilities of her own after a recent near-death experience. I wondered if she was making it up until I saw how she reacted to your presence. But what terrible business are you talking about?"

Evelyn perched on the corner of my assistants' desk, her favorite pose whenever she paid me a visit. "It's a sad story. Daphne comes from an unhappy, dysfunctional family."

I nodded. "I kind of thought so."

"There's a brother, Billy, who's two years older than Daphne. Their father drank and was abusive to their mother and the kids. When he lost his job, his wife took on a second job to pay the bills. Daphne was sixteen or seventeen when her father was murdered. Killed with a knife to the gut. Daphne told the police that Billy must have done it because she'd heard them arguing an hour or so before the murder. Everyone was shocked to hear this because Daphne adored her brother. He'd protected her since she was a baby."

"So what happened? Was Billy convicted of his father's murder?"

"He was, and then released after spending a few years in prison. His case was reopened because the knife turned up when the apartment house where the Harpers had been living underwent extensive renovations. They found Chet's blood on the knife as well as fingerprints, but they weren't Billy's."

"How sad," I said. "I wonder why Daphne accused her brother of the crime, given the family dynamics."

"Your guess is as good as mine, though I never thought the poor boy capable of killing anyone." Evelyn sent me a look that meant she was about to give me an assignment. "Carrie, Daphne's going to need your help."

"With what?" I asked, but Evelyn was already disappearing from sight.

What an eventful morning, I thought as I prepared to focus once again on library matters. I'd already met someone with psychic abilities and learned about a murder that had been committed here in Clover Ridge twenty years ago. So that was why Daphne had thought the Singleton name sounded familiar. I found it interesting that she hadn't mentioned growing up in Clover Ridge. And I wondered if her return had anything to do with her father's murder. If her brother was innocent, then the murderer had never been apprehended.

I felt a rush of excitement. Did Daphne want me to find the person who had murdered her father? Perhaps her psychic abilities had informed her that I'd helped solve a few murders, one of which had been another cold case. I quickly stifled my enthusiasm as best I could. The downside of investigating homicides was putting my life in danger, which upset Dylan and John Mathers, our police chief and dear friend. I'd all but made a lifelong promise to them that I wouldn't get involved in any more murder cases.

* * *

At five o'clock I headed downstairs and said good-bye to Susan, who worked as my part-time assistant a few afternoons and evenings a week. I found her in the small room off our large meeting room painting posters to advertise our Adopt-a-Pet program in May.

"Gorgeous!" I said, admiring the zany colorful poster she was working on, of two children petting a dog and a cat. "Let's send this one to the local paper."

Susan's thin face was wreathed in smiles. "You think?"

"I certainly do." I winked. "And it's sure to boost your sales."

At my suggestion, Susan had paid a visit to the Gallery on the Green, which was a five-minute walk from the library. Ron and Martha Mallory, who owned the gallery, had taken one look at Susan's watercolors of local scenes and immediately asked her to bring in several more to put up for sale. Next, they'd had her painting mugs, canvas bags, and polo shirts for the tourists who were expected to visit Clover Ridge as soon as the weather turned warmer. I feared it was only a matter of months before I lost my artistic assistant for good.

Upstairs on the main level, I found Smoky Joe sniffing near the front door that faced the Green, a spot he'd never paid attention to until recently. I scooped him up in my arms.

Andy Harlowe, a retired gentleman in his seventies, smiled at me as he pulled open the door. "Don't worry, Carrie. I saw your sign and wasn't about to let the little rascal run outside."

"He has spring fever," I said. "Maybe I should leave him home until it passes."

"We'd sure miss him, but better safe than sorry."

I returned to my office, placed Smoky Joe in his carrier, and left for the day. Dylan called as I was driving home.

"Tonight's meeting is on after all," he sighed, "which means I won't get home till after ten. Sorry I won't get to stop by tonight."

"I'm sorry, too. But I'm glad if it means another client for you."

"Lots of thieves roaming around," Dylan said. "If things keep up this way, I'll have to take on a junior partner sooner than I'd planned. Then my hours will be more regular."

"I'm looking forward to it. Don't forget to eat dinner."

Dylan laughed. "Rosalind makes sure of things like that. Sometimes I get the feeling she thinks I'm one of her kids."

"I'm glad she turned out to be such an efficient Gal Friday. Soon as I drop Smoky Joe off at home, I'm heading to the gym."

"Aha! Hoping to catch the eye of our handsome personal trainer?"

"As if. And even if I wanted to," I kidded, "Robby's always swamped with paying clients."

"Have a good workout," Dylan said. "Talk to you later. Love you."

"I love you, too," I said, and disconnected the call.

At home in my cottage, I fed Smoky Joe his dinner, then changed into yoga pants, a T-shirt, and sneakers and climbed back into my car. Dylan and I had joined Parson's Gym in February, agreeing it was a good way for us to stay in shape. It was located in a strip mall a short drive from the Avery property, in the opposite direction from Clover Ridge. I loved the yoga and aerobics classes but occasionally worked out in the larger room crammed with treadmills and other machines. Tonight, I decided, would be one of those times.

I grabbed a towel and put in a half hour on a treadmill at a brisk pace, then moved on to an elliptical machine, where I managed all of eight minutes before I started huffing and puffing. I climbed down still panting.

"Great job, Carrie," Robby said.

"Thanks, Robby."

Pleased by his compliment, I flashed him a smile. Robby Dowd *was* handsome, with nice, even features and thick dark brown hair. He was just under six feet, had a great build, and moved as gracefully as a cat. His good looks and pleasant, caring manner made him the most popular of the gym's three trainers. I wondered why he was checking up on me instead of working with one of his many clients.

"You're doing great, Carrie. Remember when you started out, you could barely do a minute on the elliptical?"

"I remember," I said.

"Dylan's not here with you tonight?"

I shook my head. "Late meeting. He'll probably come in tomorrow morning."

Robby nodded as if he well understood late meetings. "Why don't you work on your upper arms today?"

"Okay."

"I'll set the weights for you."

I followed him to a machine that would work my upper-arm muscles. Robby adjusted the weights and nodded.

"Three sets of ten reps," he said, as he walked away to oversee someone else's routine.

When I'd finished, he reappeared and led me to another upper-body machine that worked a different set of arm muscles.

"Thanks for doing this," I said between pulls. "Usually you're busy with your clients."

"Marcia's just finishing up, so I have some free time. I'm happy to make sure you're using the right weights."

When I was done, I went over to the stretching area.

"Stretching is essential to every workout," Robby said.

I finished my stretches and decided to call it a night. "Good night!" I called to Robby, and waved to the few people on the treadmills.

"See you soon!" he answered as I exited the gym.

I climbed into my car and realized I was famished. Eating ASAP was an appealing idea. I glanced at the other stores in the strip mall. At the far end was an Italian restaurant where Dylan and I had gotten a pizza one evening. Closer, just three doors down from the gym, was a sushi restaurant. I decided to have dinner there.

I'd finished what I'd managed to eat of my sashimi dinner and was waiting for the waitress to pack up the rest to bring home when Robby slid into the booth opposite me.

"Mind if I join you?"

"Of course not, but I'm about to leave."

He smiled. "Have a cup of tea and talk to me."

I must have looked surprised, because he laughed. "Carrie, I'm not hitting on you. I simply want to have a conversation with someone that has nothing to do with abs or weights."

I laughed, relieved. "In that case, converse away."

The waitress arrived with my boxed food and my bill. Robby ordered a tuna-and-avocado roll and a tea for each of us.

"I eat here pretty often when I work evenings, but I'd like some recommendations—restaurants where you and Dylan like to eat."

"Sure. Due Amici's one of our favorites. It's a ten-minute ride past Clover Ridge."

Robby nodded. "I've heard of it."

"I didn't realize you were new to the area."

"Kind of. I moved to Merrivale six months ago."

"Do you have a wife? A sweetheart? Parents in the area?"

"None of the above." He sounded bitter.

"Then what drew you to this part of Connecticut?" I asked.

Robby shrugged. "I tend to move around and thought this was as good a place as any—for a while. I find that gyms can often use another trainer. At least, I've been lucky so far."

Our waitress brought our tea. I sipped mine, then said, "I must have come to Clover Ridge only a few months before you."

"Really?" He seemed surprised. "You and Dylan strike me as a solid couple."

"I sure hope we're solid. I also have family here. My great-aunt and uncle live here, and I've got Singleton cousins galore—most of whom I've yet to meet."

"Lucky you." When his roll arrived, Robby used chopsticks to bring a piece to his mouth.

I glanced at my watch. "Well, I think it's time—"

"I've heard that you've solved a few murders."

I chuckled. "Somehow I've managed to get involved in a few homicide investigations. But I'm sure it won't happen again."

He cocked his head. "How can you be so certain?"

I stood and slipped on my jacket. "Because I'm determined to lead a quiet life and focus on my work and the people I love."

Robby laughed as if I'd just said the most amusing thing he'd heard all day. "Sometimes things work out very differently from how we planned."

As I drove home, I couldn't help but wonder what it *really* was that Robby Dowd wanted to ask me.

Chapter Three

My cell phone's jingle jarred me awake. I glanced at the clock as I reached for the phone and groaned when I saw the time. Who had the nerve to call me at seven o'clock on a Saturday morning?

My annoyance turned to fear. *Did Uncle Bosco have a heart attack? Did Aunt Harriet?*

"Carrie dear, good morning!"

"Mom?" I yawned. "Do you know what time it is?"

"I hope I didn't wake you. I figured there was a good chance you had to get up to go to work, and if you weren't working today, you must have a slew of errands to run."

I grimaced. As usual, my mother had an excuse for everything she did. "Is everything okay?"

"Of course—relatively speaking." My mother sounded peeved. "I thought you'd be happy to know that Tom and I are here in Clover Ridge. We arrived yesterday afternoon. There were so many problems to take care of, I didn't get a chance to call you sooner. For one thing, the car rental place didn't have the model I specifically asked for. And they'd assured me . . ."

I tuned out her litany of complaints about the rental car and then the house they were renting as I tried to wrap my head around the fact that my mother and her husband were in Clover Ridge a week earlier than expected. That meant they'd be here seven days *in addition* to the weeks or months it would take to shoot the movie Tom was in.

"But why did you come so early?" I asked, when she finally finished. "I thought you were arriving next week."

"Shooting begins a week from Monday. Most of the cast is arriving next weekend, but Tom thought it would be good to run through his lines in the locations where they'll be filming his scenes. I convinced the rental agent to let us have the house a bit earlier, and it's a good thing I did. I read him a list of the glitches I've discovered. He promised to send over a handy-man to start repairs tomorrow." She made a scoffing sound. "We'll see if he follows through."

"Well, I'm glad everything will be taken care of," I said. Smoky Joe jumped on the bed, and I stroked him absent-mindedly. "Now that I'm awake, I should start getting ready for work."

"Tom and I would love to see you tonight. I thought we'd go out for dinner—unless you already have plans."

"Dylan's working today—in his office in New Haven. We were planning to go out tonight, but I have no idea what time he'll be getting home. He might not be up for company." I knew I sounded as uncooperative as I felt. Describing my mother as difficult was like saying Mount Everest was a bit of a hike. Spending time with her always left me wrung out and unhappy.

"Carrie dear, why are you turning this into a problem? I'm your mother. Don't you think it's time I met your boyfriend?"

"You met Dylan when we were little. He and Jordan used to play together when we spent summers on the farm."

"That's not the same thing and you know it. After all, your *father* knows Dylan quite well, I understand."

I sighed, exasperated. "That's right. Dad knows Dylan because Dylan got him his job."

"Helping to catch thieves instead of being one," my mother jeered. "The perfect new career for Jim Singleton."

"Mom, please don't start. We'll go out for dinner with you and Tom tonight. I'll call or text you with the name and address of the restaurant. Say seven fifteen?"

"Perfect. I look forward to seeing you," she said. "Now I must go. Tom's calling me."

I exhaled a deep sigh of frustration as I padded to the bathroom. My mother's call had put a damper on the day. I knew better than to get pulled into her machinations, but somehow she always managed to make me feel guilty or wrong-footed. I knew I hadn't been very welcoming just now, but that was the result of our past history.

As I got dressed for work, I thought about my mother. She'd had a hard time of it, raising Jordan and me practically as a single mother. My father had come and gone. He was the greatest father when he was around—showering attention on my brother and me, the fun parent to be with—but unfortunately that wasn't very often. I had been grateful to have Jordan in my life, the one and only stable older person, though he was just four years older than me.

I had to face the fact that my mother—who used to be Linda Singleton and now went by Brianna Farrell—had never been maternal. She'd seen to it that I had food to eat and clothes to wear, but she'd never nurtured me the way my friends' mothers nurtured them—listening to their worries and hurts, cooking special dishes simply because they liked them. She'd made me feel I was a responsibility she was obliged to deal with, a responsibility she didn't much want.

I was glad when she met Tom a few years after divorcing my father. Tom Farrell was nice and easy on the eyes, with blond Tab Hunter-type looks. He was twelve years younger than my mother and apparently adored her. He liked being the center of her attention and allowed her to manage him to a large degree. She relished taking care of her handsome hubby. Tom had originally worked in finance, but when an uncle died and left him a considerable amount of money four years ago, he revved up his acting career—which until then had been limited to local acting productions—with a vengeance. They moved to Hollywood, where Tom's good looks had snagged him a few small roles.

My mother loved being married to an actor. I had gathered as much from the few notes and emails she'd sent me. It led me to believe that she'd changed. Had grown warmer. More family minded. And so a year ago I'd asked if I could come and stay with her and Tom for a short while. I'd been feeling blue and needed some downtime in a safe environment. I thought spending time with her and Tom would be ideal. Her response was brief, almost to the point of curtness, and cut me to the bone. She was sorry, but it wasn't a good time for them to have company. *Company?* Feeling even worse, I asked Aunt Harriet and Uncle Bosco if I could stay with them. They welcomed me with open arms. And I had been in Clover Ridge ever since.

I called Dylan.

"Hi, babe. I had a great workout at the gym and I'm about to leave for the office. Everything okay?"

"I just got off the phone with my mother. She and Tom have moved into their rented house in town."

"Already? I thought they were coming next week."

"Exactly. But they're here now and want to have dinner with us tonight."

"Sure. Shall I make reservations? Someplace elegant?"

"Casual's fine. I was thinking Bernie's Bistro would be a good choice, since it's on the Sound. I said seven fifteen. Let me know if they can take us then and I'll call my mother."

"Sure, but . . . Carrie, are you okay with this? You don't sound happy."

"I'm not, but we have to get together with them sooner or later. May as well do it tonight."

"All right. I'm looking forward to meeting your mother and her actor husband."

"Really? Didn't you meet her a long time ago in the summer when Jordan and I came to stay at the farm?"

"Not that I remember."

I laughed. "That's not surprising, given how much she hated coming here. Which makes me wonder why she was so eager to suggest Clover Ridge as the perfect setting for this movie."

* * *

At six fifteen Dylan and I were on our way to have drinks at my mother and Tom's place before the four of us set out for dinner. She'd invited us when I'd called to give her directions to the restaurant. The small ranch house my mother and Tom were renting was located a few blocks off the main road I took each morning on my drive to work.

Tom opened the door, a cocktail glass in his hand, and bussed my cheek. "Carrie! So nice to see you."

"Thank you. Nice to see you, too. This is Dylan Avery, my boyfriend. Dylan, Tom Farrell, my mother's husband."

Dylan and Tom shook hands and exchanged pleasantries. Two good-looking, fit men. One dark, one fair—ten years apart in age, by my reckoning.

Then why did Tom seem more boyish? Dylan's expressions varied, of course, but he always struck me as focused, resolute, and confident while Tom came across as—bland. His expression—wistful. Hopeful?

"I thought I heard the doorbell. Hello, hello! So nice to finally get to see you!"

My mother approached, a broad smile on her lips. She, too, held a glass in her hand. Her short, blonde hair perfectly framed her face, which for a woman of fifty-six was amazingly devoid of any wrinkles. Of course! A facelift. I almost burst out laughing to see we were dressed exactly the same—tunics over black leggings and knee-high boots.

"Carrie!" She air-kissed both my cheeks. "You look wonderful."

"So do you," I said, meaning it.

"And you must be Dylan!" He warranted a hug and a real kiss. "Jordan's dear childhood friend. So serendipitous how things work out."

"Nice to meet you . . ."

"Brianna." She laughed, showing white-capped teeth. "A new name for my new life. Tom, dear, why don't you take their jackets. Alas, there's no room in the hall closet—so small. Leave them in the spare bedroom."

Dylan and I shrugged off our jackets and handed them to Tom, who disappeared and returned as my mother was ushering us into the living room. I sat on the beige sofa next to Dylan, while my mother perched on one of the two armchairs covered in a garish orange-and-brown fabric.

"You just arrived yesterday," I said. "You didn't have to have us over for drinks."

"It's our pleasure, isn't it, Tom?"

"Mmm," Tom said, as he leaned against the outer wall.

"What would you like to drink?" my mother asked. "We've Scotch sours, which we're drinking, and a bottle of red wine."

Dylan asked for a Scotch sour and I opted for the wine. Tom disappeared into what I imagined was the kitchen to fill our requests.

My mother pointed to the small plate of peanuts on the coffee table between us. "Have some."

Dylan scooped up a handful of nuts. Tom returned with our drinks, and we all lifted our glasses in a toast to everyone's good health.

"Tom, tell us about the movie," I said. "It's so exciting that you'll be starring in a movie that's being shot right here in Clover Ridge."

Tom's eyes lit up. "I'm not the star, by any means, but I've got a fairly large secondary role. The film's a romantic comedy called *I Love You, I Do*. The plot is similar to Noël Coward's *Private Lives*. An older couple that divorced a few years earlier find themselves staying in the same hotel with the people they're currently engaged to—considerably younger, in both cases. They end up spending time together and realize they're still in love."

"And the two young rejected fiancés end up together," my mother added, not looking pleased. "The ending's very different from the Coward play."

Tom sighed. "Of course it is, Brianna. But it's easier to explain the similarities." He turned back to Dylan and me. "Anyway, I play the leading lady's fiancé."

My mother grimaced. "And the actress who Tom ends up with joined the cast two days ago. Tom, I hope she learns her lines and doesn't make you look bad."

Tom exhaled a huff of exasperation.

"Why was she hired so late?" I asked. "You knew months ago you were in this movie."

"Because the actress originally cast in the role is drying out in a rehab center." Tom turned to my mother. "Ilana will be great. You needn't be concerned about her learning her lines. She's a terrific actor."

"As long as she remembers she's your love interest in the movie and not in real life," my mother muttered.

What's going on here? I wondered as Tom strode off, no doubt to refill his drink.

"Anyway, *I Love You* takes place in a small country village," my mother went on, as if nothing had happened. "As soon as Tom got the part and I read the script, I realized that Clover Ridge would be the perfect setting—historic buildings around the Green, the Long Island Sound with its restaurants and marinas. Mountains in the distance. I made a few calls to find out if we could film the movie here."

Tom rejoined us in time to hear her latest comment. He rolled his eyes. "Come on, Brianna, Dirk had already decided to film in Clover Ridge."

My mother sniffed. "Maybe. At any rate, he appreciated my input."

Tom cleared his throat. "I believe his actual words were, 'We all appreciate your care and interest in the project.'"

Why are Tom and my mother squabbling? Is she really worried about this actress?

To fill the dead silence, I asked, "Who's Dirk?" I peered into my glass, surprised to discover that I'd finished off my wine.

"Dirk Franklin is the director," Tom said. "His cousin, Liane Walters, lives here in Clover Ridge. He'd spent some time here years ago and figured it would be the perfect place to shoot this movie."

"I know Liane!" I said. "She's on the library board of trustees with Uncle Bosco."

When neither my mother nor Tom responded, I exchanged glances with Dylan. He shrugged and gestured to the front door.

"Shall we move on to the restaurant?" I suggested.

My mother exhaled a deep sigh. "You know, all this traveling and dealing with repairs has wiped me out. I'm afraid I'll have to beg off for tonight. Tom and I will join you for dinner another time."

I glanced at Tom, but he'd hurried off to get our jackets.

"Of course." I bussed my mother's cheek. "Talk to you soon."

Chapter Four

"Looks like there's trouble in paradise," Dylan said as we drove to the restaurant.

"Maybe they're both irritable," I said. "After all, they just flew in from California, had a problem with their rental car, then spent the day dealing with repairs. Moving to a new home, even when it's temporary, can be very stressful."

"I hope you're right, babe, but your mother comes on like a helicopter wife, if there is such a thing. She sure didn't like that Ilana being in the movie and playing opposite Tom."

I reached for my cell phone. "I'm going to look her up."

It took less than three minutes to pull up a photo of a gorgeous honey blonde with a drop-dead figure and a smile that could have been an advertisement for a toothpaste ad. I held it up for Dylan to see.

"She's quite a looker."

"I'm checking her out on Wikipedia. Ilana Reingold," I mumbled. "Born in Doylestown, Pennsylvania. In the following TV and films . . . Oh!"

"What is it?" Dylan asked.

"Nine years ago, she was engaged to Thomas Farrell, a trader on Wall Street. The wedding was called off a week before the event. 'I love Tommy and I always will, but I need to be free to pursue my career.'" I stared at Dylan. "She and Tom were engaged, and now they end up as a couple in a movie?"

"No wonder your mom's upset."

"I feel bad for her. My mother's pretentious and manipulative, but she's had a hard time of it, being married to my father. She raised Jordan and me under difficult circumstances. I was happy when she met Tom. I spent time with them just before their wedding. It was obvious that he adored my mother and wasn't at all bothered by the difference in their ages. Naïve me—I thought they'd live happily ever after."

Bernie's Bistro was a popular place with a terrific view of the Long Island Sound and was a favorite with tourists during the summer months. We were lucky to have gotten a reservation so late, even luckier when our hostess led us to a table flanking one of the floor-to-ceiling windows that looked out on the water.

We both ordered a salad and a fish entrée. A young man stopped at our table to place warm rolls on our bread plates along with a small dish of softened butter.

I was taking my first bite when Dylan said, "Looks like I'll be flying to Texas Monday morning."

I stared at him. "I thought you were pretty much done with traveling."

"Mostly, yes, but I'm still handling some big cases involving art and jewelry heists—until Mac and I find someone we can train to take my place."

"Oh," was all I said, instead of shouting *Don't go!* like I wanted to.

"Sorry, babe. A wealthy art collector's mansion was burgled last night while he and his wife were out of the country. Three of his most expensive paintings were taken, frames and all, as well as some ancient Chinese artifacts. He called Mac and asked that I take over the case."

"How long will you be gone?"

"Difficult to say. They had a top security system in place, so either the thieves had someone on the inside working with them or they're a really clever bunch. I've got a few leads regarding similar thefts in the recent past. But I may have to fly to Europe. Lately, that's where these items end up being sold."

"Europe," I murmured.

Dylan clasped my hand in his. "I told Mac ten days is my limit, but I hope to be back home before then. I hate leaving you, and it's not good for business to abandon the two cases I'm working on here. When I get back, I'll start seriously looking for someone to train."

Our salads arrived, and Dylan began to eat with gusto. He was down to the last bite when he realized I hadn't touched my food since he'd sprung his news.

"I'm sorry about this, Carrie, really I am, but there's nothing I can do to avoid this trip. Tomorrow's Sunday and you're not working. Why don't we go someplace special— somewhere we've been thinking of visiting but never managed to get to?"

"All right." I thought a minute. "I wouldn't mind visiting the Clark Art Institute in Williamstown, Massachusetts."

Dylan smiled. "Sounds like a plan. We'll start out early, have breakfast on the road, and take the scenic route."

I reached across the table to kiss him. "Thanks. I don't mean to be a pill, but I didn't expect you to be leaving so soon. I'm going to miss you."

He pursed his lips. "Believe me, I'll miss you even more."

*　*　*

Sunday turned out to be a warm, sunny day—perfect weather for our outing. We left early, stopped for a breakfast of waffles on the way, and arrived at the museum just after noon. We wandered through the exhibits, then had lunch in town before starting back on our three-hour trip home. It was close to seven o'clock when Dylan dropped me off at the cottage.

"I'd come in, but I still have to pack. The car service is picking me up at six thirty."

I hugged him tight. "Don't forget me," I whispered in his ear.

Dylan chuckled. "As if I could."

Inside, I scooped up Smoky Joe in my arms. "Well, kiddo, looks like we're going to be on our own for a while."

My furry feline squirmed free and ran to the kitchen, where he demanded his dinner. I made a conscious effort not to sink into a pity party and told myself I would keep busy instead. Very busy. That way I wouldn't have time to sulk and be morose and miss Dylan while he was chasing after thieves.

I went into my guest bedroom that I used as an office and turned on my computer. On the library's Facebook page, I posted the news about Daphne's program and asked patrons to text, message, or email me if they were interested in attending. That done, I checked my personal Facebook page. I was reading my emails when Angela called to say hi.

"Dylan and I just got back. We went to the Clark Art Institute."

"Sounds like you guys had a fun day—driving all the way to Williamstown."

"It was a fun day, only Dylan's flying off tomorrow morning on a case. Won't be back for at least a week. Maybe ten days."

"Oh no! Poor you. I hope you won't get into trouble while he's away."

"Why would I get into trouble?" I asked, annoyed.

Angela laughed. "I didn't mean it in a bad way. Only that you always seem to find adventures."

"Murder is what you really mean."

"Okay, murder. But there haven't been any of those lately, thank goodness."

"I didn't get a chance to tell you—I've arranged to have a psychic give a talk on the various kinds of psychic abilities. She's filling in for a canceled program a week from Tuesday night. I just posted about it on the library Facebook page."

"Sounds like a winner. Just be prepared for some flack."

"Really?" I said, surprised.

"Hopefully, you'll only hear from patrons who want to attend the program. But a few might object, claiming it's the work of the devil."

"I never realized that having Daphne might be a problem. Maybe I should have run it past Sally."

"Are you kidding? A year ago Sally, Marion, and I went to a psychic for a reading. Count me in when your Daphne comes. I hope she'll give some readings."

"She said she'd be happy to."

When I returned to the library's page, I was delighted to see that several people had written to say they wanted to attend the program.

One woman had posted that she didn't think having a psychic speak at the library was appropriate. Two people had responded, telling her she didn't have to go to the program if she objected but that they planned to attend.

Yay! I silently cheered them on and added their names to my growing list.

Dylan called to say good-night. "Now don't go looking for adventures while I'm gone."

I laughed. "Funny, that's what Angela said. You'd think I had nothing to do but search out and solve a few murders."

"Sometimes it looks that way. Love you. I'll call you from the airport."

* * *

Monday morning, I arrived at the library in good spirits. Nineteen people had texted, emailed, or messaged me to say they'd be coming to Daphne's program. I sent them all notices that they were registered. Sally stopped by my office to fill me in on a few minor items.

"I have a psychic on board as a replacement program a week from Tuesday night. I have nineteen coming so far. And Angela."

"Count me in if there's room."

"We'll be in the large meeting room, so there shouldn't be a problem."

"Limit it to thirty-five, especially if she wants to do some quick readings," Sally advised. "If she's entertaining, we can always invite her to return."

When she left, I checked the Facebook page again and was pleasantly surprised to see we'd already reached the limit Sally had set. I posted that the psychic program was now full. Trish, my other part-time assistant, arrived, and we discussed which movies we intended to show during the summer months, as they had to be listed in the next newsletter. We were always planning ahead. Then my library phone rang. It was my great-uncle.

"Hi, Uncle Bosco. How are you and Aunt Harriet?"

"Fine. Fine. And you? Busy with your boyfriend, I imagine."

"Absolutely, when we're not both working. Dylan flew to Texas this morning. He has a big case."

"In that case, come to dinner tonight. No, wait, no can do. I have a seven-thirty meeting tonight at Haven House. Then a library board meeting tomorrow night. Wednesday or Thursday evening would work, though."

"I'm working late Wednesday. Thursday's good, if you're sure it's okay with Aunt Harriet."

"Yep. Your aunt said to invite you whatever night is good for you."

I laughed. "Thanks. How are things coming along at Haven House?"

"Busy, busy. We're working hard to open our doors to the homeless May first. We were lucky to hire two retired social workers who are willing to work part-time for small salaries. And a retired drug counselor offered to supervise two days a week. Some local people have been dropping off furniture. We'll take the library's offerings as soon as you can send them over."

"I'll collect a selection of books, magazines, movies, and CDs and ask Max to deliver it later this week."

"Much appreciated," said Uncle Bosco.

"Are you kidding? I'm glad you agreed to take over the running of Haven House so our local homeless population will have a place to go during the day."

"I wasn't going to let a good project like that fail just because it was started by a bunch of thieves."

We both laughed. I'd helped expose the crooks who had set up Haven House as a cover for their illegal gains, and was grateful that my uncle had offered to take over the reins.

"See you Thursday evening, then," Uncle Bosco said. "Come over when you finish work."

At noon, Angela and I walked over to the Cozy Corner Café. The lunch crowd was out in full force, but we managed to snag a table in the rear corner.

"You never told me how dinner with your mother and Tom went Saturday night," Angela said.

"We didn't have dinner with them after all."

"Oh no! Did the two of you get into an argument?"

I frowned. "No. My mother invited us over for drinks. Everything she said pissed Tom off. The worst of it is, this gorgeous actress Tom used to be engaged to just joined the cast. She plays opposite him the second half of the film. My mother begged off dinner. Said we'd get together another time."

"Your poor mom! I don't blame her."

"And guess what? It turns out the film's director is related to Liane Walters."

"Ah!" Angela said. "No wonder our board member was so eager to join forces with the Chamber of Commerce to host a luncheon for the movie's cast and crew." She eyed me meaningfully. "Along with certain important people in our community."

I laughed. "I only received an invitation because my mother's husband is in the movie. You'll get a chance to meet Tom and the rest of the cast and crew at the meet-and-greet party on the Green."

Angela's face took on an awestruck expression. "Charlie Stanton will be there. I can't wait to meet him in person."

"Who's Charlie Stanton?" I asked.

Angela shot me a look of disbelief. "Only the actor who's playing the lead in the movie."

"Oh, right."

"Didn't you ever watch *Cops and Killers*?"

I shook my head.

"Charlie played the police captain. He must be in his fifties now, but he's still gorgeous! In my opinion, he's in the same league as Tom Selleck. Those dreamy bedroom eyes."

I stared at Angela. "Who are you and what have you done with my best friend? I never knew you were such a fangirl."

Angela shrugged. "You have to admit, it's thrilling to have a movie being filmed here in Clover Ridge. We get to meet all these famous actors. You should be excited that your stepfather is in it."

I scoffed. "I think it's great, but Tom is *not* my stepfather."

* * *

Back in the library, I found Smoky Joe waiting for me outside my office.

Sally stopped by a minute later. "Carrie, a patron told me that Smoky Joe tried to leave the building when she was going out to her car."

"Thanks, Sally. It seems the good weather is calling to him."

"I wonder if maybe you shouldn't leave him home for a few days."

"I've been wondering the same thing."

I'd fed my furry feline friend and settled down in front of my computer when I heard a knock at my door. Daphne entered.

"Hi, Carrie. I hope I'm not disturbing you." She held out a paper. "I came to bring you this. I figured you'd want it right away, since the program is next week."

I took it from her. "Thanks, Daphne." I glanced at the completed form. "Looks good. I meant to call you. Your program has drawn a large number of interested patrons. It's a go."

"Really?" She beamed at me. "That was fast."

"I notified everyone via our Facebook page. We have to limit the number of people to thirty-five." I smiled at her. "But if it's a success, there's no reason why you can't come back another time."

"Thanks so much, Carrie. This means a lot to me. Say!" She sent me a questioning look. "Would you by any chance be free for dinner tonight—or one night this week? I'd love to grab a bite and talk."

I paused to think about her offer. I'd never gotten friendly with a presenter before, but I liked Daphne and her upbeat personality. "Sure. As it turns out, tonight would be fine, though I was planning to go to the gym when I leave here at five."

"I don't mind eating later. I could meet you near your gym to save time."

"Parson's Gym is close to my cottage. It's in a strip mall on the road to Merrivale. I think it's the best gym around."

"Maybe I'll check it out and ask if they have short-term memberships."

"Why don't I call you when I'm about done? There are two restaurants—sushi and Italian—in the strip mall. Take your pick."

She grinned. "I can never say no to pizza."

"Then Italian it is. See you later."

* * *

The gym was more crowded than usual, and I had to wait to use many of the machines. It was after seven when I finally met Daphne in the Italian restaurant at the other end of the mall.

"Sorry. I hope you're not starving."

"I'm fine," she assured me. "In fact, I stopped by the gym and decided to take advantage of their three-month offer."

"You'll love it! If you can afford it, take a few sessions with Robby Dowd. He's their best personal trainer." I laughed. "And cute, too."

Daphne's expression was unreadable. "I'll keep that in mind."

The hostess led us to a booth and left us to read the huge menu.

I was hungry after working out and decided to have a small salad and lasagna. Daphne stuck with her original plan and ordered a small pizza topped with chicken as well as a salad. We each ordered a glass of Cabernet. Our wine arrived in record time.

"Cheers," I said.

We clinked glasses, and I sipped. "Ah!" I reached for the piping-hot garlic knots the waitress placed before us. "This is heaven."

Daphne smiled at me. She seemed completely relaxed. "I'm so glad you were free to have dinner with me tonight. This is quite a treat for me."

"Have you met many people since you moved here?"

"Not really. I exchange greetings with some people in my apartment complex, but they all seem so involved in their own lives. I'm working part-time in a gift shop in Merrivale." Daphne gave a sad little laugh. "But the woman who owns the shop isn't very friendly. Maybe that's why business isn't very good. I have a feeling I won't be working there much longer."

"What about giving private readings?"

Daphne sighed. "It takes time to develop a clientele. Libraries are the best source for that, but some of the other libraries in the area that I approached weren't very receptive to having me speak. One librarian said there might be an opening for me to speak in June, but she had to run it by her director." She shook her head. "So far I haven't heard back."

Our salads arrived, and for the next few minutes, we were too busy eating to converse.

"I'm curious," I said, as the waitress removed our salad plates and served my lasagna and Daphne's pizza. "How did you acquire your psychic abilities? Unless it's something you'd rather not talk about."

Daphne stopped cutting her pie into wedges and looked at me. "I don't mind telling you. Do you remember I said it was because of a near-death experience?"

"Uh-huh."

"My husband pushed me down a flight of stairs. I hit my head and blacked out."

My mouth fell open. "How awful!"

Daphne pursed her lips. "Our marriage was awful. I should have left Bert the first time he hit me. When I ended up having to stay in the hospital, I got up the courage to press charges. He tried to wriggle out of it as usual, but somehow I gathered up the strength to insist that he be arrested. The judge was sympathetic and ordered a speedy trial. As soon as it was over, I filed for divorce, changed my name back to Marriott, and moved out of state."

"I'm sorry you had to go through so much pain," I said.

Daphne smiled. "Thank you, Carrie. I've learned to trust my newfound abilities. They've brought me to this part of Connecticut."

Really? You didn't happen to grow up here?

42

Interestingly, Daphne didn't pick up on my thoughts. Well, as she'd told me the first time we met, psychic ability was hit-and-miss.

She reached across the table to pat my hand. "I feel I was destined to meet you. You're so full of compassion, though I sense that your own life has been tumultuous until recently."

I wasn't in the habit of discussing my parents with strangers, but I found myself opening up. "My father was a thief. He did time in prison. Even when he was out, he never spent much time with us. I was ashamed of him and loved him at the same time. Recently he's turned his life around. We've reconnected and speak often."

"That must have been very difficult," Daphne said, "but I'm glad you've let him back into your life."

I sighed. "My mother is another story. She raised my brother and me pretty much on her own. We don't mesh very well. She divorced my father years ago and is now married to a much younger man. In fact, they're in town because Tom is in the movie they're filming in Clover Ridge."

Daphne shuddered. Her eyes widened with fear.

"What is it?" I asked.

She shook her head.

"Please tell me."

"Divination is not one of my abilities, but I sense something very bad will interfere with the making of this movie."

Neither of us ate very much after that. We asked to have our food wrapped, remaining silent as we waited for the check.

"I'm sorry, Carrie," Daphne said. "I shouldn't have said anything. I have no idea what's going to happen. Maybe I'm wrong. At least, I hope it has nothing to do with your mother's husband."

"Me too."

Daphne tried to laugh. "Well, maybe the bad thing connected to the movie will simply be a sudden thunderstorm that ruins one of their shoots."

"Let's hope so," I said.

Chapter Five

The rest of the week flew by. I was grateful that my job and other activities kept me busy so I didn't miss Dylan too much, though I wasn't happy to learn that he wouldn't be coming home for the weekend as I'd hoped and would be flying to Paris instead.

"I recovered one of the paintings and I've got a lead on a crooked setup there between a few art galleries and an auction house," he told me Thursday night when I got back from dinner at my aunt and uncle's house. "Sorry, babe. I hope to tie everything up and be home in ten days' time."

"I hope so," I said.

I'd met my mother for lunch on Wednesday and then again on Saturday. Both times, she seemed subdued. Of course, I never told her about Daphne's premonition that something bad was going to happen during the filming of the movie. For one thing, she'd scoff at it; for another, I didn't want to worry her. When I asked how Tom was, she always said he was busy studying his lines. *How long does it take for an actor to learn his lines?* I wondered, but didn't ask. Nor did I ask how they were getting along.

The only person—I use the term loosely—with whom I discussed Daphne's prediction regarding the movie was Evelyn. She had plenty to say on the subject.

"Carrie, I wouldn't worry about it too much. Psychics get flashes of insight or intuition. For all we know, she was picking up on your anxiety. After all, weren't you worried about Tom having to act opposite his old flame, who, according to her quote on Wikipedia, would always love him?"

"I suppose."

"And Daphne said she usually can't see the future, right?"

"Right."

Evelyn grinned. "See? No need to worry. Besides, I remember Daphne Harper as a flighty sort of girl. I bet she's still flighty. A tumble down the stairs or not. People don't change *that* much."

I stared at Evelyn. "You called her Daphne Harper."

"That's right. Harper is her family name."

"So you said, the day she first came into the library. I must have forgotten, because I thought nothing of it when she told me that after divorcing her husband she'd changed her name back to her maiden name—Marriott."

Evelyn looked at me with pity. "Come on, Carrie. Did you stop to think for one minute that the name of a famous hotel chain might not be Daphne's real last name?"

I shook my head. "I never considered it. I assumed she was telling me the truth. I mean, why would she make up a fake name?"

"Tsk-tsk," Evelyn said. "And to think you've managed to outsmart murderers."

"That's different! Daphne isn't a murderer. I had no reason to assume she wouldn't tell me the truth." I thought for a moment. "Though she never mentioned that she'd grown up in Clover Ridge. Or that her father had been murdered."

"Perhaps she's hiding something," Evelyn said. "Or doesn't want her ex-husband to find her."

I nodded. "That's probably it. If that's the case, she's entitled to her secret identity."

"Carrie, we all have secrets. Even you." And with that cryptic remark, Evelyn faded away.

*   *   *

Tuesday evening, I went downstairs to the large meeting room several minutes before Daphne's program was set to begin. Sally had offered to take care of attendance, so I was free to spend time with Daphne. She appeared to be both nervous and joyous.

"I'm looking forward to this evening," she said. "I feel good vibrations coming from those attending. I think I'll have many successful minute readings."

"I'm glad," I said. "Patrons have told me they're looking forward to hearing what you have to tell them."

Everyone, including Angela and Sally, was seated by seven thirty, eager for the program to begin. I introduced Daphne, who proved to be an articulate, animated speaker. She began by saying she'd never been a great believer in psychics or fortune-tellers until she had a near-death accident and found herself receiving strong intuitive impressions and bits of information about people she encountered.

"I decided to read up on psychic ability and was surprised to learn there are a variety of phenomena, from telepathy or mind reading to astral projections, which are out-of-body experiences."

Daphne gave a start when she glanced my way, and I couldn't blame her. Evelyn had suddenly manifested and was crouching in front of my seat.

"Go away! You're spooking her," I said, as softly as I could.

"All right. I'll stand at the back of the room," Evelyn said, sounding injured.

Interesting. Even a ghost was curious about psychic phenomena.

After discussing at least twelve different psychic abilities and giving examples of each, Daphne offered to answer questions. I was surprised that, while some in the audience were eager to ask a question, most of those who raised their hands wanted to share a psychic occurrence they had experienced or heard about.

About fifteen minutes before the program was to end, Daphne announced that she would go around the room and give what she called minute readings. "Please understand that this is not something I can control in any way, so please don't be angry if I'm unable to sense something as I walk past you. It may only mean that your life is moving tranquilly along—for the moment."

The audience laughed, and I knew for sure that I would ask her to come back to do another program. I was surprised that no one, aside from Evelyn, had recognized Daphne as someone who had once lived in Clover Ridge. Of course, people changed over twenty years. It was even possible that no one present had known her as a teenager.

I decided to stop daydreaming and listen instead to what Daphne was telling patrons as she stopped at their seats.

"I get the sense that you'll have visitors staying with you very soon," she told one elderly woman.

"Yes! My son and his family are coming to visit this weekend!"

When she got to Angela, she said, "You're about to have a joyous celebration with friends and family."

"I sure am!" Angela said.

Daphne was approaching the back row when she suddenly froze as if she'd been wounded. "You!" she exclaimed. "Why are you here?"

A man who had been leaning against the back wall dashed out of the room. I followed him into the hall, but he was racing up the steps and fast approaching the main level. Daphne came to stand beside me. She was close to tears.

"Daphne, what is it? Who did you see?"

"My ex-husband. How did he find me?" She looked at me. "I'm sorry, Carrie. I didn't mean to ruin the program."

"Do you feel up to returning to your audience?"

She tried to smile. "Yes, I want to. I need to move on with my present life."

I put my arm around her and led her back to the room.

The room was abuzz with chatter. I walked up to the front and said, "I'm sorry about that. Daphne thought she'd seen—"

"A ghost!" someone called out.

"Something like that," I said. "But there are a few minutes left, so if Daphne feels she'd like to continue . . ." I glanced at her.

"Yes, I would," she said staunchly.

The audience quieted down and the program resumed. I allowed it to run a few minutes over.

As the room emptied out, Daphne apologized again for the interruption. "I've no idea how Bert knew I'd be here tonight." Her fear had turned to anger. "Too bad he ran off. I'd like to give him a piece of my mind."

"Not to worry," I assured her. "I'm sorry he managed to get in. He certainly wasn't on my list of patrons scheduled to attend."

As Daphne gathered up her notes and her pocketbook, I sensed that something beyond her ex's unexpected appearance was causing her distress. I wished she trusted me enough to tell me the real reason she'd returned to Clover Ridge.

Did her move back have anything to do with her father's murder? I wondered, then immediately told myself to stop thinking about murders. One would think I had an obsession with murders, both solved and unsolved.

*   *   *

The third Saturday in April turned out to be sunny and warm, with not a cloud in the sky—the perfect day for the Welcome to Clover Ridge luncheon and ensuing meet-and-greet party for the movie people. The luncheon, to which I'd been invited, was being held at the Inn on the Green, one of the largest and oldest buildings on the side of the Green around the corner from the library. Lunch was scheduled from noon till two to give forty or so town bigwigs like the mayor, Uncle Bosco, and members of the Chamber of Commerce the opportunity to chat with the movie cast and crew.

At two o'clock the group would move to the Green itself, where townsfolk could mingle and talk to the celebrities for the next two hours. The town center was bound to be as jam-packed with people and cars as Times Square on New Year's Eve. Though I wasn't scheduled to work that day, I pulled into the library parking lot before eleven o'clock to be assured of having a place to park. As it was, I managed to snag the last available spot. I spent the next forty-five minutes doing paper-work in my office, then walked on over to the luncheon.

"Straight back through the hall, the room on the left," the hostess informed me. Most of the round tables were filled up when I arrived, I noticed with dismay. I should have gotten there earlier. I waved to Uncle Bosco, who was sitting with Aunt Harriet, Mayor Al Tripp and his wife Dolores, John and Sylvia Mathers, and a woman I didn't know. Relieved to see an empty chair, I was heading to their table when my mother called out to me.

"Carrie, over here!"

Uncle Bosco and I exchanged glances. My great-uncle wasn't fond of my mother, hadn't been since she'd married my father, his nephew. Still, his advice to me when I'd gone to dinner at his and Aunt Harriet's two nights before was to "suck it up." Not quite the expression you'd expect from someone approaching eighty, but apt nevertheless. "She'll be leaving Clover Ridge just as soon as this movie business is finished." Unlike most of Clover Ridge's residents, Uncle Bosco consid-ered the moviemaking event an invasion of our village.

My heart beat faster as I walked toward my mother and the table full of movie people. *They're just people. So what if they're in movies?* Telling myself this did nothing to calm my nerves.

My mother stood and kissed my cheek. "You're here at last!" she declared, making me even more uncomfortable. After all, the luncheon was to celebrate the movie people, not someone like me. "Everyone, this is my daughter, Carrie Singleton. She lives here in Clover Ridge, where she oversees the adult activities of the public library."

That's one way of describing my job.

I smiled. The people at the table smiled back at me. All except Tom and the beautiful blonde at his side, who had never stopped their private conversation. Until my mother reached over and poked him in the ribs.

"Carrie dear, I want you to meet the important members of the cast and crew of *I Love You, I Do*." She gestured to the heavy-set middle-aged woman with long black hair sitting across the table. "This is Hattie Fein, a wizard at makeup and hair." My mother smiled graciously at the striking brunette in her midfifties. "Serena Harris, our leading lady. Next to Serena is Ronnie Rodriguez, chief cameraman par excellence; Dirk Franklin, film director; and TV and film actor Charlie Stanton."

My mother glared at the beautiful blonde, who sat studying her very long, very bright fuchsia nails. "Ilana Reingold. And of course you know Tom."

"Welcome to Clover Ridge. I'm so happy to meet you all," I said.

Everyone but Ilana murmured words of greeting. Since all eight seats were taken, I said, "And now I'd better dash off and find a place to sit, since they're about to start serving lunch. I've never eaten here, but I'm told the food is excellent."

Dirk, skinny and agile as a teenager though he had to be in his late forties or early fifties, sprang up from his seat.

"Sit here, Carrie. I only stopped by to discuss something with Serena and Charlie." He rolled his eyes. "My dear cousin Liane insists on making me the dancing bear at her table."

We all laughed, and I felt considerably more relaxed as I took the seat he'd just vacated. Charlie helped me move the heavy chair closer to the table.

"Thank you," I said.

"You're most welcome."

Charlie gave me a broad smile, and I could see why Angela had gone star-struck over him. He was still a very handsome man in his late fifties or early sixties—tall and rangy, with broad shoulders and a large, square face that smiled easily. He reminded me very much of James Garner, a favorite old-time actor of mine.

"My best friend Angela would give her eyeteeth to be sitting here next to you," I told him. "She works with me in the library and is one of your biggest fans."

"I must meet this young lady, if she's as pretty as you."

I felt my cheeks grow warm. "Angela's very pretty," I said, "and getting married in June."

"If I could have your attention, please," came a voice over a very loud mic.

We all turned to the front of the room, where Liane Walters was standing. She thanked all of us for coming and the movie cast and crew for choosing Clover Ridge as the setting for *I Love You, I Do*, and introduced the people who had arranged and paid for the luncheon. Then she introduced the cast and crew. As each person stood, the applause was tremendous.

Then Dirk took the mic to say a few words. "Our sincere and heartfelt thanks to those of you who arranged our luncheon and the meet-and-greet afterward so we can get to know the residents of Clover Ridge. We're honored to have the opportunity to film *I Love You, I Do* here in your village. When I was a kid, I used to visit my cousin Liane and fell in love with this place. Clover Ridge has everything to recommend it—a marvelous green surrounded by centuries-old, picturesque buildings, parks and mountains close by, and miles of waterfront on the Long Island Sound."

He stopped for applause. "I'd like you to know that I'm on the hunt for extras for our movie. I need women and kids under ten for one of our shopping scenes. I'll be interviewing townspeople later on, out on the Green."

Mark and Tacey would love to be in a movie! I hoped my cousin Randy and his wife Julia were planning to bring their young children to the meet-and-greet.

Charlie leaned over to whisper to me, "God bless him, Dirk can go on for hours. Sometimes I think he gets us more angels than our producers, though it's their job to find backers."

"Have you worked with Dirk before?" I asked.

Charlie nodded. "This is my third project with him. Dirk is low-budget and considered an indie director, but he sure has his pulse on what the public wants."

We chatted a bit, and it was only when our salad plates were cleared that I realized how much I enjoyed talking to Charlie Stanton.

"So tell me, what's life like here in Clover Ridge?" he asked.

"Typical small-town life, I suppose, which suits me. I've only been living here since May of last year, when I came to stay with my great-aunt and uncle." I pointed to the table where they were sitting. "My uncle's on the library board, and I ended up getting the position of head of programs and events."

"And your love life? Is there a special someone in your life?" Somehow the way Charlie posed the question didn't seem intrusive.

I grinned. "I have a boyfriend. Dylan's an investigator for art and jewel thefts. In fact, he's away on a case now, but I'm hoping the new office he's in charge of will handle cases that will keep him closer to home."

Charlie nodded. "I like the idea of settling down in one place where the store owners know you and your neighbors look out for you."

"You've been acting for quite some time," I said. "Did you know the people involved in this movie before?"

"I met Tom and your mother last weekend."

He gestured with his chin at Serena to my right, who was deep in conversation with Hattie. We watched as Hattie rubbed her fingers along Serena's left cheek.

Charlie moved closer to me so he could whisper in my ear. "Serena's a fine indie actor and still hoping to make it in Hollywood. The poor dear is obsessed with wrinkles, real and imaginary. She had to stop those injections because it gave her a frozen look. And she won't go through with another facelift—not since the results of the last one put her into hibernation for the best part of a year."

I rapped his arm. "You are outrageous!" I said, laughing.

"It's the truth. She'll probably ask me to block her left side in every scene we play together regardless of how the script is written. What's more, I adore her and will do as she asks."

Our waitress placed my salmon and veggies in front of me. A minute later she brought over Charlie's dish.

"I should have ordered the same as you, but I can't resist filet mignon when it's on the menu." He winked. "Please don't tell my wife. I promised to avoid meat and go easy on the desserts."

"I didn't know you were married."

"To the love of my life." He winked again. "I bet there are plenty of things you don't know about me."

"I don't really know anything about you," I said.

"That's a relief," he said. "It can get tiresome, talking to strangers who think they know you inside and out because of what they've read about you on the internet. Anyway, Elinor and I have been married for thirteen years. Alas, we have no children. She is my third and last wife. The previous two were short-term mistakes."

We started to eat. My salmon was perfectly prepared and as tasty as it looked. As was the medley of three kinds of squash.

"This is fantastic. Here, have a taste." Charlie held out a forkful of filet mignon.

He was right. "Excellent. Dylan and I will have to come here one night. I don't know why we never have before."

I offered Charlie a bite of my salmon, which he devoured with gusto. "Another winner, for sure."

A sudden noise startled me and brought all nearby conversation to a halt. My mother was on her feet, having knocked over her chair. Her face burned red with rage. "At least have the courtesy to answer me when I ask you a question."

Tom's response was too low for me to hear, but whatever he said only infuriated her further.

People were staring, but my mother ignored them. I suddenly remembered how she'd yell at Jordan or me when she was angry at us, not caring if we were in a store or some other public place.

"Don't tell me you're discussing the movie. This is about making a play for your old girlfriend. The same girlfriend who dumped you years ago."

There was a communal intake of breath.

"This is better than live theatre," Charlie whispered in my ear.

"Please, Brianna, you're blowing this all out of proportion," Tom said, as he placed his hand on my mother's arm.

She brushed his hand aside. My mouth fell open as she picked up her water glass and tossed its contents against his chest. "Oh!" she said, as if surprised by her own actions, then ran out of the room.

I'd started to get up when I felt Charlie's hand on my shoulder. "Let them settle it themselves," he said.

"You're right." I was relieved that Tom had followed my mother out.

I glanced up to see how Ilana was reacting to the scene she had helped bring about. She seemed oblivious to the stares and whispers as she tossed back her blonde mane and asked the waitress to refill her wineglass.

Order in the dining room was restored and people returned to their meals and conversations, though I was sure most of the conversations now revolved around what had just taken place. Our waitress cleared our plates. Ilana's had hardly been touched. Dirk came over to talk to her, perching on the edge of the chair Tom had so recently vacated. She pursed her lips, displeased by what he was saying. Still, she stood and followed him out of the dining room.

"What's Ilana like?" I asked Charlie as our waitress filled our coffee cups.

Charlie laughed. "What you see is what you get. Ilana is a terrific actress—on stage, in films, and in life. She loves men and we love her—at least for a while. Most of all, she loves drama of the sort you just witnessed."

"I know she and Tom were engaged once. But that ended years ago. Now Tom's married. To my mother."

Charlie shrugged. "All men are fair game to our fair Ilana, especially her former lovers. She started in on Tom the first night we all met for dinner. I think he was shocked at first, then flattered. And now he's hooked."

"Oh no! Until Tom got a part in this movie, he and my mother were in a good place."

"And perhaps they will be again. Ah, here comes our dessert. I can't wait to taste the molten chocolate cake. It's one of my favorites."

Serving dessert must have been the signal that the other diners could descend on the movie people, and descend they did. Soon I was surrounded by fans waiting their turn to talk to Charlie. I quickly finished my cake and waved good-bye to him. I stopped by Liane's table to thank her for inviting me, and then Uncle Bosco beckoned me over.

"What in tarnation made your mother mad enough to storm out of here like a tornado?"

I grimaced. "She was angry at Tom for fawning over Ilana Reingold and acting like she wasn't there."

Uncle Bosco shook his head. "That woman never fails to make a spectacle of herself. One of these days she'll find herself in serious trouble, and it will be her own doing."

Chapter Six

At two o'clock I walked across to the Green, which was already mobbed with local residents eager to meet the movie people. The event planners had set up tables and chairs, but most people preferred to mingle on foot as they sipped lemonade or liquor-free punch and munched on cookies. Though the streets along the four sides of the Green had been closed to traffic, I could hear the horns of frustrated drivers a few blocks away as they crept along slowly as snails in their search for a parking spot.

Dirk and the four actors starring in *I Love You, I Do* sat on a raised platform in a spot well shaded by trees. With them were Liane Walters, the mayor, and Artie Pohl, a big bear of a man who was the president of the Chamber of Commerce, as well as three men I didn't recognize. At two fifteen, Artie stood and tested the mic.

"Can I please have your attention," he boomed. The chattering quieted down. "We're thrilled that Firestone Productions has selected our town for the filming of their movie *I Love You, I Do*. In a moment you'll have a chance to meet the actors and the people responsible for the making of this movie."

When the applause died down, Artie moved on to introduce Dirk, Charlie, Serena, Tom, and Ilana, as well as the three men, who turned out to be the screenwriter and producers. After a few more speeches, a reporter and a photographer from the local TV station took over. As the photographer snapped pictures, the reporter asked the movie people questions about the film they were making. Then they joined the fray and began asking local people how they felt about a movie being made in Clover Ridge.

I was working my way through the crowd to get to Tom, wanting to ask him if my mother was all right, when I felt a tug on my arm. I turned to find an excited Angela.

"There's Charlie Stanton! He's even better-looking in person. But look at that line of fans waiting to meet him."

"I don't blame them. Charlie's very friendly," I said.

Angela's eyes popped. "You talked to him?"

"Sat next to him at lunch."

"Oh. My. God!"

"Angela, I need to talk to Tom for a minute. Then I'll introduce you to Charlie."

There was a small group of people around Tom. I waved to him, and he called me over.

"Excuse me. Family business. Tom's my—a relative," I said as I passed several angry faces. Somehow I couldn't bring myself to say *stepfather*.

"What is it, Carrie?" he asked, when I was close enough to talk quietly.

"I just want to make sure my mother's okay. I didn't see her after you guys left the inn."

"Brianna's fine. She drove back to the house. I'll catch a ride later with someone."

No doubt that someone is Ilana. "Thanks. I was worried."

"No need. Everything's okay," he said, clearly annoyed by my concern. "Talk to you later."

I returned to Angela, who was waiting for me a few feet away. "What was that all about?" she asked.

"My mother and Tom had a fight. He's obsessed with Ilana Reingold." We turned to look at Ilana tossing her long hair and laughing with fans.

"Who could blame him?" she said.

Charlie, who was sitting between Ilana and Serena, caught my glance and beckoned me over. I grabbed Angela's hand, and we walked up to him.

"Hey! Where do you think you're going?" more than one person called out. I felt bad about pushing ahead, but Charlie had called me.

"Charlie, this is my friend Angela Vecchio. I told you she was dying to meet you."

"So you did. Nice to meet you, Angela. Carrie tells me you're getting married soon."

Angela's red color deepened. "Carrie told you that?"

"She sure did."

"See you later," I told her, but she never heard me. Charlie winked at me as I waved good-bye.

The Green was mobbed with people, which made walking difficult. I exchanged greetings with several patrons and was surprised when Rob Dowd from Parson's Gym called out my name.

"Hi, Rob. I didn't know you were a movie fan."

He shrugged. "Why not see what the fuss is all about. Besides, it's a great day to be outdoors."

"Have fun," I said, making a dash for a vacant chair I'd just spotted at one of the tables.

I dialed my mother's cell phone. She picked up on the fourth ring. She sounded groggy, as though she'd been sleeping. "Hi, Mom, it's me. Are you all right?"

"I just took a sleeping pill."

"In the middle of the day?" I asked.

"Well, I didn't sleep well last night, and figured since Dirk called a meeting for after the shindig on the Green, I might as well get in a nap. We'll probably all go out for drinks and dinner later on."

"Oh. Okay. I was worried about you after you took off during lunch."

She made a laughing sound. "That's sweet of you, honey, but we're good. Tom swore to me there's nothing between him and Ilana. He was so very sorry he'd upset me."

"Well, all right," I said. "Talk to you soon."

I slipped my cell phone back into my pocketbook, a bit unsettled by mother's response. I certainly hadn't been happy to see Tom exchanging whispers with his old love either, and his apology didn't ring true. I supposed my mother wanted so much to believe him that she'd swallowed it whole.

I realized I was thirsty and joined the line to get a cupful of lemonade. Angela found me a few minutes later. She was still dazed from having spoken to Charlie Stanton.

"He's really nice."

"Told you."

"I'd better get back to work," she said.

"I'm thinking of heading home," I said. "I was going to stop by my mother's house, but she's taking a nap."

"When is Dylan coming back?" Angela asked.

I released a deep sigh. "I don't know. Soon, I hope, because I miss him."

"Of course you do." Angela hugged me and walked back to the library.

I noticed that the platform now stood deserted because the movie people were scattered about the Green with the rest of us. Charlie and Serena were holding court at one table, Ilana and Tom at another. So many people! I was delighted to see my cousin Randy, his wife Julia, and their children, Mark and Tacey.

"Hi, Cousin Carrie!" Four-year-old Tacey came zooming into my arms.

I swung her around. "Wow, you're getting heavy."

"That's 'cause I'm bigger. I'm going to kindergarten in September."

"I kind of figured we'd run into you here," Randy said, giving me a bear hug. "I told Julia my cousin Carrie's always where the action is."

"That's right." I grinned at Randy, having learned to take his teasing in stride. "In fact, I even had lunch with the movie people and the bigwigs at the inn."

"Good for you," Julia said.

"I'm so glad I ran into you. Dirk Franklin, the director, is looking for local people to have walk-on parts in the movie."

Eight-year-old Mark's eyes lit up. "You mean I could be in the movie? How cool is that!"

"We have to find out what's involved, buddy," Randy said. "And what exactly the director is looking for. Could be he wants a bunch of ninety-year-old people. Or little babies who go goo-goo."

"Daddy, you are so silly," Tacey chimed in.

"Actually, he wants women and kids—about your age," I said to Mark and Tacey.

"Great! Let's go find the director," Mark said. "He'll hire us. I know he will!"

Julia and I laughed as we exchanged glances. She shrugged. "I know, my quiet son has taken on an entirely new personality."

I scanned the crowd, hoping to catch sight of Dirk. I spotted him some distance away.

"There's Dirk," I said. "Come with me and I'll introduce you. Then hopefully we'll have some thespians in the Singleton family."

"What's a thespian?" Tacey asked.

"An actor!" Mark announced.

"However did you know that?" Julia asked.

"Because of the movie, our class got to talking about movies and plays and acting. The word simply came up," Mark explained airily.

I left my cousins happily chatting with Dirk, who seemed very interested in signing on Julia and the children. *Time to head home*, I thought, as I started walking to my car. I smiled at Daphne as we were about to cross paths.

"Daphne, how nice to see you. Did you come out to—"

A stocky man about five foot nine pushed his way between us. His face was set in a furious grimace as he clutched Daphne's upper arm. "And here you are, hiding in plain sight."

"I'm not hiding," Daphne said. She tried to shake free of his grip, but he held on.

"Let go of her!" I said.

His dark eyes looked me up and down. "Get lost. This is between me and my wife."

"Bert, stop it! You're hurting me."

Frantically, I looked around. John Mathers stood several feet away, conversing with a group of people. I was about to run and get him when Charlie and Serena walked by.

"Charlie! Come here! Please!"

In one glance he'd figured out the problem and approached Daphne and the man I assumed was her ex-husband. Charlie removed Bert's hand from Daphne's arm and clenched Bert's shoulder.

"I don't think the lady's buying what you have to sell."

"Is that so?" Bert was furious at the interference. He stared up at Charlie, who had a good six inches on him, and tried to shake free of his grip, but Charlie held firm. "Look, buddy. This is a private matter. Between me and my wife."

"I'm not your wife," Daphne said. "Not anymore."

"I'm telling you to take a walk," Charlie said.

Daphne's eyes widened as she stared at Serena, then back at Charlie, no doubt thunderstruck that Charlie Stanton had come to her rescue.

Serena tugged at Charlie's sleeve. She was statuesque and considerably taller than she'd appeared sitting down. Even so, she barely reached Charlie's shoulder. "Keep out of this, Charlie. Don't get involved. Dirk won't like it."

"Are you kidding? This guy's bad news. I know the type."

I raced over to John. "Sorry," I interrupted the group's conversation. "John, I need you. There's a situation."

Given our past history of solving a few murders together, John knew I wasn't one to get upset over nonsense and followed me without a word.

Bert had calmed down by the time we broke through the ring of people that had gathered around him and Daphne, Charlie, and Serena.

"Ah, the law has arrived," Charlie said cheerfully. "Serena, I think this is where we exit the scene."

They left. Daphne looked like she wanted to take off too.

"What's going on here?" John asked, his stern gaze on Bert.

"Nothing," he mumbled. "I just was talking to my wife. My *ex-wife*, that is."

John's expression was considerably softer when he turned to Daphne. "Do you want to talk to him?"

"I do not. Not now. Not ever."

John nodded and returned his attention to Bert. "I think that's pretty clear. What's your name and where do you live?"

Bert mumbled something too low for me to hear. Whatever it was, it pissed John off.

"I'm Lieutenant John Mathers of the Clover Ridge Police Department. If you don't care to show me some identification, I'll haul you off to our local jail for assaulting your ex-wife. Now, if you don't want to spend a night there, I advise you to comply with my request."

Bert whatever-his-last-name-was let out an exaggerated sigh as he pulled out his wallet and showed John his driver's license. John took a photo of it with his cell phone and handed it back to Bert.

"Thank you, Mr. Lutz. Now do us all a favor and drive back to Ohio."

Bert ignored John and pointed a finger at Daphne. "We're not finished, you and I. You'll be hearing from me."

He swaggered off.

"I'd like to leave now," Daphne said.

"Of course," John said. "Please call the station if he bothers you again."

Daphne nodded and walked briskly away. I followed after her. "Daphne, would you like me to come with you?" I asked.

She shook her head. "No, Carrie. Thank you for getting Lieutenant Mathers, but right now I need to be alone. To figure out what I'm going to do."

Going to do? "This must be very upsetting, especially after he showed up at your program Tuesday night."

Daphne thrust back her shoulders. She wore a look of determination I'd never seen from her before. "I'll be all right. Please don't worry about me."

Easier said than done, I thought as I headed for my car and what I hoped would be a peaceful evening at home in my cottage.

Chapter Seven

Dylan finally arrived home Monday night, exhausted and exhilarated. It was close to eleven when he stopped by the cottage to bring me up to date on his case. He'd tracked the thieves to Vienna, where INTERPOL and the Austrian police had captured them. He'd managed to retrieve the two remaining paintings and most of the Chinese artifacts. Best of all, he was home to stay—until the trial, which was months away, when the thieves would be extradited to Texas.

We sat on the living room sofa, our arms around each other. Smoky Joe welcomed Dylan home by plopping down on his lap.

"As soon as I have the New Haven office under control, I'm hiring someone to help me with cases. And Mac agrees we need someone to take my place in the field. That means finding the right person, training him or her, et cetera. It will take time, babe, so be prepared that I'll probably have to take off a few more times before I can stay put."

"As long as you're here now," I said, and yawned.

"I'm keeping you up," he said, getting to his feet.

"Sorry, but I have to be up really early in the morning. My mother called to tell me that several of Tom's scenes are being filmed on the beach behind the inn where the two couples are supposed to be staying. They're scheduled to start shooting at seven, but she said to get there as early as I can make it, because once word gets out, the place will be flooded with spectators."

"I'm beat, too. We'll catch up over dinner tomorrow night."

The next morning my alarm clock woke me at five thirty. I stumbled to the bathroom, aware that the sun still had yet to rise. I decided to leave Smoky Joe home for the day, since I didn't want to leave him in the car while I watched the filming and it didn't make sense to drive all the way home to get him before work when the library was a few minutes' drive from the waterfront.

I wasn't familiar with the seven miles of Clover Ridge shoreline that ran along the Sound, though it was only a few miles from the Green. It had never been developed or beautified, though it was popular with fishermen and boaters, many of whom docked and winterized their boats at one of the two marinas. The few seafood restaurants built along the strip were modest, but the three or four small inns were supposedly "hidden treasures" known to very few.

My mother hadn't been kidding when she said, early hour or not, the place would be mobbed with spectators. Cars were parked helter-skelter along both sides of the two-lane road that ran parallel to the Long Island Sound. I parked as close as I could to the Clever Clam—or I should say the Tarleton Arms, where the two couples in the movie were on vacation. Because the forecast for the day was warm and sunny, Dirk had decided to film as many outdoor scenes set on the back lawn and stretch of beach as they could get in. My mother had said he'd be starting with a scene between Tom and Ilana, followed by one with Tom and Serena.

As I approached the inn, I noticed the three large equipment trucks beyond it. Those watching crowded together on the lawn and faced the water.

My mother had told me to go inside the inn and tell whoever was on duty who I was. A woman at the desk said, "You can go inside. They're in makeup."

I walked through the narrow hall, observing that the movie people had taken over all the downstairs rooms. One room was filled with costumes, another with equipment. I entered the third room, where Hattie Fein, the makeup woman, was attending to Ilana while a skinny young man sporting black leggings, a black T-shirt, and a long black ponytail worked on Tom.

"There you are!" my mother said as she approached me from the corner of the room. "I was beginning to think you weren't coming." She sounded harried.

"It's pretty hectic out there," I said. "So many people have come to watch."

"Didn't I tell you? That's why I said to come early."

I came as early as I could. "Can I be of any help?" I asked.

Ilana must have heard me, because she called to me, a fake smile on her beautiful face. "Hi there, Tom's stepdaughter. I'm dying of thirst. Could you pretty please get me a Diet Coke from the kitchen? And make sure it's cold?"

"Sure." I glanced at Serena, Tom, and Charlie. "Would anyone else like something to drink?"

Serena smiled as she shook her head.

"I wouldn't mind some ginger ale," Charlie said. "Thank you, Carrie."

Pleased that he remembered my name, I turned to Tom. "Anything for you, Tom?"

"Nothing, thanks."

I left the room and went to find the kitchen, which I figured was located at the back of the inn past the staircase. I returned with the cans of soda and handed them to Charlie and Ilana.

"Thanks, Carrie," Ilana said. She sipped some soda, then held out the can to Tom. "Want some?"

"Sure." Tom took the can from her and drank. Was it my imagination, or did their fingers touch?

I glanced at my mother. She looked as though she was about to burst into tears. I pulled her into the hall.

"That woman is awful! I'd like to take her soda and pour it over her head," I whispered.

My mother shrugged. "Tom claims it's just her way and she means nothing by it. Yesterday she made a big play for Charlie. Only he made a joke of it. He stroked her head and treated her like a puppy."

Dirk strode into the room. "All right. Everything's set up and we're ready for your scene," he said to Tom and Ilana. "Remember, this is the scene where you run into each other at the water's edge. Tom, you've gone out for a walk. Rachel, the woman you're to marry, is resting in your room. Same for you, Ilana. Your lover Austin is tired after driving four hours and you need some fresh air."

"And I don't want to waste one minute of this delightful weather," Ilana said, beaming at Tom. "And neither do you."

Dirk gave a few more directions, and then he, Tom, and Ilana went outside.

"Follow me," my mother said as she also exited the inn. "You'll be able to see it all from where we'll be standing."

Outside, there was a buzz of activity. Ronnie Rodriguez, the cameraman, had his huge camera contraption ready to start shooting. Dirk went to talk to the extras while someone walked over to the crowd behind the rope, no doubt telling them to remain silent.

"I'm surprised at how big the set is," I said to my mother, taking in the terrace, lawn, and stretch of beach.

"In the scene they're about to shoot, Luke and Vicki—the two characters Tom and Ilana are playing—walk along the water for a bit, then sit down on the terrace and have a drink," my mother explained.

Dirk gave Ronnie some last-minute directions, then got into his moving chair. "Action!" he called.

I was spellbound as I watched Tom approach Ilana as she stood on the beach, staring at the water. Though their voices were low, I could make out the words and follow their conversation. What struck me the most was how different Luke and Vicki were from Tom and Ilana. Luke was more open and less sophisticated than Tom. And Vicki was completely devoid of Ilana's flirty personality. I thought the scene was going along great when Dirk called out and stopped the action. He conferred with the two actors. I saw them both nod. The camera moved back, as did the sound techs with their boom mics, and the scene began again.

More than an hour later, Dirk called the scene a wrap and called for a break. My mother seemed very pleased. "Only three takes and they got it done," she said.

"But the actual scene isn't even ten minutes long," I said.

"That's movies," she said.

We followed Dirk, Ilana, and Tom inside the inn. I glanced at my watch. I had to leave for work soon.

Dirk, Ilana, and Tom huddled in a corner of the makeup room, then Dirk turned his attention to Serena, who'd been chatting with Hattie Fein. My mother approached Tom.

"That went wonderfully," she said.

"Thanks, Brianna," Tom said.

"I agree," Ilana chirped. "Such a romantic scene. Two people meet and have no idea they're about to fall in love." She rubbed Tom's back. "It reminds me of the way we met."

Tom looked at her quizzically. "Really? We met at a party. At Chris Tankeroff's house. It was his wife Tandy's thirtieth birthday party."

"Of course! You'd brought that pretty little assistant who had one drink and became violently ill."

"Not from the drink. She had an allergic reaction to one of the hors d'oeuvres."

"Whatever! You were so cute, looking after her. Trying to find a doctor among the crowd. That's when I knew I had to get to know you."

"That's quite enough, Ilana!"

I stared at my mother. Her humiliation had gelled into a cold fury.

"Mom, ignore her. Please! Deal with her later," I begged, as Ilana let loose a silvery laugh as fake as the color of her blonde hair.

"You had your chance with Tom years ago, and you threw it away."

Ilana batted her eyelids. "We're merely reminiscing. Right, Tom?"

"Tom!" my mother said, a note of desperation in her voice. "Do something."

"What would you like me to do?" Tom asked.

My mother made a scoffing sound. "Stop playing into her fantasy. It's humiliating. It's not fair to me." Her eyes filled with tears.

I put my arm around her and tried to lead her away, but she shrugged free. I suddenly realized that all chatter in the room had ceased. Members of the cast and crew were staring at the trio, entranced as if they were watching an action film.

"Say something, Tom."

"This is embarrassing, Brianna. It would have been better if you hadn't . . ."

"Come?" My mother's voice was shrill. "You wanted me to come until *she* became part of the cast."

Ilana turned to my mother and flashed her a smile. "Brianna darling, try to relax. Tom's a big boy—"

My mother slapped her. People gasped. "You've gone too far, Ilana. Stick to the script or something very bad will happen to you!"

Chapter Eight

My mother cried the entire ride back to her rented house while I did my best to comfort her. I offered to spend the day with her, but she told me she'd be fine and I should go to work. I was upset that she was upset but glad that for once she was sharing her feelings. Her statements were all over the place and often contradicted each other.

"I never should have married Tom," she said between sobs. "We're too different. When we first met, the age difference didn't matter. He enjoyed being the focus of my attention. But lately it's become clear to me that he wants a much younger woman."

Like Ilana, I thought but didn't say.

She blew her nose loudly, then went on. "I thought he loved me. No, I know he did. But now I wonder if he's been pining for Ilana all these years."

"She's some piece of work," I said. "Too bad she ended up doing this movie playing opposite Tom."

"Dirk originally wanted Ilana for the role, but she was tied up."

"I see," I said, as I drove down my mother's block. "Would you have tried to stop Tom from taking the role if you'd known Ilana was in the movie?"

"Of course not! Tom was elated when he got this part. I was happy for him. I had no idea that Ilana would behave this way." She turned to me. "You saw for yourself—she's all over Tom, like he's a bowlful of rocky road ice cream she wants to devour."

Tom? A bowlful of rocky road ice cream? "She's unbelievable, I agree. But it's up to Tom to tell her to cut it out. What does she hope to gain from her behavior?"

"Isn't it obvious? She wants Tom." My mother sniffed. "Although he claims she's just acting that way for fun. Sometimes I can see his point. Other times I worry that he wants to get back together with her." She shook her head in frustration. "I'm not sure what's real and what isn't anymore."

I rubbed my mother's back. "I'm sorry you're going through this. She has no right to humiliate you."

"I shouldn't let her get to me. I blew up in front of everyone. Now I'm so embarrassed."

That realization brought a new bout of tears.

As I pulled into the driveway of their rented house, my mother met my gaze. "Ilana's ruined my relationship with Tom. She ruined my life. If only someone made her disappear."

* * *

I left my mother sipping tea and watching a soap opera on television and drove to the library, surprised that despite all that had transpired since my visit to the movie set, I was going to arrive at work on time. I felt bad for my mother. I'd truly thought she had found happiness with Tom, but after seeing him with Ilana, I doubted there was much hope for their future together.

But maybe I was being too pessimistic. After all, what did I know about marriage and how much stress one could endure? The question was, did Tom still love my mother?

I turned on the radio to a local station that played soft rock. At the end of a song, the announcer came on.

"There's no update to report on the homicide we told you about earlier. All we know is the victim is a woman named Daphne Marriott, age thirty-seven. She was found strangled inside her rented apartment in Clover Ridge."

"Daphne!" A chill snaked down my spine.

"As we reported earlier, a neighbor—Andy Fazio—said his dog started acting strangely—whimpering and pawing at the door—when they passed the victim's apartment early this morning. Andy knocked several times. When Miss Marriott didn't respond, he turned the knob. The door was unlocked. He walked in and found the body lying on the living room floor.

"Lieutenant Mathers said the police are investigating and asks anyone with information to call the following number."

My hand shook as I switched off the radio. Daphne was dead. Murdered. I pulled over to the side of the road and gulped down gallons of air. Tears welled up at the horror of it all. I had just lost someone who, with time, would have become a close friend.

Underneath my sorrow I was beset with guilt. The last time I'd seen Daphne had been Saturday afternoon when she was being manhandled by that awful ex-husband of hers, Bert something-or-other. That was days ago. I should have called to find out how she was. To make sure she was okay instead of taking her at her word.

Could Bert have killed her? He could very well have hung around Clover Ridge. Perhaps they had argued. He'd been angry. Was he angry enough to choke her?

I parked in the library's lot and entered the building.

"What? No Smoky Joe today?" Max asked as I pulled open the door.

I shook my head. "I went to watch a scene being filmed this morning." It seemed so long ago. "Max, did you hear? Daphne Marriott, the psychic who came to speak here last week, was murdered."

"I heard as I was driving over," Max said. "A real shame. She seemed like such a nice lady, too."

Surprised, I asked, "Did you get to talk to her?"

"Just for a minute or two after her program. But I told my wife about her, and Dolly made an appointment to see her." He grimaced. "Her mom died last summer, and Dolly misses her terribly."

"Did Dolly think it was worthwhile, going to see Daphne for a reading?"

"Oddly enough, she did—not that the psychic lady had much to say about her mother." Max smiled. "But she told Dolly that she and I have a sound marriage and that she's doing a fine job with our two boys."

He made a clicking sound with his tongue. "Such a pity. Who would want to kill someone like her?"

"I don't know, Max, but I intend to do my damnedest to find out."

Max chuckled. "Don't let Lieutenant Mathers hear you say that."

"I intend to call him the minute I get to my office to tell him everything I know about Daphne."

My message to John's direct line at the police department went to voice mail. Next I called his cell phone. He picked up immediately.

"Hi, John, it's me, Carrie. I just heard the news about Daphne on the radio."

"Terrible business. I was going to contact you—soon as I finish talking to a person of interest."

"Her ex-husband Bert, I suppose."

"I wish. Herbert Lutz is in the wind. I've got an APB out for him."

"Do you know about Daphne's history?"

"I know Lutz was abusive."

"Further back. Daphne's originally from Clover Ridge."

"She told you all this?"

"Actually, someone here in the library mentioned it." That part was true. "I can't seem to remember who."

"Carrie, I'll be over in fifteen minutes."

John appeared at my office twelve minutes later. He kissed my cheek, pulled out the desk chair Trish and Susan shared, and sank into it. He rubbed his eyes then, elbows on knees, he hunched forward and looked pensively at me.

"Carrie, please tell me why, though you've been living in Clover Ridge less than a year, you somehow manage to have a connection with every homicide victim?"

I shrugged. "I get to meet a lot of people through my job in the library. That's how I met Daphne."

"And her history?"

"Her maiden name is Harper, not Marriott."

"Is that so?" I could see the wheels spinning in his head.

"Someone recognized her when she first came into the library a few weeks ago and told me about her family's history."

"Which is?"

"Her father was an abusive drunk. He was murdered—stabbed with a knife, I believe. Daphne told the police she heard her brother Billy arguing with her father. Her brother was arrested for the crime. Later he was exonerated."

I looked at John. He was rubbing his forehead and deep in thought. Finally, he met my gaze. "Chet Harper. I remember the miserable SOB. He was a mean drunk. Took his anger out on his family. I went to the apartment more than once when neighbors called."

"What I don't understand is why Daphne accused her brother of killing their father. The way I heard it, she and her brother were close. He protected her from their father as best he could."

John grimaced. "That was the work of my predecessor. Good old Mitchell Flynn. He wanted to close the case ASAP and didn't give a damn how he did it—as long as he could provide a viable suspect and help get his friend elected commissioner. Once Daphne said Billy finally gave their father a bit of his own treatment a week before the murder, Mitch worked on her until she admitted the two men might have argued that evening."

"Even so, saying they argued the night of the murder is a far cry from committing a murder," I pointed out.

"I know. Unfortunately, Billy Harper had a lousy lawyer. The jury saw him as a sullen young man who had had his share of beatings and was probably no better than his father. I'm glad he managed to prove he was innocent and was released from prison."

"Where was Daphne's mother when all this was going on?"

"Good question." John nodded reflectively. "At the time her husband was being stabbed to death, Pattie was at work. Afterward, she just seemed to fall apart. It was as if she'd run out of whatever it was that had given her the strength to work two jobs. She left town a few days after Chet was murdered. As far as I know, no one's heard from her since."

"So she couldn't have murdered her husband since she was at work."

"We checked. Her alibi held up." John shot me one of his penetrating looks. "Why all these questions, Carrie? Are you thinking Daphne's murder is related to her father's all those years ago?"

"I have no idea," I admitted. "But why would anyone want to kill her?"

"You mean, besides her ex-husband?"

I shuddered. "I wouldn't want to run into him in a dark alley. But if Billy didn't kill his father, that's an unsolved murder."

"Don't I know it. But getting back to the present, tell me how you got to know Daphne."

"She came to the library because she was interested in doing a program. She told me she'd acquired psychic abilities after a near-death incident. We liked each other and went out for dinner, which was when she told me that the near-death experience was when her husband pushed her down the stairs."

John scoffed. "Big surprise that she'd pick an abuser for her husband."

"At least she had the good sense to end the marriage," I said.

"Uh-huh, and a lot of good it did her. As you saw for yourself, her husband found out where she was living and came to hound her."

"Last Tuesday evening he showed up at Daphne's library program as well."

"Interesting," John commented.

"After you sent him away, I asked Daphne if she wanted me to stay with her, but she took off. Maybe if I'd—"

"Carrie, please don't go there. You're not to feel guilty. You couldn't have prevented this."

I released a deep sigh. "I suppose you're right. I really liked Daphne. I felt that over time we'd become close friends."

"Did she happen to mention why she'd moved back to Clover Ridge after all these years?"

I shook my head. "Since she'd never told me she was from here originally, I certainly couldn't ask."

John got to his feet. "Thanks for the info. Now I have another lead to check out." He met my gaze. "Carrie, I know you liked Daphne and hate like hell what happened to her, but promise me you won't go looking for her murderer."

I fluttered my eyelids. "Would I do something like that?"

John wasn't amused. "Let me hear you say it."

"I won't go looking for Daphne's murderer." *Though I'll find out what I can.*

"Thank you."

Evelyn appeared as soon as John closed the door behind him.

"Of course you'll try to find the person who murdered Daphne. I told you that girl needed your help."

"I should have gone home with her on Saturday after her ex showed up and practically assaulted her. But she brushed me off, and I was concerned about my mother—"

Evelyn exhaled a huff of exasperation. "Carrie, my dear. I didn't mean you should have acted as Daphne's body-guard. But you do have a knack for finding overlooked facts and ferreting out secrets. And I'll help you the best I can."

"Do you think Daphne's murder has something to do with her father's all those years ago?"

"It wouldn't hurt to look up old newspaper articles about Chet Harper's murder. Maybe you'll find a piece of informa-tion that will prove useful."

"Did you know the family?"

Evelyn shook her head. "Not really. I knew the kids by sight and their mother Patricia just to say hello to. She seemed like a nice woman. Harried. Always in a hurry, probably because she worked two jobs. I suppose she had no time for any of life's pleasures."

"I think I'll check out the old newspapers like you sug-gested. I'd love to go through old police reports, but I can't see John letting me do that."

Evelyn laughed. "Not after that warning he gave you. But cases that old might be available to the public—as long as they're no longer active."

"I'll look into that."

I quickly sat down at my computer, intent on doing some research. I clicked on the library's database and started browsing through local newspapers dating back twenty-two years, a few years before Chet Harper was knifed to death. I wanted to see if there were reports of any fights he might have gotten into. I bit my lip when I came across an article about my father being arrested for a heist, though at that point he hadn't lived in Clover Ridge for some time.

And then I found something. There was an article in the *Clover Ridge Tribune*, a weekly paper that was still going strong, from a few months before the murder. Chet Harper had been in a bar fight with a man named Lester Brown. The bar owner broke it up as the police came on the scene. No arrests were made.

Who on earth is Lester Brown? I'd never heard the name, though I knew a Priscilla Brown—a buxom woman in her sixties—who attended all the library's musical events. I typed in her name, curious to see what came up.

"What are you working on so feverishly and intensely?"

I spun around. My part-time assistant Trish Templeton had entered the office.

"Hi, Trish. Did you hear that Daphne Marriott, the psychic who spoke here last week, has been murdered?"

"I did. Sorry about that. I know you liked her a lot. Is what you're looking up related to her murder?"

My mouth fell open. "Am I that predictable?"

Trish laughed. "Carrie, I can read you as easily as one of my kids' books. You want to find the person who killed your new friend."

"I do. And I'm wondering if her death is related to her father's murder here in Clover Ridge twenty years ago."

Trish squinted at me. "What on earth are you talking about?"

I filled Trish in on Daphne's background. Her eyes grew rounder with every fact I provided.

"Daphne Harper. I remember her. She was a few years ahead of me in school. A pretty, quiet girl. I'd heard that her father was a drunk and beat his wife and kids."

My pulse quickened. Why hadn't I thought to question Trish? She'd grown up in Clover Ridge and knew practically everyone in town.

"What do you remember about her father?"

Trish shrugged. "I never had a conversation with him, if that's what you mean. But I think my dad might have known him—from work."

I bit my lip as I thought of Roy Peters. The last time I'd asked him for information involving a murder, Roy had suffered a beating and landed in the hospital. "Do you trust me to ask him a few questions?"

Trish eyed me skeptically. "I suppose, since this goes back twenty years. I can't imagine whatever happened then could have any connection to Daphne's murder."

"Of course Daphne's killer might be her abusive ex-husband. He was bothering her on the Green last Saturday. I had to call over John Mathers to chase him off. But I just found an old article in the local paper about a fight her father had with a man named Lester Brown."

"Lester Brown," Trish repeated. "Call my dad. He'll tell you all about Lester Brown."

Chapter Nine

To my surprise and delight, Roy Peters was happy to hear from me. He was retired from his job with the local telephone company, which had since merged with a larger corporation that also provided TV and Wi-Fi services for our growing number of electronic gadgets that were quickly becoming essentials.

"Hi there, Carrie. Looking for some help solving another murder?"

I laughed. "Roy, you know me too well. I don't know if you heard that a woman was murdered out at the Baxter Garden Apartments."

"Heard it on the news. Sad business. Can't see how I can help you, though."

"It turns out that the woman grew up here in Clover Ridge. Her name was Daphne Harper. Her father was Chet Harper."

"I remember him. A nasty drunk. He worked for the phone company until he got fired. Got into more brawls than you have fingers and toes. Finally, someone had had enough and knifed him."

"Did you know anyone he fought with?"

"Let me think. This is going back years. Some of the guys he drank with and fought with are gone—dead or moved away. Why are you so interested in Chet?"

"I'm wondering if Daphne's death is connected to her father's. I got to know her a bit, and though she didn't say so, I have the feeling she came back to Clover Ridge partly because of her father's murder."

"Hmmm. Well, there was Les. Lester Brown, for one. He was a foreman, and Chet often worked under him. Still, they were pretty good buddies until Chet took it into his head that Les had a soft spot for his wife, Pattie."

I was getting somewhere! "What was Pattie like?"

"Pretty. Soft-spoken. Not strong enough to cope with the likes of Chet. She had to work two jobs to pay their rent. I also think she took a second job to put distance between herself and his fists."

"Do you think it's true—that she and this Lester were having an affair?"

Roy scoffed. "Who knows? Chet claimed she was hardly ever home and he once saw her getting into someone's car late at night."

"But why Lester Brown?"

"I suppose because he was a good-looking guy, divorced, and always flirting with every woman he came across, married or not."

"Does he still live and work in town?" I asked.

"If I remember correctly, he took a job at the Verizon store in the mall. I think he moved to an apartment a few years ago. Hey! Coincidentally, I think it was the Baxter Garden Apartments."

"Quite a coincidence," I agreed. "Thanks, Roy. You've been very helpful."

He laughed. "Good thing there was no chance of anyone hearing us talk about this murder. Just don't mention my name to Lester if you find him—in case he killed Chet's daughter."

"Of course not," I agreed. "Good-bye, Roy. Be well."

What to do? What to do? Should I call John and offer him this information, or find a way to talk to Lester Brown myself? *Both*, I decided.

The library phone extension rang. It was Angela. "Shall we go to the Cozy Corner Café or someplace else for lunch?"

"Are you up for some sleuthing?" I asked my best friend.

"Am I ever! Where are we going?"

"To find out what we can about a man named Lester Brown. Turns out he got into a fight with Daphne's father shortly before he was murdered. Lester lives in the same apartment complex Daphne moved to. Could be she confronted him, accused him of murdering her father, and he killed her too."

"I'm game," Angela said, "but how do you plan to do this?"

"Trish's dad said Lester's working over at the mall. I thought we'd go to the Verizon store and, if we're lucky, have a little chat."

"I'm in," Angela said, "but first let's stop at the Cozy Corner Café for sandwiches and eat them on the way."

"Good idea."

I called John's cell phone and told him what I'd read about Lester Brown in the old news article.

"Thanks, Carrie. Kind of you to share this information."

Was that a note of sarcasm I detected? Had John already known about Lester Brown? "Oddly enough, one of our older patrons said he lives in the Baxter Garden Apartments where Daphne was murdered. Makes you wonder if they crossed paths and she accused him of having stabbed her father."

"It's possible, I suppose."

"Anyway, I thought I should let you know."

"Much appreciated. I prefer this to your going off questioning suspects on your own."

* * *

The mall was a short drive out of town. It had been built a few years ago and was an attractive place to shop. I parked near the Verizon store and, as I feared, it was full of customers buying, updating, and learning about their cell phones during their lunch hour.

Angela let out a sigh of disappointment as we entered the store. "This was a waste of time. There's no way we'll get to talk to this Lester, let alone find out anything."

"Don't be so negative," I said. I glanced around the large room, searching for a good-looking man in his sixties. Since most of the employees were younger, Lester Brown was easy to spot. "I bet that's him—helping that young woman with the long brown hair," I said to Angela. "I'm going to check out the demo cell phones near where they're standing."

I ambled over to the phones, pretending to be engrossed in studying the difference between two choices. From their conversation, I gathered that Lester had successfully solved the young woman's problem with her phone's camera. He was about to call out for the next person waiting for tech support when I tapped his arm.

"I don't mean to jump the line," I said in my most polite voice, "but does this phone—or any of these phones—have an alarm? If someone should break in and attack you . . ."

"I don't think any of them do," Lester said. "But if you're looking for an alarm, they sell them on Amazon."

I pressed my hand to my chest. "Of course! How silly of me! I'm just so upset. I just heard about that woman being murdered. Strangled in her own apartment." I shuddered. "It's so close to where I live."

He pursed his lips. "I just heard. Bad business, that. But no need to panic. Just don't open your door to strangers."

"I can't help but worry since this happened at the Baxter Garden Apartments. I live only a few blocks away. Alone. Except for my bird."

"I see." Lester's dark-brown eyes studied me—at first with curiosity and then with amusement. And suddenly he was laughing.

"Hey, aren't you that librarian—the one with the library cat who's always getting involved in crime investigations?"

I felt my face growing warm. "Maybe I am. Carrie Single-ton. And you're Lester Brown."

He nodded. "I am. I suppose you're here to find out what I know about the murder, since the woman was found a block from my apartment."

"Her name was Daphne Marriott. You might have known her as Daphne Harper."

Lester's mouth fell open. "Chet and Pattie's daughter."

"Yes."

"I had no idea—you said she was living at the Baxter Apartments."

"Yes."

He was gazing off into space. "Funny. I thought I saw her once—in the supermarket a week or two ago. She grew up to look exactly like her mother."

Unless Lester had done a stint at the Actors Studio or the Yale School of Drama, his shocked expression struck me as genuine. It was time to learn what I could. "Did you have an affair with Daphne's mother?"

Lester's eyes lit up, and I caught a glimpse of the sexy, virile man he had been in his younger days. "I did not, as I told her husband repeatedly. Had to give him a licking before he'd believe me. Poor Pattie. She had a miserable life with that SOB."

"Do you know who killed Chet Harper?"

"I have no idea. I felt sorry for their son, Billy. The cops pinned it on him, but I never thought he did it." Lester sighed. "Why? Do you think Daphne's murder has something to do with her father's stabbing twenty years ago?"

I sighed. "I wish I knew."

Chapter Ten

Dylan called me on my cell as Angela and I were driving back to the library. "I've been tied up all morning and just found out that your friend Daphne was murdered. I'm so sorry, babe."

I sighed. "Me too. John stopped by earlier to find out what I knew about Daphne." I glanced at Angela. She was checking her phone for texts, but I had to be careful what I said. Angela was my best friend, but I'd never told her about my relationship with Evelyn. If and when I did, it wouldn't be in a car. I'd told Dylan about my friendship with a ghost when we were driving home from a restaurant and he'd nearly crashed into some bushes.

"Someone in the library told me her story—that her abusive souse of a father was knifed to death twenty years ago."

"I remember that!" Dylan said. "Her brother was charged and convicted of the crime."

"And was exonerated. Daphne said she was drawn to Clover Ridge but never told me why. I think it was connected to her father's murder."

"Tell me you're not starting to investigate," Dylan said.

Angela must have heard him because she burst into giggles.

"Well, I happened to run into someone who got into a fight with Daphne's father shortly before he was murdered."

"Carrie!" Astonishing how Dylan managed to sound angry, exasperated, and frightened simply by saying my name.

"Please don't worry. After talking to Lester Brown, I got the definite sense that he had nothing to do with Daphne's murder—or her father's. Though it is a coincidence that he lives in the same apartment complex as Daphne."

"Damn it, Carrie—you can't rely on your 'definite sense' to decide if someone's a murderer. Criminals lie. They deceive. Tell John about this Lester fellow—that he lives where Daphne was renting and about the fight he had with Daphne's father. It's his job to interview everyone connected to Chet and Daphne Harper."

"I already told John about Lester, thank you very much. I'm sure he'll interview him. And you don't need to worry about me. I just went to the Verizon store where he works. I had Angela with me."

"That's supposed to make me feel better?"

I decided that was a rhetorical question and didn't bother to answer. "Don't forget I'm making dinner tonight. What time do you expect to be home?"

"Six thirty at the latest. I'll call if I'm running late."

I disconnected, unhappy that I'd caused Dylan grief.

"You shouldn't have told him where we went," Angela said.

I shook my head. "I don't want to keep secrets from Dylan. It's like lying and only serves to put distance between us. I'd rather he got angry at me."

Angela chortled. "You'll find out soon enough that some things are better off not shared. I have a list of things I don't tell Steve if I don't want him to blow a fuse. You have to use your judgment when it comes to sharing."

Back at the library, I answered some emails and a few phone calls. Trish headed downstairs to set up the movie for the afternoon, and I walked over to the hospitality desk to put in an hour of signing people up for programs and answering their questions. I missed Smoky Joe—seeing him scampering around the library, pausing to visit with patrons. This was one of the very few days I hadn't brought him to work.

I called my mother to find out how she was feeling, but she never answered. Either she was sleeping or she'd gone out for a walk. I felt bad that the experience of coming to Clover Ridge so she could be with Tom while he was shooting a film had blown up in her face. Ilana's behavior was awful, but even worse was that Tom had done nothing to support my mother. For the first time that I could remember, I felt protective toward her. I didn't like seeing her hurt.

Though my mother and I hadn't been in touch on a regular basis for years, I'd gathered from what she'd told me that her marriage to Tom had been a happy one until now. When had this change in their relationship come about? Was it permanent, or just a phase because he was finally appearing in a movie with well-known actors?

I'd no sooner returned to my office than the phone started to ring.

"Carrie Singleton, programs and events."

"Hello, Carrie. This is Robby Dowd—from Parson's Gym. I need to talk to you as soon as possible."

"Robby, hi." I knew I sounded as puzzled as I felt. "What's wrong?"

"I can't explain on the phone. I hate to bother you at work, but—it's really important. A matter of life or death. Death, actually." His voice caught on a sob.

"Robby—"

"I could get to the library by five thirty."

"I'll be gone by then."

"Dammit, I wasted hours down at the station, and now I'm tied up at the gym until five—if I want to keep my job. Please, Carrie. I have to talk to you ASAP. I swear I'll explain everything, but it's complicated and not something I want to discuss over the phone."

I thought quickly. "The gym is only a short distance from my cottage. Why don't I meet you there? Say five twenty if the traffic's not too bad. Is there someplace we could talk privately?"

"Yes! My boss Greg's office. He won't mind."

"I can only spare half an hour, Robby. Dylan's been out of the country and he just got home last night. Unless you want to tell me now—?"

"Thanks, Carrie. See ya later."

He hung up before I could ask another question.

For the next few hours I carried out my library responsibilities, often wondering what could be troubling Robby. Was the station he was referring to the police station? Of course. What else could he have meant? I suddenly remembered sensing he wanted to discuss something with me a few weeks ago.

Evelyn popped in, and I told her about Robby's strange phone call.

"He sounds like he wants you to help with an investigation."

"What investigation?" I asked.

"You'll find out soon enough." She disappeared just as Susan opened the door to my office.

Then Dylan called to tell me that a new client had stopped by and now he expected to be home closer to seven o'clock. "I'll call if I'm further delayed."

"That's fine," I said. I considered telling him I'd arranged to meet Robby but decided I didn't want to upset him. I'd tell him afterward over drinks.

"How was watching them film this morning?" he asked.

I laughed. "I feel as though that happened days ago. Tom's former fiancée—the actress he ends up with in the movie—kept coming on to him in real time. My mother got upset and said a few things she shouldn't have. Tom was hopeless. He did nothing to stop Ilana from acting like a bitch in heat. I drove my mother back to their rented house. When I called later, she didn't answer the phone."

"It sounds like they're having serious problems. Babe, don't get involved. There's nothing you can do."

"I know. It's frustrating, wishing I could help."

Dylan chuckled. "I can imagine. You love to get in the middle of situations and make them right."

"I guess. I should know by now that the world doesn't work that way."

I left the library at five sharp, eager to hear what Robby wanted to tell me. I couldn't imagine what he thought I could do. Solve some secret problem he had? He knew Dylan was an investigator. Maybe he'd been robbed of something valuable and wanted to ask my opinion before hiring Dylan to retrieve whatever had gone missing.

The gym was full of people. Robby was engrossed in conversation. I waved to him, and a minute later he came over. He put his hands on my arms and met my gaze.

"Carrie, I owe you big-time for this."

"I'll take a few private sessions in payment," I said as a joke.

"You got 'em." He directed me down the hall to the offices. "Greg's gone for the day. He said I could use his office."

Instead of taking the large chair behind the desk, Robby sank into one of the two visitors' chairs and covered his face with his hands.

I turned the other chair so I'd be facing him and sat down. "All right. What's this all about?"

He remained silent for a minute or two. When he looked up, tears were streaming down his cheeks. "My sister is dead. Murdered."

I blinked, trying to take in what he was telling me. "Daphne was your sister."

He nodded.

"Then you're Billy. You went to prison for killing your father."

"How do you know? Did Daphne tell you?"

"No, someone recognized her when she came to the library and told me about your family. But I had no idea that you—"

"Did you know she helped put me away? I was furious with her at the time. Refused to talk to her during the trial or later when she came to visit me in prison, until it dawned on me that Flynn, that SOB, had manipulated Daphne—worked on her until she all but admitted to seeing me knife the old man. Eventually I made it my business to get a lawyer to look into my conviction—a good lawyer this time."

"And you changed your name."

He let out a bark of laughter. "Of course! Who wants to hire an ex-con, even after he's been proven innocent? I wasn't taking any chances. Besides, I didn't have the stomach to put up with the stares, the question in people's eyes when they heard the name Billy Harper.

"I changed my name legally. Dowd is my mother's maiden name. But when the police came by today wanting to talk to me, I told Greg who I really am."

"I'm curious," I said. "If you don't want anyone to know your history, why did you come back to this area?"

Robby snorted. "Good question. I was drawn back, but if you notice, I chose not to live or work in Clover Ridge. Just close enough to look around—"

"Like you did on Saturday."

He nodded. "It sounds stupid when I say it out loud, but—" His expression grew stronger, more resolved. "Carrie, I didn't kill my father, but someone did. Though twenty years have passed, I keep hoping I'll learn something that will tell me who murdered him. I have to know, even if that person has died."

"Daphne said she was drawn to Clover Ridge too. I think it was for the same reason." I held his gaze. "And possibly because she sensed you were here and needed to ask your forgiveness."

"She told you that?" Robby asked.

"Not in so many words, because like you, she didn't reveal her true identity. But tell me, why were you brought down to the police station?"

Robby frowned. "That's easy enough. The police went through Daphne's things and found my phone number."

"Did they think you killed her?"

"I wouldn't be surprised. I have no alibi for the time she was murdered, but they don't have any evidence that I'd ever been to her apartment, so they couldn't hold me."

"When did you find out that Daphne was living in the area?" I asked.

Robby leaned back and stretched out his legs. He seemed calmer now that he was telling me his story. Amazing how sometimes just talking helped to reduce stress.

"She came to the gym to sign up for a month-to-month membership. At the time, I was working with one of my clients. We caught sight of each other, and—" He gave a little laugh. "We each got the shock of our lives. We arranged to have dinner that evening when I finished work and ended up talking for hours."

I nodded. "I'm glad the two of you got to reconnect before she died."

"Before someone murdered her, you mean." His voice grew hard. "That's why I called you, Carrie. I want you to find the person who killed my sister."

Chapter Eleven

I stared at Robby. "I'm not a detective, Robby. Lieutenant Mathers is very good at his job. He's also a good friend of mine. You can count on him to do everything in his power to find the person who killed Daphne."

"Right. Yeah. Excuse me if I don't have the faith you do in the Clover Ridge Police Department. The last guy railroaded me straight to prison."

"John Mathers is nothing like his predecessor!"

"Maybe. I sure hope that's the case, but I've read about you, Carrie Singleton. You've solved a few murders in the area. And you knew my sister."

"I did, and I'm so sorry about what happened to her. I think in time we would have become good friends."

"More reason to find the person who killed her."

I exhaled loudly. "Dylan and John Mathers have told me in no uncertain terms not to investigate her murder."

Robby laughed. "And you plan to listen to them?"

"They're concerned about my welfare," I said, hating how prissy it sounded.

Robby reached over to rest his hand on my shoulder. "Carrie, I don't want you to do anything reckless, but you have a way of finding out things."

I nodded. "I confess I want to help find the person who murdered Daphne. The most likely suspect is her ex-husband. Did she tell you about him?"

"Daphne said he showed up at her library talk—scared her half to death. And he hassled her at that event on the Green." Robby grimaced. "Her ex is one lucky SOB. If I'd caught him with his hands on my sister, he would have ended up in the hospital with a few broken bones."

"I was there and ran to get Lieutenant Mathers. He ordered Bert Lutz to leave town." I shrugged. "I've no idea where he is now. I know John—Lieutenant Mathers— wants to question him."

"Any more ideas?" Robby asked.

I snorted. "I shouldn't be telling you this, but I looked up old newspaper articles from around the time of your father's murder and saw there was an article about a fight he'd had with a man named Lester Brown."

Robby nodded. "I remember him. They were friendly for a while until my father got it into his head that Les was interested in my mother."

"Do you think he was?"

"I doubt it. Les Brown was a big flirt. And I certainly didn't get the sense that my mother cared at all about him."

"What was your mother like around the time of the murder?"

Robby tilted his head to one side as he thought. "She was busy working most of the time. But I remember thinking how weird she was acting—happy one minute and singing a song, then suddenly turning anxious. Frightened."

"Do you think she was seeing anyone?"

Robby shot me a disapproving glance. "That's a funny thing to ask."

"I suppose it's difficult to imagine your mother having an affair, even though your father was abusive."

"Sorry. I have no business censoring your questions. The answer is, I have no idea. Part of me is shocked to think of my mother committing adultery. Part of me wishes she'd had a bit of happiness during those dark years."

He pressed his lips together as he thought. "I never saw any signs of her having a lover, but Daphne told me that a few times she'd passed a man leaving our apartment complex when she was coming home from school. She had a feeling he'd been seeing our mother." He scoffed. "Of course, the man could have been seeing another woman who lived in our building. But I remember a few times when the phone rang, Mom rushed to answer it. She had the strangest expression on her face when she hung up."

"Are you in touch with your mother now?"

Robby shook his head. "No, and neither was Daphne. Daph was horrified when she took off without a word to either of us. Of course she wasn't around at the time of my trial either, which I sorely resented at the time. I think she's remarried and living somewhere in Oregon. I suppose she hated her life with my father so much, she didn't want any reminders of it, and that included Daphne and me."

"I'm sorry," I said. "I know what it's like to come from a dysfunctional family."

"There's one more thing I want to share with you. Recently, Daphne picked up strong vibes from someone who knew our mother."

"That's not surprising," I said. "I'm sure there are plenty of people in Clover Ridge who knew her."

Robby laughed. "Of course, but this is where her new-found psychic abilities kicked in. Daph was out in a public place when she received a very strong sense that someone she'd passed had known and loved our mother very much."

"Was it the man she'd seen a few times leaving your apartment complex?" I asked.

"She wouldn't say. She wanted to make sure before she told me any more."

"How could she make sure? Did she know his name? Where he lived?"

Robby shook his head. "I have no idea. She wouldn't tell me."

"Then Daphne was murdered," I murmured. "That's no coincidence."

He shot me a look of pure anguish. "But why would someone who loved my mother all those years ago want to kill my sister?"

"Did you tell all this to Lieutenant Mathers?" I asked.

"Are you kidding? Do you know how it sounds? Besides, I was pissed at the way they questioned me—as if I'd hurt my own sister."

I nodded. "And you'd like me to find out who did."

"Yes. With all my heart."

* * *

It was close to six thirty when I finally walked through the front door of my cottage. Smoky Joe was happy to see me and led me into the kitchen, where I dropped off the items I'd bought for that night's dinner and fed him a large supper. While he was chomping away, I wandered into the living room. His displeasure at having been left home all day was evident—throw pillows on the floor, a chewed-up magazine; even some papers I'd left on the coffee table had been scattered about.

"Sorry, Smoky Joe," I told him when he joined me in my bedroom after eating his fill. "I know you hate to be left here on your own."

I changed into jeans and a T-shirt, then headed back to the kitchen to prepare dinner for Dylan and me. I set the kitchen table, then heated up the barbecued chicken and roasted veggies I'd bought after meeting Robby, and dressed a salad with my homemade dressing. All the while, my mind reviewed the events of the day.

It was hard to believe it had been just this morning that I'd stopped by the movie set to watch them film a few of Tom's scenes. My mother's interchange with Ilana had upset me, but more disturbing was learning that Daphne had been murdered.

Daphne is dead! Robby is really her brother, Billy Harper. And he wants me to find out who killed his sister. This was both something I wanted to do and something Dylan and John wanted me *not* to. Why was life so complicated?

I exhaled loudly. Maybe there was no mystery here. Sometimes the most obvious solution was the right one. Bert Lutz had probably murdered Daphne. The spouse was always the most logical suspect, and Bert was a hothead and a wife-beater. I'd seen for myself how angry he'd been when he'd accosted Daphne on the Green, furious because she had dared to leave him.

Still, I couldn't help wondering if Daphne's murder was connected in some way to her father's. A farfetched possibility, since that was now a very cold case. Suspects might have moved away or died. Chet Harper had had a violent temper and must have set someone off. Discovering who had murdered him was close to impossible. Neither Roy Peters nor Lester Brown, two people who had known him, could give me any leads.

Dylan came over at seven thirty bearing an expensive bottle of white Bordeaux. "Mmm," I said, taking it from him when I left his warm embrace. "This will go very well with dinner. I'll open it now."

"Allow me to do the honors," he said, following me into the kitchen. "Smells good. What have you created this evening?"

I laughed. "Barbecued chicken and roasted veggies. Straight from a new market," I said, and was relieved when he didn't ask why I hadn't gone to Gourmet Delight.

Over dinner, Dylan told me about the new client who had stopped by his office. "He's a software inventor and thinks one of the three people working for him might be stealing his secrets."

"Sounds intriguing," I said. "How do you plan to catch the thief?"

"I'm working on it. First I have to familiarize myself with the kind of software material Terry's working on. Then I want to understand the working conditions—how they all work together, who has access to Terry's files and how secure they are."

"In other words, you need to gather information and then you'll start investigating."

"I suppose you could put it that way." Dylan laughed. "It's still a far cry from chasing after stolen artwork and jewelry."

I cleared our dishes and turned on the coffee. Dylan stretched his arms overhead. "It's good to be home."

"I hope you stay here a while."

"Me too." He opened his arms, and I slipped onto his lap for a long and satisfying kiss. I loved Dylan and believed we were together for the long haul, which meant I had to get something settled, and the sooner the better.

I stood when the coffeemaker began to make noises and set out mugs and plates for our dessert.

"I stopped by the gym before coming home," I said as I poured coffee into Dylan's mug.

"Really? That must have been one fast workout."

I reached inside the refrigerator for the milk container. "I went there to talk to Robby Dowd."

"Did you start dating him when I was out of town?" Dylan teased.

"He wanted to talk to me about Daphne."

"The woman who was murdered?"

"Yes. Robby's real name is Billy Harper. He's Daphne's brother."

"Oh."

I set the container of milk on the table harder than necessary. "Before you start to lecture me, I need to say what's on my mind."

I drew in a deep breath, hoping I wasn't setting myself up for an impasse in our relationship.

"Robby called me at work and said he needed to talk to me. At that time I had no idea he was related to Daphne."

"But why did he call *you*?"

"Because he knew that I'd helped solve other homicides. He wants me to find the person who killed his sister."

Dylan pursed his lips. "I see."

"I know you hate when I get involved in an investigation because you're worried something will happen to me. I tell you I won't do it again—but I do, and—well, I'm sorry." *That didn't come out as planned.*

"Then you'll explain to Robby that you're a librarian and he should talk to John."

"I already told him to talk to John." I forced myself to meet his gaze. "But I'm sick of apologizing. I'm going to help Robby."

Dylan gaped at me as if I'd just told him I was going to the moon.

I reached over and rubbed his arm. "Dylan, I love you and I love that you care about my safety, but I'm not a child. I can't have you trying to stop me from doing something I believe is important."

I put up my hand to stop him from speaking. "I don't want us to fight over this. I promise to use good judgment and will try not to do anything rash or put myself in danger."

Dylan took my hands in his. "I'm an investigator. I deal with thieves and worse. I've seen men shot and knifed, and I've been in plenty of tough spots myself. It's hard for me to see you involved in another murder investigation. Even before you knew that Robby was Daphne's brother, you went to check out that man who had fought with their father shortly before he was stabbed to death."

"I did. I promise to be more discreet in the future."

Dylan shook his head. "There's no point in arguing with you, Carrie. You're going to do what you feel is right, and I can't change that. All I ask is that you please be careful. I don't want anything to happen to you."

Chapter Twelve

That night Dylan fell asleep holding me close. Though he'd respected my wishes and refrained from berating me for getting involved in another homicide investigation, I knew that he feared for my life. But he seemed cheerful enough when the sun rose on a lovely April morning.

"Since I don't have anything urgent to take care of at the office and you start late today, why don't we have breakfast out?"

"Sounds like a great idea," I said. "Did you have anyplace in mind?"

"There's a cute B and B north of here that serves the best waffles and French toast. I went there with my parents a few times."

"That was years ago," I said. "Are you sure they're still in business?"

Dylan grinned. "Uh-huh. I called them yesterday."

"Sneaky!" I said, bopping him on the head with a pillow.

He bopped me right back. We got into a pillow fight until Smoky Joe jumped on the bed meowing for his breakfast.

"I'll feed you in just a minute," I told him. "And don't worry—I'm taking you to the library as usual. I have to remember to bring some cans of cat food and some more kitty litter. We're running low on supplies."

Half an hour later, Dylan and I were in his BMW, heading for the Westcott Inn. I studied his profile as he drove. His face muscles were relaxed, his mood contemplative.

"Do you have any idea how you plan to start your investigation?" he asked.

I laughed. "None whatsoever. After that big buildup last night, I have no idea where to begin. I have two thoughts, though—either Daphne's ex-husband murdered her, or her death is connected to her father's murder twenty years ago."

Dylan nodded. "A sound deduction."

"Really?" I was pleased by his compliment.

"Sure. Daphne was strangled. There was no evidence of sexual assault or signs that her assailant was after money or valuables."

"Sounds like you spoke to John about it," I said.

"I did."

"Were you going to tell me?"

He shot me a shamefaced grin. "I was, until you mentioned you'd gone to speak to someone you thought might have murdered Daphne's father."

"John put out an APB for Bert Lutz," I said. "I'll know soon enough if and when he's brought back to Clover Ridge for questioning."

"And what are you planning to do about tying Daphne's murder to her father's?"

I shrugged. "Good question. I read through the old newspaper items. The only thing that caught my eye was the argument Chet Harper had with Lester Brown. He seemed to think that Lester was having an affair with his wife. Lester said Chet was way off base on that."

"Maybe she was having an affair, only it wasn't with Lester."

I nodded. "Robby said that Daphne told him she'd picked up vibes from someone recently who had deep feelings for her mother. She was going to check him out."

Dylan rolled his eyes.

"I know. Pretty flimsy information. If only I could speak to Patricia Harper and ask her who this person is. Though of course that doesn't mean he killed her husband."

"Robby's not in contact with his mother?"

"Nope. He said she remarried and lives in Oregon. Oh— and that Dowd was her maiden name."

Dylan patted my knee. "We investigators have our arsenal of tools to track down people who try to fly under the radar. I'll see what I can find out about Patricia Harper née Dowd now Mrs. Something-Else who's living in Oregon."

I leaned over to kiss his cheek. "Thanks so much, Dylan. I can't believe you're helping me with this."

He pursed his lips, pretending to be angry. "Neither can I. But to tell you the truth, I'm overwhelmingly impressed by you, Miss Carolinda Singleton."

"Thank you, my love, but I've told you—I changed my name to Carrie fifteen years ago."

"You'll always be Carolinda to me."

"So much for changing things legally," I said wryly.

We stopped at a light, and Dylan turned to face me. "You have changed, Carrie. You blow me away."

"Really?"

"Without a doubt! You seemed so tentative that October morning you came to look at the cottage—unsure of yourself and your place in the world. And now you're a confident, well-respected member of the community."

I laughed. "I'd just gotten my job at the library. I didn't have enough money to pay what I imagined the rent would be. And then you let me have the cottage at a ridiculously low rate."

"I think I was beginning to fall for you even then."

"And now?"

"I know I'm the luckiest guy around."

"How lucky am I? I now live at the cottage rent-free."

Our fingers entwined, and we rode the rest of the way without speaking.

* * *

The Westcott Inn was a pretty, sprawling, white wood-framed house with a red front door. We entered the narrow hall, and a smiling woman in her midforties led us to a table beside a window in the dining room. I gazed out. Just beyond the lawn, three horses were grazing in a meadow.

"Like it?" Dylan asked.

I took in the muted woven carpet, the knickknacks on the mantel above the fireplace, and grinned. "Can't wait to come back."

"Let's first see how you like the food here," Dylan advised.

Only two of the other six or seven tables were occupied—one with two older women, the other with a couple about our age.

"I imagine this place is very busy during the summer," I said.

"And most weekends," Dylan said from behind his large menu. "I'm having blueberry pancakes."

"And I want French toast with strawberries and honey."

"Good choice."

Our waiter, a slender college-aged young man, approached with a broad grin. "Good morning! My name is Eric. Would you like to start with orange juice? Coffee?"

"Coffee, please," I said. "With cream."

"Orange juice for me," Dylan said. "And we're ready to order."

"Great!"

We told him what we wanted to eat, and he sped away to place our order. I leaned back in my chair and gazed out at the horses.

"Happy?" Dylan asked.

"Very. As long as we're home by twelve fifteen, I'm all yours."

"I have nothing pressing right now. I plan to start interviewing for an assistant in a week or two."

I suddenly remembered. "I haven't spoken to my mother since I drove her home from the film shoot yesterday. I want to make sure she's okay."

I reached inside my pocketbook for my phone and called my mother's cell. It went to voice mail. "I'm beginning to get worried."

"Could be she's watching another shoot and has her phone off," Dylan said. "Why don't you try her again after we eat?"

"Good idea."

Eric brought over Dylan's juice and my coffee and the rest of our order a few minutes later. My French toast filled a large platter.

"Wow! I'll have to take half of this home," I said. But a few minutes later I was finishing off the last of the toast.

Eric was pouring me a coffee refill when my phone played its jingle.

"Maybe that's her," I said.

It was John Mathers, sounding grim. "Carrie, your mother's here at the precinct. I brought her in for questioning."

"Questioning? For what? Why?"

"Ilana Reingold was found murdered this morning. Looks like she'd been struck over the head with a heavy object."

A cold fear washed over me. "Where did this happen?"

"Dirk Franklin, the director, found her in her room at the hotel where most of the cast and crew are staying."

"How awful! But why do you think my mother has anything to do with it?"

"Several of the cast heard her threatening Miss Reingold yesterday, and she doesn't deny it."

"I was there and heard her myself, but she didn't mean it *literally*. She was hurt and angry because Ilana kept flirting with Tom, my mother's husband, and frustrated because Tom acted like nothing was wrong. He and Ilana were engaged several years ago." As I spoke, I realized how incriminating my words sounded.

"Right. That's what the director told me. I'm about to interview the other actors."

"John, this is my mother you're talking about. She wouldn't kill anyone."

"Sorry, Carrie. I advised her to get a lawyer. She said she doesn't know any lawyers in the area."

I swallowed. "Is Tom with her?"

"No, he brought your mother here then took off. I'm not sure where he went."

"I'll be there as soon as I can."

I told Dylan what happened. He went in search of Eric to ask for our bill.

"I can't believe John likes my mother for the crime because she got angry at Ilana yesterday for flirting with Tom," I said as we exited the inn's long driveway.

"Well, unless he has solid evidence to prove she's a viable suspect, I doubt that he can book her."

"She needs a lawyer. I have to call Ken Talbot. He doesn't handle criminal cases, but he has a friend who does. I can't remember his name."

"Phil Demuth. His office is in the same building as Ken's."

"I forgot that Ken is your lawyer too. Do you happen to have Phil Demuth's phone number?"

"Yes. I'll call his office if you like, but Phil's probably in court."

Dylan instructed his phone's virtual assistant to contact Phil Demuth's office. His receptionist answered the call.

"Hello, Irene, Dylan Avery here. Is Phil in, by any chance?"

Irene said Phil was in court and was expected back in the office at two PM. Dylan explained the situation and asked her to have the lawyer call my mother ASAP. He asked me for my mother's cell number, which he then rattled off to Irene. He thanked her and ended the call.

"There's nothing more you can do for your mother now except give her moral support when we get to the precinct."

I reached over to hug him. "Thanks. I'm glad you're going with me. I can't imagine where Tom disappeared to at a time like this."

Dylan shook his head. "Me neither."

I let out a huff of exasperation. "How can John think my mother's guilty? Anyone could have killed Ilana. Most of the actors are staying at that hotel, but she and Tom aren't."

Dylan patted my thigh. "You'll find out more when we get to the station. Bizarre that two women were murdered a day apart in Clover Ridge."

"I'm wondering—is this a man who hates women, or are there two murderers wandering around town? Daphne and Ilana come from two different worlds. They didn't even know each other."

"As far as we know," Dylan said.

Chapter Thirteen

Thoughts of my mother whirled around in my head as we drove to the police station. *Of course she didn't kill Ilana!* When I was growing up, she'd been critical and manipulative. She'd screamed a lot, but she'd never hit Jordan or me when we'd done something that angered her. It wasn't like her to get physical, much less strike someone with an object.

Dylan parked the car in the lot behind the precinct. When we walked in, Gracie Venditto, the police department's dispatcher, was sitting at her desk.

"Hi, Carrie. Here to see your mom?"

I nodded. "And now you've met both my mother and my father." *As suspects in murder cases.*

Gracie shrugged. "It happens."

I leaned over the desk and whispered, "Is she very upset?"

Gracie shot me a knowing look. "She's calmed down some."

"Good."

"She'll be happy to see you. Let me find out if John has finished talking to her."

I let out a sigh of relief. "You mean she's not being charged?"

"I don't think so. Not now, at any rate." She gestured to the row of chairs behind me. "Have a seat. I'll be back soon."

I sat down, and Dylan went off to use the men's room.

"Hey there, Carrie."

"Oh, Charlie! I didn't see you there." I moved to a chair next to Charlie Stanton.

He smiled. "Of course not. You're worried about your mother."

"I am. I'm sorry Ilana's been murdered, but I'm sure my mother didn't do it."

"Really?" He cocked his head. "From what I've read, anyone can be capable of killing when sufficiently provoked."

"What are you doing here?"

Charlie let out a belly laugh. "Waiting to be questioned. We all are. Dirk and Serena are ensconced in other rooms." He winked. "I suspect the police want to make sure we don't collaborate on our alibis."

I glared at him. "This isn't a joke, Charlie! A woman's been murdered and they think my mother killed her."

His expression turned solemn. "I do apologize, Carrie. My morbid sense of humor arises when I'm upset. I'm very sorry that Ilana's been murdered. I've known her for years. We all have. Which is why, I suspect, we are all about to be thoroughly interrogated."

"Carrie," Gracie called out as she came over to where I was sitting. "They're waiting for you in John's office."

I walked down the narrow corridor and entered the open doorway. Dylan followed me into the room and leaned against the back wall. My mother sat hunched over in a chair. Her face was red and blotchy from crying. I was glad to see Tom in the other "guest" chair. He got to his feet and gestured to me to take his seat, which I did.

"Hello, Carrie. Dylan." John was standing behind his desk. "We're just about finished here."

"Good! Does that mean my mother can leave?"

"Yes," John said. "As long as she remains in the area while our investigation continues."

My mother reached for my hand. Surprised, I clasped it in mine. "Thanks so much for coming, Carrie. This has been a terrible ordeal."

"I can imagine," I said. "Dylan contacted a lawyer. He's in court now, but he has your cell phone number and will be calling you soon."

"Thank you." She squeezed my hand and turned to smile at Dylan.

"Brianna, why don't I drive you back to the house so you can rest?" Tom put an arm around her shoulders. "You've had a rough morning."

My mother shook herself free of his embrace. "And where will you be? Where are you off to *this* time?"

Tom winced. "I'll stay with you a while, but as soon as everyone's given their statement, we're having a meeting—to discuss what just happened and decide if and how we might proceed with the project."

My mother glared at him. "Go to your meeting, Tom." She turned to me. "Carrie, would it be all right if I stayed with you? I promise I won't be any bother."

"Brianna, what are you saying?" Tom asked.

"You've made it perfectly clear that you don't want me in your life any longer," she said. "I'll stay with my daughter. And if she won't have me, I'll get a hotel room until I'm free to leave this awful place."

I stared at my mother, stunned by her request. We hadn't lived under the same roof in more than twelve years. My memories of our time together were not pleasant.

But then I'd been a difficult teenager—often acting out and irritable. Now I was an adult, old enough to feel sympathy for this unhappy woman whose life was in shambles. She was my mother and she needed my help.

"Of course you can stay with me, Mom," I said. "Dylan and I will bring you to my cottage and get you settled. In fact, I'll call the library and let them know I won't be coming in today."

My mother smiled at me. "Thank you, Carrie. I appreciate your letting me stay with you, but I don't want you to change your plans in any way. Tom can drive me to the house we've rented so I can pack my bags, then drop me off at your cottage."

"I'll be gone for hours," I began.

"I'll manage," she said. Her tone was firm, but the look she sent me was a plea for understanding. "Please. Let's not argue."

I got it. She *wanted* to be alone—at least for now—and not have to answer the many questions I was bound to ask. I was scheduled to work late that day, but I'd leave the library at five instead.

"Okay. I'll see you later." I gave Tom directions to the cottage and the door key and security system code to my mother. "I'm afraid I'm low on groceries, but we'll manage."

My mother pursed her lips. "In that case, Tom and I will stop at the supermarket and pick up a few items."

"Whatever you say, Brianna," Tom said. He sounded resigned.

* * *

"What have I done?" I asked Dylan the moment we exited the precinct. My good intentions had been replaced by a feeling of panic. "I can't remember spending one hour with that woman when we weren't arguing over something."

My heart was pounding. "And I have no idea how long she's planning to stay. What if she decides to leave Tom and wants to live with me? I couldn't bear it!"

Dylan burst out laughing.

I stopped in my tracks and glared at him. "What's so funny? I'm terrified she'll try to run my life. And what if she *is* a murderer? What then?"

Dylan pulled me close. When I tried to speak, he put his finger to my lips. He held me until my racing heart slowed. Finally, he released me.

"You don't have to be terrified of your mother. You're an adult now, Carrie. Linda or Brianna or whatever she's calling herself these days has no wish to take over your life. You did the right thing, letting her stay with you. She's distraught— from being a suspect in a homicide case and because she might be heading toward her second divorce."

"You think so?" I asked.

"I do. It has to be devastating."

"It seemed to come about so suddenly. I mean, I thought she and Tom were getting along."

"So she led you to believe. They might have been at odds for some time. Even when you asked to stay with them."

"I never considered that."

Dylan chuckled. "And keep in mind—if things get too grim, you can come and stay with me."

I kissed him. "Good to have a backup plan."

I was feeling considerably better when Dylan dropped me off. I placed towels in the guest bathroom and carried my computer from the guest room, which I used as my office, into my bedroom. I put Smoky Joe in his carrier and we set off for the library. I saw how happy he was to be there after spending the previous day alone in the cottage. He dashed from room to room, stopping to accept pats and words of adoration from patrons, his bushy tail held high. He really was a social creature!

"Isn't today a late day for you?" Sally remarked when I stopped by her office. "It's barely eleven o'clock."

"Did you hear? This morning one of the stars in the film they're shooting was found murdered in her hotel room."

"No!" Sally looked concerned. "Another murder. What's happened to our sleepy village?"

"I don't know," I said, "but my mother was questioned, along with everyone connected to the film. She'll be staying with me, so I came in early and would like to leave at five, if that's okay."

"Of course it is," Sally said, as I'd hoped she would. "Susan will be here, and we don't have anything special scheduled tonight."

When I got to my office and sat down at my desk, I couldn't focus on work. Trish came in and found me staring at my computer screen. I told her Ilana Reingold had been murdered.

"I heard about it on the radio driving over here." She shuddered. "It's scary to think someone's going around killing women in Clover Ridge."

"Unless there are two murderers," I said.

"That's even worse—isn't it?" Trish said.

"I suppose. Are things running smoothly here in the library?"

"The lights kept flickering during the Zumba class. I called Max and he found the problem—a bad fuse. Would you like me to check on the other programs in progress?"

"Thanks, but I'll do it. Might as well, since I can't focus on anything that requires concentration."

The current-events group was having a heated discussion about the increase in property taxes. The Friends of the Library were discussing their next book sale. I returned to my office just as Trish was leaving.

"Sally asked me to man the hospitality desk for the next hour," she said.

"All right. I'll start laying out the June-July newsletter."

"Marion just emailed us the news regarding the children's section. I texted Harvey. He's sending us his tech-related info later today."

I beamed at my super-efficient assistant. "Thanks, Trish."

She grinned back at me. "No problem."

Trish knew that things had been kind of cool between Harvey Kirk and me since he'd come to think I'd suspected him of having murdered someone—which I kind of had.

My office phone rang as Trish left the office. It was Angela. She sounded hurt.

"Why didn't you tell me about the murder and your mother and everything?"

"I was going to—over lunch. Sally told you the news?"

"She did."

"John suspects that my mother may have killed Ilana. She was furious at the way Ilana was making a play for Tom and said so yesterday in front of everyone."

"Oh no! Do you think it's possible she killed Ilana?"

I let out a deep sigh. "I like to think she didn't, but how can I know for sure? Angela, she asked to stay with me, and I told her she could. Tom's dropping her off at the cottage as we speak."

"But why? Are things that awful between them?"

"Maybe. He hurt my mother terribly by ignoring her and going along with Ilana's outrageous behavior. The odd thing is, Ilana's flirting was so over the top. Now that I think about it, I wonder if it wasn't all an act."

"What do you think she was after?" Angela asked.

"You mean besides winning Tom back? I have no idea."

We agreed to meet at noon at the back door to walk over to the Cozy Corner Café as usual. Nothing had changed, but I felt better after talking to my best friend.

I pulled up the June-July newsletter on the computer and smiled at the masthead that Susan had drawn: an adorable sketch of children swimming in a lake with adults watching them from the shore. That girl was so talented!

"What's this I hear about another murder?"

I looked up. Evelyn was in her usual position—perched on the corner of Trish and Susan's desk.

"Can you believe it?" For the fourth time that morning I related the little I knew about Ilana's murder.

Evelyn listened closely. When I'd finished, she said, "That was kind of you—letting your mother stay with you, given your past history."

"I don't know how smart it was, but I had no choice. She was very upset and didn't want to stay with Tom. He was clearly taken aback by her decision."

Evelyn gave a snort. "A good move on your mother's part. It gives Tom a chance to stew over what life would be like without her."

"Hmm. I never thought of that," I said.

Evelyn cocked her head. "Do you think your mother murdered Ilana?"

"I find it hard to believe. The only reason John suspects her is because she threatened Ilana yesterday—in front of all of us."

"Letting off steam," Evelyn murmured.

"That's what I thought. I mean, who threatens someone, then goes ahead and kills them? Too obvious."

"Your job is to find out more about Ilana. Who knew her before coming to work on this movie? Who had reason to want her dead?"

"Actually, Charlie, Dirk, and Serena had all worked with her on previous movies."

I felt a chill as Evelyn stepped closer to me. "Talk to your mother. She's an excellent source of information."

Chapter Fourteen

S moky Joe moved about so frantically inside his carrier, I nearly dropped him before we reached the cottage door.

"I know. You smell the great outdoors and long to go roaming. Sorry, pal, but I can't let you do that."

"Meow!" he answered, sounding very unhappy indeed.

I set him free in the hall and followed him into the kitchen, where I found my mother humming along to a sixties song on the radio as she set the kitchen table—for three.

"I'm glad you're in a much better mood," I said as I fed Smoky Joe his dinner.

"I'm feeling a bit calmer. Phil Demuth called, and we had a long chat. He says the police can't charge me based solely on what people heard me say to Ilana the other morning."

"Well, that's a relief." I gestured to the table. "Is Tom coming for dinner?"

"No. I told him we need to spend some time apart to think about our marriage."

My mother cocked her head at me. "Do you know where he disappeared to as soon as he delivered me to the police station? To call Ilana's brother to break the news to him." She grimaced. "Turns out he and Tom had gotten pretty close when Tom and Ilana were dating."

"I'm so sorry," I said.

She dropped into a chair and sighed. She'd put on lipstick and eye shadow as usual, but her air of despair made her look all of her fifty-six years. "A few of my friends told me I was a fool to marry a man twelve years younger than me, but Tom and I were madly in love. Yes, madly in love." A smile hovered around her lips. "In fact, it was Tom who insisted we make it official. He was so attentive. So caring."

"I saw how Ilana was behaving," I said. "It was so—blatant. Almost as though she was acting."

My mother nodded as she thought. "Funny, that crossed my mind—afterwards. But I'm more concerned about Tom's behavior. He was like a puppy dog, lapping it all up." Her lip curled. "If I were going to kill someone, it would be Tom, not Ilana."

Time to change the subject. "Then who's coming to dinner?"

"Who do you think? Dylan, of course. He called to see how I was holding up. I told him I was making dinner and invited him to join us. He'll be here as close to six thirty as he can make it."

"Oh!" For a minute I was too surprised to say anything else. "I'm glad you did. With our work schedules, Dylan and I don't get to have dinner together very often during the week."

My mother fixed her gaze on me. "Carrie, it was nervy of me to invite myself to stay here, but I was desperate. I promise it won't be for long. And while I'm here, I don't want to keep you from your boyfriend."

"Good to know. Anything you'd like me to prepare?"

"Not a thing." She stood. "I'm going to lie down for half an hour; then I'll add a few ingredients to the salad and heat up what dishes need heating up that I bought in that fantastic gourmet place in town."

*   *   *

I changed into jeans and a T-shirt, then plopped down on the living room sofa to watch the local news station. I clicked on the closed captioning and turned down the volume so it wouldn't disturb my mother. A young Latina reporter questioned Dirk and Serena outside the hotel where Ilana had been murdered early that morning. They expressed shock and sorrow that someone they had known and worked with over a period of years had been so brutally murdered while they slept a short distance away in their rooms.

Someone they had known and worked with over a period of years. That sounded interesting. It must have struck the reporter as interesting as well, because she then asked if they knew if anyone else Ilana had worked with would have reason to kill her.

Dirk let out a false laugh. "In our business, egos can get easily bruised. Tempers flare. But deep down we movie people are practical realists. After any burst of emotion, we move on and work together as a team to create a movie our audience will love. That's our job. Our purpose in life."

Wow. He's as good a spin doctor as he is a director.

"I see," the reporter said. "So you don't think anyone Miss Reingold knew might have murdered her?"

"Of course not! We all loved Ilana."

The reporter turned to Serena. "Do you feel the same way, Miss Harris?"

Serena frowned. "I feel the deepest sorrow for Ilana and her family, and frankly fear for my own safely. I am terrified that a crazed serial killer is going around murdering women. What kind of a place is Clover Ridge? Poor Ilana was the second woman to be killed in two days. I've asked your police chief to place an officer outside our hotel, but he claims there isn't enough manpower to do that."

Serena glared at Dirk. "I'm hoping the studio will provide a private guard until the murderer is apprehended."

What a diva! But I couldn't blame her. I'd be petrified in her situation.

"Are you planning to continue filming your movie?" the reporter asked Dirk.

"There is the possibility that we will. A good deal depends on whether I can find a suitable replacement for poor Ilana. It won't be easy, but I have started interviewing actresses for the role." Dirk released a deep sigh. "Tomorrow morning we're holding a brief memorial to celebrate Ilana's illustrious life. Sadly, none of us will be attending her funeral, as it's being held in her home state of Pennsylvania."

He put on a brave face. "But movie people are resilient. Firestone Productions hopes to carry on with this project. If I can find the right person for the part, I intend to see it through." He glanced at Serena. "As does everyone involved. We'll soldier on as usual."

I chuckled as I clicked off the TV. Dirk made his cast and crew sound like a troop of Marines ready to go into battle. Though most of it was blatant PR, I found it interesting that he was already on the hunt for Ilana's replacement. Despite Dirk's claim that they were quick to get past personality clashes, it was obvious that Ilana had had a volatile personality. She might have offended someone grievously.

She'd broken off her engagement to Tom, which meant I couldn't leave him off the list of suspects. Especially if she happened to have rebuffed him a second time.

At six fifteen my mother appeared. She'd changed into another blouse and pants and looked well rested.

"That's a great bed you have in your guest room," she said. "Much more comfortable than the one in the house Tom and I were renting." She grinned. "Maybe I'll stay here indefinitely."

My expression must have revealed the shock her words had given me, because she burst out laughing. "I'm only teasing, Carrie. But that nap was the best sleep I've had in ages."

I hesitated, then said what I was thinking. "You and Tom haven't been getting along?"

"Not for some time. I thought it was because he wasn't getting any parts. Oh, a bit part here, a commercial there, but nothing like this movie. I even broached the possibility of his going back to his old job." She grimaced. "That blew up in my face. And then he was asked to audition for the role of Luke in this movie. He was thrilled, but it didn't help things between us. When I heard he'd be playing opposite Ilana—frankly, I was worried."

"Why? Did you think Tom was still in love with her?"

My mother shrugged. "The truth is, until recently, I'd never given it much thought. I met Tom a few years after their relationship had ended. After *she* ended it."

"I figured it would be her doing," I said, not wanting to tell my mother that I'd Googled Ilana. "Did Tom ever say why she broke it off with him?"

"Only in general terms. They had a whirlwind romance. The successful financier and the beautiful actress. They got engaged and were planning their wedding when Ilana got cold feet. She grew more and more distant. She finally told Tom she wasn't ready to get married—though she was no kid at the time. He was devastated, but he insisted he was over her. And we were happy!" My mother said the last sentence emphatically, as if she wanted to convince me—or herself.

I wrapped my arms around her and hugged her tight. "I'm sorry, Mom. Stay here as long as you like and decide what you want to do with the rest of your life."

My mother reached up to kiss my cheek. "Thank you, Carrie. I never expected that you would turn out to be my safe haven." She glanced down at her watch. "Oh my! Enough of this chitchat. Dylan will be here soon. Let's have dinner ready when he arrives."

She had made some wonderful selections at Gourmet Delight—fish baked in what smelled like heavenly sauce, a platter of asparagus covered with slivered almonds, whipped potatoes, and a salad of baby greens with honeyed walnuts, strawberries, and goat cheese. There were Italian pastries for dessert.

"What a treat," I exclaimed.

"Let's not forget the mini croissants." She gestured with her chin. "They're on the counter."

"I love these!" I removed them from the paper bag and slid them into the toaster oven to warm up.

Dylan showed up a few minutes later. He took me in his arms and kissed me, then gave my mother a peck on the cheek, which pleased her no end.

Who is this woman and what has she done with my mother?

Dylan handed me a bottle of wine. "A chilled Chablis," he said.

My mother lifted it deftly from my grasp. "I'll do the honors. You and Dylan sit down and start on the pâté."

"I didn't know—" I shut up as I watched her remove a dish of pâté from the refrigerator.

Dylan's eyes were gleaming. "Is that from Gourmet Delight? I love their pâté."

"I do too," I said, "though it's so expensive."

My mother waved the corkscrew in her hand. "An occasional indulgence is good for the soul."

"Why are you in such a good mood?" I asked. "You spent the morning being interrogated by the police and you're taking a break from your husband."

"The truth?" She paused to fill our three wineglasses. "Because I feel free. As though I'm on vacation. All the stress that built up this past month is gone—at least for now. My lawyer assured me that they can't charge me based on my outburst, and I believe him. As for Tom—I'm very hurt and disappointed, but maybe it's time to call it quits on our marriage. He was very sweet when he drove me here, but I think he's secretly relieved that I decided to move out of our rented house."

Dylan lifted his glass. "Here's to you, Linda—er, Brianna. You're one hell of a brave woman."

"To you, Mom." I sipped my wine.

"Thank you both," my mother said. She smiled at Dylan. "Linda will do. I've decided my Brianna days are over."

I giggled. "Whatever made you change your name in the first place?"

My mother shrugged. "I thought it made me sound . . . younger. Silly, isn't it?"

I smeared pâté on a croissant and took a bite. Ah, heaven!

"My lawyer also said my best chance of avoiding all future charges regarding Ilana's murder will be when her killer is found—the sooner the better."

"Lieutenant Mathers is an excellent detective," Dylan said. "He's recently solved some homicide cases."

My mother grinned. "Imagine my surprise when Phil told me that my own daughter had played a major role in solving those cases."

I glanced at Dylan, who was frowning. To downplay the situation, I said, "I only did some checking; asked a few questions."

"Linda, Carrie isn't a trained investigator," Dylan said. "She came close to getting herself killed when she tracked down one of those murderers."

"You're a trained investigator, Dylan. I'm sure you can give my daughter some advice on how to stay safe while chasing down clues." My mother looked at Dylan, then at me. "I'd feel so much better knowing that someone close to me was actively looking for the person who killed Ilana Reingold."

Chapter Fifteen

As quickly as my mother had opened the subject of wanting me to investigate Ilana's murder, she closed it by serving the rest of our meal. We were too busy eating to say much besides how wonderful everything tasted. That is, my mother and I commented on each dish. Dylan remained silent. I knew it bothered him that my mother, who was supposed to care for and protect me, didn't hesitate to put me in harm's way.

But how could I not get involved? Regardless of what her lawyer had told her, my mother was a suspect in Ilana's murder. I didn't want to see her brought up on charges if she was innocent. And if I'd told Billy Harper I'd try to find out what I could regarding Daphne's murder, how could I do less for my own mother? Besides, the two cases might very well be related.

Still, I couldn't help wondering if she'd known all along that I'd investigated murders in the past and had arranged to stay with me so she could urge me to find Ilana's killer. For once, I didn't mind her scheming. I was eager to solve this case.

When we finished eating, I helped my mother clear the table. She loaded the dishwasher while I put on a pot of coffee and arranged the Italian pastries on a platter.

"Let's have our dessert and coffee in the living room," I said, "while you tell us everything you know about the people in the cast and crew and their relationship to Ilana," I said.

I placed cutlery, napkins, mugs, and dishes on a tray and asked Dylan to set it down on the living room table. I followed behind, carrying a tray of milk, sugar, a fresh pot of coffee, and the pastries. "Don't worry," I whispered. "I won't do anything stupid. I promise."

"You better not," he growled back. "As for her—it's one thing for you to decide to look into a case; it's another for a mother to deliberately put her daughter's life in danger."

We sat down on either side of the table—Dylan and me on the sofa, my mother in a chair—and I poured coffee into our mugs.

My mother bit into her cannoli, sipped her coffee, then said, "Tom was thrilled when he got a call from his agent that Dirk Franklin, who is based in New York, wanted him to try out for the role of Luke in his next indie film. Now that I look back, I can only wonder if Ilana asked Dirk to call him."

"She'd worked with Dirk before?" Dylan asked. At last he was no longer pouting and was showing interest in the case.

My mother cocked her head. "They'd all worked with each other before—Serena, Charlie, Ilana, the crew." She laughed. "The men had their own special connections with Ilana."

"How exactly?" I asked.

"Interludes. Affairs. Whatever you want to call it. Tom said she'd been with Dirk and Charlie. Even Ronnie Rodriguez, the cameraman."

"What about Serena Harris?" I asked.

"From what Tom told me, there was no love lost between the two women, though years ago, when Ilana first started in films, they were friends."

"What was Ilana into—what did she like to do when she wasn't working on a film?" Dylan asked.

My mother pursed her lips. "She liked to party and have a good time."

"Was she on drugs?" I asked.

My mother shrugged. "I have no idea. She liked to gamble. Tom said she had him go with her to Las Vegas for three, four days at a time. He'd get bored and go back to the room while she stayed at the tables till the wee hours of the morning."

"Ilana and Tom were engaged once. Do you think she was trying to get him back?"

"It sure looked that way, though now that I've had time to think about it, I'm not so sure."

"So what do you think she was up to?" I asked.

My mother sipped her coffee. "Years ago Tom told me he doubted that Ilana was capable of love. He thought she'd learned to pretend to have feelings but never actually felt anything."

"Then why was she making a play for Tom?" Dylan asked. "Was it a game for her? Out of malice?"

My mother finished off her cannoli. She appeared to be deep in thought as she chewed and swallowed. "Those are good questions. I'm sorry, but I don't have an answer for you."

"Did she need money?" I asked. "Maybe she thought that Tom was wealthy since he'd been in finance."

My mother laughed. "He was—years ago. Sure, he still kept his hand in the stock market, but we've been living on what he earned in previous years. We manage to pay our bills and not much else."

Dylan leaned forward. "I hate to ask you this, but do you think your husband killed Ilana?"

"I doubt it, though Tom was out when I woke up this morning. He claims he went for a walk, but the car felt warm when we got into it to drive to the precinct. I have no idea where he went or why he lied to me."

"Had they argued?" I asked.

My mother shrugged. "I don't know."

"What about Charlie Stanton and Dirk? Did they have any issues with Ilana that you know of?"

"I heard her arguing with Dirk yesterday afternoon, but I think it was about something in the script." She shook her head. "Surely no director would kill off one of his actors because she had a complaint about her lines."

"I would hope not."

The landline phone rang. I headed to the kitchen to answer it.

"Hi honey," my father greeted me. "What the hell's going on in Clover Ridge? Two murders in two days! I sure hope you're not trying to solve them."

"Hi, Dad. It turns out I knew both victims. Mom was questioned about the second one. Ilana Reingold was in the movie playing opposite Tom. In fact, years ago Tom and Ilana were engaged to be married."

My father whistled. "Some coincidence, eh? But why were they questioning your mother?" He sounded concerned.

I explained why, then added, "Mom's pissed at Tom. She's staying here with me." I lowered my voice, though my mother couldn't possibly hear me from where she was sitting in the living room chatting with Dylan. "I think that marriage is over. Kaput."

"That's too bad," my father said, not sounding sad at all.

"Ilana kept coming on to Tom. I saw for myself how he was eating it up. Of course Mom was upset, but Tom didn't seem to care. I can't blame her for wanting at least some time apart."

"But why did you invite her to stay with you? You and your mother have never gotten along."

"She asked to stay with me. I suppose I felt sorry for her, so I said she could."

"Caro, I hope you know what you're doing."

"Me too."

For a minute, there was silence. "I'm worried about you—and your mother, strange as it may seem."

"You are?"

My father exhaled a lungful of air. "I'm thinking Linda needs me there—for moral support."

I felt my blood pressure rise. "I don't think so, Dad. Bad idea." *Where is this coming from?*

"It's the right thing to do. Your mother's really hopeless in a crisis."

"But why do you care? And—and what about your girlfriend?"

"What girlfriend?"

"The one you've been seeing? The one—never mind."

My father laughed. "Now don't you go concerning yourself with my love life. I'll check out flights and get back to you, let you know when I'll be arriving."

"But Dad—you can't stay here!"

"Of course not, honey. I'll bunk down at Dylan's house. Talk to you soon."

As soon as I returned to the living room, Dylan knew I was upset about something.

"Um, Dylan, can I speak to you—in private?"

My mother shot me a questioning look. "Is it about Ilana's murder?"

"No, something else."

Dylan followed me into my bedroom. I closed the door and in whispers told him that my father was flying to Clover Ridge and planned to stay with him.

"Sounds like he still cares about your mother."

I sat down on my bed and held my head in my hands. "That's all we need! My mother's married, remember?"

Dylan laughed. "Right! To Tom, who she's thinking of leaving."

"It isn't funny. It's as screwy a plot as the movie they're making—if they ever finish it."

Dylan took me in his arms. "We'll straighten it all out. I'll call your dad and try to head him off."

"Meanwhile, let's not say anything about this to my mother. She deserves a peaceful night's sleep before Jim Singleton shows up."

Dylan left, and after straightening up the kitchen, I told my mother I was off to bed. She said she'd stay up and watch some TV, then go to sleep.

The phone didn't ring, so I had high hopes that Dylan had been successful. Then, just as I was drifting off, I heard a ping on my cell phone and read Dylan's text.

Sorry only managed to delay his arrival one day. Sweet dreams, my love. Talk to you in the a.m.

*   *   *

I woke up the next morning and checked on my mother. She was in the kitchen, making herself a cup of coffee with the Keurig machine, which I hardly used anymore.

"Morning, Mom. How did you sleep?"

"Fine. Where do you keep your paper towels?"

I pointed to the pantry. "In there. Have you seen Smoky Joe?"

"The cat? I let him out."

"You what!"

"He was scratching at the front door, so I let him out. Why? What's the problem?"

"Smoky Joe isn't allowed outside."

"Well, excuse me! How was I supposed to know?"

"I'm sorry. You're right. I never got to mention it with everything going on."

"When we had Jasper, he always went outside."

"And got into cat fights and nearly got run over twice."

"It's so isolated here, there's no danger of a car hitting him. Don't worry, Carrie. He'll be back soon."

I dashed out the front door and looked around. Of course there was no sign of him. "Here, Smoky Joe! Come home!"

I circled the house, calling to him. "Come home, Smoky Joe. I'm going to feed you!"

He'd been longing to go outside ever since the weather had turned warm. I tried not to focus on the fact that I wouldn't be searching for him now if my mother wasn't staying with me. No point in dwelling on that. I was worried about my little kitty. Smoky Joe was probably hungry, unless my mother had failed to mention that she'd also fed him this morning. In which case, he could very well be gone for hours.

"No luck?" she asked when I came back inside.

"No."

"He'll come home when he's good and ready."

"It's almost time for me to leave for work. I can't have him wandering around outside until I get home!"

"I'll try to entice him inside with some treats."

The irritation I'd been suppressing finally escaped. "Who knows if that will work. Smoky Joe hardly knows you!" I made a face, the same face I used to make as a teenager when she did something that frustrated me.

"There's that expression I remember so well!" she said. "I'm not totally useless, Carrie; really I'm not. I'm capable of luring your cat back into the house."

Her cell phone rang before I could reply. She pursed her lips as she listened to the caller.

"Yes, Tom, I'm aware that you must be upset. You can only imagine how I've been feeling this past week."

She stared at the ceiling as Tom replied. "No, I don't want to talk to you this morning or anytime today, so don't stop by Carrie's cottage." Another pause. Then, "I'll be perfectly fine here enjoying the peace and solitude on my own after what I went through yesterday."

Frowning, she listened for a minute. "Yes, I'll call if I change my mind, but I won't." She ended the call.

"Will you be okay on your own?" I asked. "I could come home at lunchtime, if you like."

"There's no need, Carrie. I'll be okay—I'll watch some TV and think about my future."

Just then I heard a loud meow coming from outside. I hurried to the front door and opened it. Smoky Joe tore into the house and headed for the kitchen.

My mother was grinning. "See, I told you he would be back when he was good and ready. I suppose he didn't want to miss his day at the library."

"Or his breakfast," I said as I got a can of cat food from the pantry.

"I think we can take this as a sign that things are looking up," my mother said. "The police will figure out who murdered Ilana, and I'll come up with a plan for the rest of my life."

Chapter Sixteen

I pulled into a spot in the library parking lot, eager to immerse myself in library programs and events instead of in family crises. With my mother as my houseguest and my father due to arrive in Clover Ridge tomorrow, my personal life was beginning to seem like a soap opera even to me.

When Angela stopped by my office, I told her my father was coming to Clover Ridge to give my mother moral support. I certainly wasn't expecting her reaction. Her eyes twinkled as she beamed at me.

"Oh, Carrie. That is the most romantic thing I've ever heard! Jim still loves your mother after all these years."

"I don't think that's the case, Ange. At least I hope it isn't the case."

"What's wrong with you? Having your parents get back together is the dream of every child of divorce."

"Perhaps a child of ten or even seventeen. I'm thirty years old, in case you've forgotten. As for my parents, they've been—"

The library phone rang, cutting short this ridiculous discussion. It was Sally asking me to stop by her office. Angela took off, and Evelyn decided to accompany me on my short walk to Sally's office.

"It is rather odd that Jim wants to come here for your mother's sake."

"So you've been eavesdropping," I complained. "Have I no privacy?"

Evelyn chuckled. "Guilty as charged. I must say, Carrie. Your life is constantly full of surprises."

"Lucky me," I grumbled.

When I reached her office, Sally handed me a list of movies she thought our patrons would enjoy seeing. She'd recently started watching foreign and indie films and asked if she could make suggestions regarding the movies we showed to our patrons.

"These look wonderful," I commented as I scanned the titles. "I really must go to the movies more often."

Sally laughed. "Carrie, your life is like a movie. Speaking of which, what's happening with the movie they were filming now that poor Ilana Reingold's been murdered?"

"I heard Dirk Franklin say on the evening news that they hope to go ahead with the movie. He's looking for a replacement for Ilana right now."

Sally waved a dismissive hand. "Yesterday's news."

I stared at her. "What are you talking about?"

"Liane Walters called me this morning. Dirk's been brought in for questioning again. She's terrified John Mathers is about to charge him with the murder."

"I had no idea," I said.

Back in my own office, I wondered about the latest development in the homicide investigation. Dirk Franklin a murderer? He was slender—actually slight—and had struck me as totally nonthreatening. I shook my head, annoyed with myself for even thinking someone was incapable of murder because he didn't look the part. From my own experience, I ought to have known better than to judge someone guilty or innocent based on his demeanor. John must have had good cause if he was questioning Dirk again.

My office phone rang. "Hello, Carrie. It's Robby. Robby Dowd."

"Hi, Robby." I felt a moment of panic. Was I supposed to have gotten back to him? With all that was happening, I couldn't remember. And why was he still using the name Robby Dowd? I supposed because I was the only person around who knew his real identity.

"I called to see if you've found out anything new regarding my sister's case—or my father's."

"Sorry, I've been occupied with family matters. My mother's husband's in the movie they're filming here in town."

"And Ilana Reingold was murdered only a day after Daphne. They had me down at the station yesterday for one of their 'interviews.'"

"They can't think you had anything to do with Ilana's murder!"

"That's the thing about having been in prison, whether you've been exonerated or not." He scoffed. "I'd never even spoken to the woman, much less known who she was, until I stopped by the Green when they had that meet-and-greet event with the movie people on Saturday."

"I can't see any connection between the two murders, or with your father's twenty years ago," I said.

"Me neither," Robby said. "Daphne never mentioned knowing Ilana Reingold. They didn't exactly travel in the same circles."

"I haven't got a clue," I admitted. "They weren't murdered the same way. But there is something I did—I asked Dylan to find your mother. That would be helpful, don't you think? Maybe she'll tell us who she was involved with all those years ago."

"If she really had a lover. Thanks, Carrie, but I'm beginning to think that idea is nothing more than grasping at straws."

I hung up, sadly agreeing with him.

Later that day, driving back from lunch with Angela at our favorite Indian restaurant, I called my mother. "What have you been doing?" I asked.

"I went for a walk along the river. I'd forgotten how lovely this area is, especially in spring."

"Has Tom called?"

"Several times," she said. "He's desperate for me to come back to our rented house, but I'm not ready to do that. I don't know if I want to live with him any longer."

To change the subject, I told her that Dirk had been brought in for questioning again.

"Better him than me," my mother said.

I had to agree with her. "I'll be home around five twenty."

"See you then."

Back at the library, I found Tom pacing outside my office.

"Sorry to barge in here like this, Carrie, but I need to talk to you about your mother."

I bet you do. Tom's eyes were bloodshot, his hair, usually gelled into place, was disheveled, and his shirt was half in, half out of his jeans.

"You look as though you haven't been sleeping," I said as I opened the door and ushered him inside.

"How can I sleep with everything that's been happening— Ilana murdered, Brianna staying at your place? I'm a total wreck!"

Trish rolled her eyes. Without uttering a word, she left what she was working on and exited the office.

"Tom, it's not my place to interfere in your relationship with my mother." I sat down.

"Please, Carrie. You have to make her see reason."

"What reason? You humiliated her by acting like you and Ilana had the hots for each other."

"That was it! We were acting. I told Brianna, but she refused to believe me."

You did? "Why would you do that?"

Tom sank into the other chair and exhaled loudly. "She was trying to make Dirk jealous."

I found it difficult to picture Dirk in bed with Ilana, the seductress. "Ilana was in love with Dirk?"

Tom lowered his eyes. "Not exactly, though they had been romantically involved."

"So . . . I don't get it."

Tom cleared his throat. "Dirk recently inherited a bundle of money. Ilana wanted Dirk to marry her. She was in debt and desperately needed the cash."

Ah! Got it. "How did she rack up so much debt?"

"Gambling."

"And Ilana thought by playing up to you, she'd made Dirk jealous and he'd ask her to marry him." I frowned at him. "Sounds awfully pathetic to me."

"I know, but she was desperate, and I'd agreed to help her."

"Why?"

"Why?" he echoed. "Because she asked me to."

"From what I saw, you were beginning to fall for her all over again."

He nodded. "Just a little. Ilana had that way about her."

"My mother saw it too, no matter how much you insisted it was all an act."

Tom met my gaze. "But I love Brianna. I need her in my life."

"From the little she told me, you haven't been getting along for some time."

"I was feeling down for a long time, but it had nothing to do with Brianna. My career was stuck. Outside of a few bit parts, I wasn't getting any acting roles. But then this came along."

"And so did Ilana," I said wryly.

"Will you tell Brianna that I love her and I miss her?"

"Yes," I said, "but I get the impression she's trying to decide what she wants for her future." A devilish impulse prompted me to add, "My dad heard she was questioned about Ilana's murder and he's concerned. He feels obliged to come to Clover Ridge to give her moral support."

Tom's expression turned to one of pure anguish. "Jim Singleton's coming here?"

I nodded. "Do you have any idea why the police questioned Dirk again?"

"I ran into him just before I drove here. The poor guy was trembling. The cops found out that he and Ilana had been seeing each other. Not only that—they questioned him about his previous visits to Clover Ridge."

"On Saturday, Dirk mentioned that he used to come here to visit his cousin, Liane." I thought a minute. "Did the police say why they were interested in his previous visits?"

"They wanted to know if he'd been romantically involved with anyone around twenty years ago."

I told Tom once again that I'd give my mother his message, and he left my office somewhat calmer than when we'd started our conversation. I turned on my computer but found it difficult to settle down to work. For one thing, the fact that Tom obviously still loved my mother came as a surprise. I now had a better understanding of his behavior, not that I condoned it. Ilana had asked him to pretend to want her back, he'd kind of fallen for her again, and now she was dead. He hadn't treated my mother right and he knew it. And now he wanted things to go back to the way they were.

I had no advice to offer my mother. Only she could decide if she wanted to stay married to Tom. I wished my father wasn't coming to Clover Ridge. Much as I loved him, he had no horse in this race. He could only complicate matters.

Surely my parents weren't about to fall in love with each other all over again—like the plot of this movie. That was fantasy. They had both moved on to new lives, other relationships.

Then it occurred to me—maybe I wasn't being fair to my father. He had changed more than my mother had these past few years. He was now a law-abiding citizen with a good job.

Maybe he *was* only acting as a Good Samaritan when I'd told him my mother had been questioned as a murder suspect and it looked like her marriage was on the rocks. Only a few months ago *he* had been a murder suspect. At any rate, there was nothing I could do to stop him from coming now.

I was pulled from my thoughts when my cell phone sounded its jingle. My heart sank as I read the name: *Phil Demuth.* My mother's lawyer.

"Hello, this is Carrie Singleton."

"Hi, Carrie. Miss Singleton. Phil Demuth here. I'm in the Clover Ridge police station with your mother."

I heard voices—too low to make out any words. "Why? What happened?"

"As we speak, your mother is being questioned again regarding the murder of Ilana Reingold."

"But why? I thought after yesterday she was cleared."

"So did I. But they got the results of the fingerprints found in Miss Reingold's hotel room. Your mother's prints were on the door handle."

Chapter Seventeen

I told Trish I was going to the police station and raced to my car. Minutes later I stormed into the precinct. Gracie raised her eyebrows when she saw me red-faced and out of breath.

"John's in his office with your mother and her lawyer."

"Is she being charged?"

"No clue. It's been a full house today. I can't imagine John's charging the whole bunch of them. We haven't enough cells."

"Can I join them, do you think?"

"I'll find out."

Gracie left and returned a few minutes later. "John said he's almost through interviewing your mother. She'll be out very soon."

Thank God he isn't holding her! I released a lungful of air. I was too tense to sit, so I paced the small waiting area. Why were my mother's prints in Ilana's room? She'd never mentioned going there.

My mother looked subdued as she walked toward me. Her lawyer, a Paul Giamatti look-alike in a gray three-piece suit, followed a few paces behind. She murmured something to him, and he approached.

"Carrie, pleased to meet you. I'm Phil Demuth." We shook hands.

My mother gave me a shamefaced smile. "Sorry to drag you away from work, Carrie."

"How did you get here?" I asked.

"Phil drove me."

"I can drop her back at your cottage"—he glanced at his watch—"if we leave right now. I'm meeting a client at my office in forty-five minutes."

"Is there anything I should know?" I asked him.

"Linda's not being charged, though Lieutenant Mathers might want to speak to her tomorrow."

"I'll drive her home," I said, and turned to my mother. "Wait here. I want to speak to John before I leave."

John was on the phone when I entered his office. He cut his conversation short when he saw me.

"Sorry, Carrie. Your mother's prints were on Ilana Reingold's doorknob and a few articles inside her room."

"That doesn't mean she murdered her."

He exhaled loudly. "Of course it doesn't, and—off the record—she's not my number-one suspect in this homicide. The trouble is, when I questioned her yesterday, she never mentioned entering Ilana Reingold's room."

"She's been staying with me. I'll drive her home now."

"Good. She worked herself into quite a state when I questioned her."

"Probably because she's having marital issues on top of all this."

"So she said."

"She doesn't know it, but my father's flying in tomorrow. To give her moral support."

John burst into a loud guffaw. "That's all we need—Jim Singleton on the scene."

In the car, I told my mother we'd swing by the library so I could collect Smoky Joe, then head for home.

"I am so sorry, Carrie. I never wanted to be a burden to you," she said.

"Why did you go to Ilana's room?"

Silence.

"Mom?"

"Why do you think? To tell her to stop flirting with Tom. I told her she had her chance to marry him years ago, but instead she broke it off and broke his heart."

"What did she say to that?"

My mother pursed her lips. "She laughed at me. She said Tom still loved her and she could have him back anytime she wanted. I was furious. I wanted to hurt her. I picked up the vase . . ."

My heart began to pound. "And you hit her with it?"

She shook her head. "No, but I wanted to. Believe me, I wanted to."

"Then what happened?" I asked.

"Ilana seemed to change course. She said it would all be over soon and then I could have Tom back."

"She wanted to make Dirk jealous," I said.

"How do you know that?" my mother demanded.

"Tom came to see me at the library. He's miserable and he wants you back."

"What does he think—he can flit from me to Ilana and back again?"

"I think," I said slowly, "that he was flattered when Ilana asked him to show interest in her and it got out of hand."

My mother turned to study my expression. "It sounds like you're advising me to go back to Tom."

"Only if you want to."

"I don't know if I can trust him," she said softly.

I drew a deep breath. "I have to tell you something. Dad's coming to Clover Ridge."

"Jim is?" Was that *pleasure* I heard, mixed in with her surprise? And why was she patting her hair? "I haven't seen him in years."

"He's concerned about you and wants to be supportive. He's flying in tomorrow."

"He's actually coming here because of me? There's no need for that," my mother said.

"Which is what I told him, but I couldn't change his mind. He's going to stay with Dylan."

I pulled into the library parking lot and turned off the engine. "Be right back," I said.

"I don't mind spending time in the library while you finish your day's work."

"Really?"

She nodded. "I'll find some magazines to read or chat with some of your colleagues. It will be a relief to talk to someone not connected to the police or those movie people."

"Well, all right, if that's what you want—but Mom, they're bound to ask you questions about the movie and Ilana."

My mother shot me a knowing look. "Carrie dear, I'll be fine."

And she was. I left her chatting with Angela, who offered to show her around the library during her break. After greeting Susan and giving her an abbreviated version of my trip to the police station, I buckled down to some much-needed paperwork. I finally came up for air at four thirty, when I left my office to check on my mother and found her sitting at a table in the coffee shop with Marion, the children's librarian, and Katie, who ran the coffee shop.

"Your mother's been regaling us with stories about you when you were little," Marion said.

"Really?" I said, wondering what on earth she'd remembered or had made up to tell them.

"Carrie dear, you're so lucky to be working in this library," my mother said. "Your coworkers are by far the nicest group of people I've met in a long time."

Katie beamed at me. "And we feel the same about Carrie."

"Thank you," I said. "Mom, we'll be leaving for home in half an hour. Please come to my office at five o'clock."

"I'll be there!" she said with a grin. Socializing with my colleagues seemed to have cheered her considerably.

My mother was practically euphoric on the drive to my cottage. She went on and on about how proud she was of me. I had finally settled down. I had a good job and a wonderful man in my life. She finished by saying, "Who knows? I might become a grandmother in a couple of years."

Who is this woman and what has she done with my mother? "Mom, what put you in such a good mood?" I asked.

"Aren't you glad that I am?" she asked, sounding peeved.

"Well, sure—I guess. I'm just surprised that you seem so happy after the harrowing day you've had, being questioned again by Lieutenant Mathers."

"Carrie dear, I know I didn't murder Ilana Reingold, and I have confidence in Phil Demuth."

Oh no! A thought struck me like a bolt of lightning, and I didn't like it one bit. "Mom, please tell me your good mood isn't because Dad is coming."

"And what if it is? I'm deeply touched that Jim's coming all this way because I've been interrogated in a homicide case."

"What about Tom?" I asked.

"What about him?"

"I'm just wondering if perhaps you should give him another chance."

"We'll see about that. Anyway, enough about this. I'm tired, and I'm going to close my eyes until we're back at your cottage."

* * *

While my mother rested in her room, I watched the local news on the living room TV. There were no new developments regarding the two homicides.

Dylan called me from his car. "I'm on my way to the airport to pick up your dad."

"You're kidding! I thought he was arriving tomorrow."

"He changed his plans. Talk to you later."

At six thirty, I was heating up last night's leftovers when my mother came into the kitchen. She opened the cupboard and started setting the table.

"Wine or water?" she asked.

"Whichever you prefer."

"I think water tonight."

"Then water it is," I said.

She reached for the tumblers and placed two on the table.

We chatted as we ate. I was surprised. There were no criticisms. No bragging. "This is nice," I said when I'd swallowed the last of my dinner.

"It is, isn't it?" My mother put her hand on mine. "I quite like having a daughter."

I frowned. "Why didn't you like having a daughter years ago?"

My mother studied my face. "I loved you and Jordan—really I did—but I didn't have the stamina to deal with your father and raise two kids on my own. I'm sorry, Carrie, for not being the kind of mother you would have adored."

I nodded. "I suppose I wasn't the easiest daughter in the world."

"You weren't, but I was the adult. I should have tried harder."

Something inside me urged me to get up and hug her. "I'm glad I have you now."

She wrapped her arms around my waist and squeezed. "Me too."

Chapter Eighteen

M y mother and I were having coffee and dessert in the
living room when the doorbell rang.

"Caro, honey!" My father enveloped me in a bear hug as
soon as I opened the door. Peering over his shoulder, I shot
Dylan a questioning look.

"Jim wanted to surprise you both."

"He sure did," I said, then concentrated on observing my
parents.

My father was holding my mother at arms' length, a devilish grin on his face. "Linda! Why, you don't look a day older
than when I last saw you."

My mother blushed. "Thank you, Jim. You're in pretty
good shape yourself."

Indeed, my father looked handsome and trim and considerably younger than his fifty-eight years—just one of the many
benefits of going straight and getting a job he loved.

I rolled my eyes at Dylan as my father hugged my mother
considerably more gently than he'd hugged me.

"What are we in for?" I whispered.

"Don't ask me. They're your parents."

My mother and father sat side by side on the sofa. Were they . . . ? Yes, they were holding hands. I was longing to yank their hands apart when Dylan murmured, "Leave them be."

I was shocked by my impulse. Equally shocked that Dylan had known what I was thinking.

With their foreheads bent toward each other so that they almost touched, my parents conversed in low tones. I heard my mother mention Tom a few times, my father asking about the murder.

"Did you have dinner?" I asked Dylan.

"I grabbed something at the airport, but I can eat."

"Dad, want something to eat?"

"Whatever you have, Caro, would be nice."

"And to drink?" I asked over my shoulder as I walked into the kitchen.

"Why don't we open a bottle of wine?" my mother said.

"Now?" I asked. "It's almost nine o'clock."

"A nice red would suit me," my father called out.

"Got it," Dylan said, and hurried to open a bottle.

I took leftovers, cheese, and bread from the fridge and placed them on the kitchen table. I put out plates, cutlery, and wineglasses. My parents were still engrossed in conversation when they joined Dylan and me in the kitchen.

Dylan and my father piled food on their plates and started eating. In between, Dylan and my father fell into conversation about a case they'd both worked on.

"I'm so glad you finally have a legitimate job that you like," my mother said to my father.

"Like?" he roared. "I love working with Mac and Dylan."

I smiled at my father, pleased that he was happy and looking so well.

Jim winked at me, then covered my mother's hand with his. "Linda, I hope you take your time deciding what you want to do—about your marriage and your future."

"Right now my main concern is not being charged with killing Ilana Reingold. My lawyer thinks they don't have a solid case against me, but I've started to worry again."

"All I can say is, John Mathers is an upstanding lawman," my father said. He turned to me, "And your own daughter is an excellent detective. When I was a suspect in a homicide a few months ago, she made it her business to find the real killer."

Three pairs of eyes regarded me with various expressions. My father beamed at me with pride and my mother studied me with speculation, but Dylan was the first to express what he was thinking.

"While Carrie has proven to be a remarkable detective, she is not a *trained* investigator. If you'll remember, Jim, by chasing after that killer, she managed to put herself in harm's way—which is not something we want."

"Of course we don't," my father agreed.

Time to redirect the conversation. "I thought the police were looking at Dirk Franklin as a possible suspect."

"They were," my mother said, "because of his personal relationship with Ilana and because he's been visiting his cousin here in Clover Ridge since he was a kid." She frowned. "Though I can't see what that has to do with anything."

Dylan and I exchanged glances.

"Come on. Out with it," my father coaxed.

"A man named Chet Harper was murdered twenty years ago," Dylan said. "His son was tried and convicted for the crime but later exonerated. Chet Harper was the father of the young woman who was killed the other day."

"The day before that young actress was murdered," Jim mused.

"And the old homicide was never solved." My mother scoffed. "Sounds like your police chief is looking to tie up three murders with a neat ribbon."

Dylan frowned. "Linda, John Mathers isn't that kind of a cop. If two or all three of the murders are connected, he'll find the link. Otherwise, he'll keep an open mind."

"You're saying there might be two killers," my father said.

"Possibly three," I said, "if we include Daphne's ex-husband. Still, I can't help wondering if her murder is related to her father's all those years ago."

"What do you know about the twenty-year-old murder?" my mother asked.

"The man was an abusive drunk," I said. "He beat his family and got into bar fights. Someone knifed him one night when he was home alone."

"Sounds like there must have been plenty of people who wanted to kill him," my father said, "yet they never came up with the right person."

"Could his wife have murdered him?" my mother asked.

"She was at work."

"I still don't understand why Lieutenant Mathers was so interested in the possibility that Dirk might have been in Clover Ridge when this man was murdered all those years ago," my mother said.

"Because the police suspect that Chet's wife had a lover who might have killed Chet because he'd been mistreating her," I explained.

My mother laughed. "I can't see Dirk in the role of gallant lover."

"Why not, Mom? This was twenty years ago. Dirk would have been in his midthirties."

My mother pressed her lips together as she thought. "Well, why doesn't the man's widow tell the police who this person was?—unless she's no longer alive."

"She left town right after the murder, moved to the West Coast, and changed her name," Dylan said.

"Her son Robby Dowd—that's what he goes by now—recently came back to the area to find his father's murderer. He happens to work in the gym Dylan and I belong to."

My father chuckled. "Now there's a bit of good detecting right there. Carrie, how did you find out this Robby Dowd was Chet Harper's son?"

I felt my cheeks grow warm. "Robby told me himself. He knew I'd been involved in a few homicide cases, so he asked me to help him find his sister's killer—possibly the same person who murdered their father. He thought his mother might have had a lover, but he can't ask her because he has no idea where she's living. I asked Dylan to try to track her down."

"So without this woman's testimony, there's no way of knowing who her lover was," my father said.

"*If* she had a lover. *If* he's still alive," my mother said. "Lots of ifs in this story."

Dylan cleared his throat. I sensed his hesitation about what he was about to share. "The woman once known as Patricia Harper is very much alive. She remarried some years ago and is presently living with her husband across the sound on Long Island."

I grinned. "That's brilliant. Good job, Dylan!"

"Actually, Rosalind, my secretary, deserves all the credit. All I did was show her some of the various ways to locate people who don't want to be found," Dylan said.

"Have you told John?"

"Not yet," Dylan said. "I will, of course, but right now he's concentrating on the two current homicides."

"I know Robby will want to see his mother ASAP."

"Maybe that's not such a great idea," Dylan said.

"Why shouldn't he?" I asked. "Don't you think he deserves some answers? His mother took off, leaving him and Daphne when the police were already treating him as a suspect."

"Of course he deserves answers. That woman has a lot of explaining to do."

The doorbell rang, startling us all.

"Who on earth could that be at this time of night?" my mother said as I headed to the front door.

Dylan followed me into the hall. "Ask who it is before you let anyone in."

"I plan to," I said, pissed that he thought it necessary to state the obvious. "Who is it?" I called out.

"It's Tom, Carrie."

I cracked open the door. My mother's husband loomed in the doorway. He looked more disheveled than he had when he'd shown up at the library. What's more, he now reeked of liquor.

"I want to speak to my wife."

"Now isn't the best time."

"It is for me," he said as he pushed his way inside.

Chapter Nineteen

"Tom! What are you doing here?" my mother asked as she joined Dylan, Tom, and me in the hall.

"I need to talk to you, Brianna."

"It's late, and you should leave."

Tom strode past us and glanced at my father, still sitting at the kitchen table. "It doesn't look like you're about to go to sleep anytime soon. In fact, I'd say you're having a party."

"Not a party exactly." My father came to stand with us. "Just some old friends getting together."

Old friends, my foot. I couldn't remember if Tom and my father had ever actually met, so I made the introductions as any good hostess would. "Tom, this is my dad, Jim Singleton. He's spending a few days here in Clover Ridge. Dad, Tom Farrell."

"A pleasure," Jim said.

Tom ignored my father's outstretched hand and glared at my mother. "So, Brianna, we run into a few problems and you call on your ex for comfort and consolation?"

"Don't be ridiculous! I didn't invite Jim to come here. And please stop calling me Brianna. My name is Linda."

Already sloshed to the gills, Tom was totally incapable of dealing with the scene he'd encountered when he'd entered my cottage. He opened his mouth, but no words came out. Feeling sorry for him, I took his arm and escorted him into the kitchen. "Why don't you sit down and have something to eat?"

He nodded. "Thanks, Carrie. I never had dinner."

I viewed the contents of what remained in my refrigerator and brought containers of chicken salad and tuna salad and more bread to the table. I grabbed the half-empty bottle of wine and slipped it into the pantry. Wine was the last thing Tom needed.

My father and Dylan returned to their places at the table and resumed eating. My mother hovered in the hallway. I beckoned to her and pointed to my seat. She made a face but sat down.

Silence reigned as I put on a large pot of coffee. I had a feeling the evening was far from over.

"I understand you're here to make a movie," my father said to Tom.

Tom nodded. He swallowed what he was chewing, then said, "We were making great progress; then one of the actors was murdered."

"How terrible," my father said.

"Tom's costar and former fiancée," my mother said.

"Nothing like keeping it in the family," my father said.

Was that supposed to be humorous? I glared at him, but Jim didn't notice. If anything, he seemed to be enjoying himself. Having made an effort to be social, he returned to his conversation with Dylan, for which I was grateful, as it filled the silence looming between my mother and Tom.

When the coffee was ready, I poured everyone a mug, then said, "Tom, I know you came here to speak to my mother. You can go into the den and talk to her there."

My mother shot me a look of reproach. "Carrie, it would have been appropriate to ask *me* if I want to talk to Tom."

"Sorry, but I'm caught in the middle, seeing you're both here in my house. Please talk to Tom, find out what he wants, then . . . I don't know. Do something!"

"Thank you, Carrie," Tom said softly as he got to his feet. He seemed calmer, more in control of himself. "Brianna, Linda—whichever you prefer—I'd like you to hear me out."

My mother nodded. She followed Tom into the den and closed the door behind them.

Five minutes passed. Ten. The door remained closed. Finally, Tom walked out, shaking his head. I hurried to him. "Are you all right?" I asked.

"As good as can be expected." He looked morose but completely sober as he headed for the front door.

My mother waited until he was gone before she joined Dylan, my father, and me in the living room.

"Do you want to tell us what just happened?" my father asked as she sank into one of the chairs.

My mother could be very private when she chose, and I expected a snippy reply. Instead, she released a deep sigh. "Tom just admitted he'd been unfaithful to me with Ilana. He apologized for having lied to me and begged me to forgive him."

"Why on earth did he feel it necessary to tell you now?" my father demanded. "After all, the poor woman's dead."

"Because he's expected down at the precinct first thing tomorrow morning for another interview." My mother cringed, and I knew how hard it was for her to share all this with us. "Tom thinks they must have found his fingerprints in Ilana's room—on the nightstand or the bed linens, if they can get them off fabric."

"I believe they can," Dylan said softly.

"Anyway, he figured that word would get out somehow, and he didn't want me to hear about his . . . indiscretion as a bit of gossip."

I moved to stand beside my mother and put my arm around her shoulders. "That must be a shock to your system."

She blinked back tears. "Especially after he swore repeatedly that nothing happened between them."

"Did Tom say when it happened?" Dylan asked.

"It was the night she was murdered. After I had words with Ilana, I went back to the house we were renting, took a sedative, and fell asleep. Tom said he was too restless to watch TV. Since it was only a little past nine o'clock, he drove to the hotel to see who was around. He found Ilana in the lobby chatting with Serena. She invited him to her room for a drink, and it—just happened." My mother rubbed at the tears streaming down her cheeks. "Just happened, my patootie. He said when it was over, he was horrified by what he had done. He got dressed and left."

"What time did he leave?" Dylan asked.

"Tom wasn't sure, but he said he was back at our place at eleven fifteen."

"Do you think Tom killed Ilana?" I asked.

169

My mother glared at me. "Don't be ridiculous, Carrie. Of course he didn't."

"They could have argued," Dylan said. "After all, she'd broken things off once, and suddenly she was coming on to him to make Dirk jealous. It's enough to make any guy crazy. Add liquor to the mix."

My mother shook her head. "Tom's not one to explode in anger. He internalizes his pain. Don't think for one minute that I plan to go back to him, but I know he didn't kill Ilana."

"Then who did?" my father wondered. "Someone in the cast or crew?"

"Could be, since she opened her door to whoever it was after Tom left," Dylan said.

"Except I don't see how that ties in with the other murder," my father said.

My mother rose to her feet. "This has been an exhausting day. I'm going to bed."

* * *

My mother was still asleep when I was ready to leave for work the following morning. I considered calling Sally to say I'd be taking a personal day so I could stay home with her, but I decided I couldn't neglect my job because of my mother's marital problems. Besides, weird though it seemed, my father had come to Clover Ridge to offer her his support and I, for one, was glad he was here.

I called Jim's cell. He picked up immediately.

"Morning, Caro. Your mother up yet?"

"Still sleeping."

He chuckled. "Linda does love her beauty sleep. Dylan's gone for the day. I'm about to run out and buy some fresh bagels to bring over to your place for our breakfast."

"In that case, I'll leave the alarm off and the side door unlocked. And Dad . . ."

"Something bothering you?"

"You're not . . . er . . . thinking of getting back together with Mom."

"Of course not, honey."

"She's still married. And you two are so very, very different. Like water and oil."

My father let out a deep sigh of exasperation. "Caro, I'm simply trying to be there for your mother when she needs a shoulder to lean on. I like to think in some small way it helps make up for all the times I wasn't there and should have been."

Is this my father talking? "All right, Dad. Talk to you later."

* * *

Though the day was expected to eventually turn sunny, it was drizzling when I brought the cat carrier into the library. As soon as I released Smoky Joe, he took off to visit with his many friends. I walked over to the circulation desk to say hello to Angela and give her an abbreviated version of last evening.

"It sounds like a sitcom," Angela said with a grin. "Do you think your parents will get back together?"

I shuddered. "My father says no, and I can't even imagine such a thing happening. They're two very different people in very different places in their lives. My mother just learned that her husband was unfaithful to her and that he might be charged with murder. As for Jim, I suspect he has a girlfriend he's keeping under wraps."

"Do you think Tom killed Ilana?"

"I don't. Trouble is, I can't imagine who did."

"My money's on Dirk," Angela said. "He was in a relationship with Ilana and he used to come to Clover Ridge to visit relatives."

"Still, there's no evidence that he was here twenty years ago when Chet Harper was murdered." I sighed. "From what I can see, there are no clues leading to any one person. There are no clues, period. John seems to focus on one suspect after another, but he can't make his case."

Angela raised her eyebrows. "Maybe it's time you did some investigating on your own."

"I plan to—from a safe distance. My days of chasing after suspects are over," I said, then headed to my office.

I'd no sooner turned on my computer than the library phone rang. It was Robby.

"Hi, Carrie. Have you learned anything new regarding my sister's murderer?"

"Sorry, no. I've been caught up in the other homicide that may or may not be related to Daphne's murder. For a short while, my mother was a suspect because movie people overheard her threaten Ilana Reingold. And now my mother's husband is being questioned by the police as a possible suspect. Though I can't see how this is connected to Daphne."

Robby sighed. "Me either. I'm calling to tell you that the police have released Daphne's body. Her cremation is this afternoon. I've arranged a memorial service in her honor. I hope you'll attend."

"I'd like to very much. When is it?"

"Sunday, two days from now. At the Quaker meeting house down the road from the gym. I'll text you the details."

"Robby, Dylan's secretary was able to track down your mother."

Robby released a few deep breaths. "Really?"

"Yes. She's remarried and is living on Long Island. Last night we had a rather upsetting gathering at my house and I forgot to get the information from Dylan. I'll call you back as soon as I speak to him."

"Thanks, Carrie. I can't begin to tell you how much this means to me. I need to talk to my mother. Find out why she abandoned Daphne and me when we needed her."

"Robby." I hesitated, knowing he wasn't going to like what I was about to say. "She may not know herself why she left. Or give you the answer you want to hear."

"She owes me an explanation," he said stiffly.

"Do you want to hold off on Daphne's service—until you contact your mother so you can offer her the chance to attend?"

"No," he said firmly. "Given how she ran out on us, she's not welcome at the service."

"I understand. I'll send you your mother's address and whatever else Rosalind was able to find out."

As soon as I ended the call, Evelyn appeared. She shook her head in mock amazement. "My goodness, Carrie. There's never a dull moment where your family's concerned."

"You heard me talking to Angela."

She nodded. "I was passing by and happened to hear you mention your father, and so I stopped to listen to the rest."

"Right now Tom's being questioned down at the police station while my father's having breakfast with my mother," I said. "Jim insists he's only being a Good Samaritan."

"Could be that's all there is to the matter," Evelyn said. "Besides," she said, perching on the edge of my assistants' desk, "he's not the only one who's been looking after your mother."

For a minute I didn't know to whom she was referring. "You mean me."

"I do."

"I feel sorry for her. Tom finally admitted that he betrayed her with Ilana. She says their marriage is over, but I don't know if that's true. Tom still loves her. And my mother's been badly hurt. She's not in any condition to make such a huge decision."

Evelyn was grinning at me.

"What's so funny?" I demanded.

"Nothing. I'm smiling at your compassion. Your loving-kindness."

"Well, she is my mother," I said begrudgingly. "And lately she's been too upset to criticize me or put on airs."

"Perhaps, but I think you and your mother are learning to relate differently to each other."

"Could be," I admitted. I smiled. "I'm glad she's back to being Linda again."

"The good solid name she was born with."

"I suppose you heard my conversation with Robby."

Evelyn nodded. "I did. Dylan's secretary located his mother. I suppose Robby is pleased that she's been found. That should make for an interesting conversation."

"If she agrees to speak to him. Robby's intent on asking his mother why she took off when she did. She may not be willing to talk about that."

"There are more important matters at stake," Evelyn said.

"Yes. Finding out if she had a lover. And if so, what was his name."

"I'm thinking that you're the one person who can ask her that delicate question." Evelyn sent me an enigmatic smile and faded before I could protest.

Chapter Twenty

I called Dylan to get the information about Daphne and Robby's mother. He was on the phone with a client, but Rosalind was happy to fill me in on how she'd tracked down Patricia Harper.

"Very clever of you," I said, when she had told me all the details.

"It's all thanks to that boyfriend of yours. Dylan told me where to look, and I followed my instincts. Both helped me find what you wanted." I heard papers rustling, then, "Patricia Harper now calls herself Sheila Rossetti. Rossetti is her married name. Here's her address in Medford."

I jotted down the address and phone number and thanked Rosalind. Then I called Robby's cell phone, but it went to voice mail.

"Call me when you're free," I said. "I have your mother's new name, address, and phone number."

That taken care of, I worked on the June-July newsletter for an hour. I'd just finished laying it out and getting it ready for the printer when my father called.

"Caro, I'm down at the precinct with your mother. I think you should know. Tom's in deep doo-doo."

"Why? Because his fingerprints were found in Ilana's room? He expected them to show up, given that they'd spent time there together." I sighed. "I hate to say it, but it looks like John is getting desperate. First Dirk, then Mom, and now Tom's in the hot seat."

"Unfortunately, there's no doubt he was there that night."

"Which, knowing Tom, I'm sure he didn't deny."

"There's more, Caro."

My heart began to race. "Tell me, Dad."

"Tom was seen talking to your friend Daphne Marriott."

"Really? Who saw him?"

"Serena Harris said she saw them in conversation last Saturday at the meet-and-greet on the Green."

"So? I'm sure plenty of people stopped to speak to Tom that day."

"Serena also saw them talking the night Daphne was murdered. She told your friend John that Tom and Daphne were having an animated conversation in the street near Daphne's apartment."

"How did Serena know who Tom was talking to?" I said.

"She had no idea who the woman was until she saw Daphne's picture in the newspaper. Tom is insisting he never spoke to Daphne after the event on the Green. He remembers going out for a walk the night Daphne was murdered, but the only person he says he exchanged words with that evening was a woman walking a dog. Daphne didn't have a dog."

"Dad, Tom needs a lawyer."

"Your mother called Phil Demuth to represent Tom. Phil said he would, but if he does, he can no longer be her lawyer in case there's a conflict of interest."

"Mom agreed to it?"

"She sure did. She's terribly upset about this latest development. She wants to do everything she can to help Tom."

"Is John planning to arrest Tom?"

"We don't know. Meanwhile, Linda plans to remain at the precinct as long as Tom's being questioned. I'm staying with her."

"Thanks, Dad. Would you like me to come down there during my lunch hour?"

"No, honey. I'll keep you posted on what's happening."

"I'm so glad you're here in Clover Ridge."

"I am, too. Family has to support one another."

I laughed. "Interesting that you consider Mom and Tom family."

"The concept of family has taken on an elastic meaning these days. Gotta go. Talk to you later."

Trish joined me in the office, and I brought her up to date on what was happening regarding my mother and Tom and the murder cases.

"Do you think this Serena is telling the truth?" Trish asked when I'd finished.

"I don't see why she has any reason to lie."

"Still, I think John needs more than that to hold Tom for the murder."

After Trish left to bring the newsletter to the printer's, I was about to lock the office and set out for the Cozy Corner Café with Angela when Robby called me. I gave him the information regarding his mother's whereabouts.

"Thanks, Carrie. I appreciate this." I heard the hesitation in his voice and waited to hear what he wanted to add. "I was wondering—would you be willing to come with me when I talk to her?"

"I'd be happy to, though it will have to be when I'm off from work. I'm afraid I can't take any more personal days."

"Of course. Let me know what day is good for you," Robby said. "I'd like to speak to my mother next week, if possible. I'll reschedule my appointments accordingly."

"I'll let you know as soon as I get my work schedule for next week. I should have it in a day or two."

*   *   *

Later that afternoon, while Susan and I were discussing the artwork for the August-September newsletter, my father called to say that John was allowing Tom to leave the station.

"That's good news," I said. "It means John doesn't have enough evidence to hold him."

"He told Tom not to leave the area."

"I'm not surprised."

"Er . . . Carrie, I'm driving your mother to the cottage so she can pack up her things. She's moving back to the house she and Tom are renting."

"You're kidding!"

"That's what she wants, and I'm not about to argue with her."

"Do you think she's doing the right thing?"

Jim let out a deep exhalation. "Honey, when it comes to romance, I don't even try to venture a guess. From what I've seen of your mother and Tom, they seem to need each other."

"All right. Whatever." After a minute, I asked, "Does it upset you—Mom going back to Tom?"

My father roared with laughter. "Not in the slightest."

"Dad, you have someone stashed away in Atlanta, don't you?"

"Honey, I gotta go. Talk to you soon."

"It's a good thing you have a key to the cottage. Don't forget to shut off the security system."

"Will do. It's the first thing I do when I enter a home."

"Ha! Is that supposed to be a burglar joke?" I asked.

When Dylan called shortly after, I gave him the news about my mother and Tom.

He laughed. "Well, I can't say I'm surprised."

"Why do you say that?" I asked.

"A certain type of woman is inspired to great dedication and sacrifice when the man she loves is in trouble."

I thought a moment. "I suppose you're right. Besides, I think my mother and Tom truly love each other."

"And need each other," Dylan added.

"Mmm," I agreed.

"Like you and me, babe."

I grinned. "So nice to hear you say that."

"Hey, you want to go out for dinner tonight? I was thinking some nice quiet place. Nothing fancy."

"I'd love to. Things have been too hectic lately."

"I'll pick you up at six thirty, quarter to seven—depending on traffic. I'll call on my way home."

"Looking forward to it."

Hardly an hour had passed when my mother called to tell me she'd moved back into the rented house. "Thanks so much for putting me up, Carrie."

"It was my pleasure," I said. "Though it was under difficult circumstances, I'm glad we got to spend time together."

I disconnected and looked up to find Susan laughing. "What's so funny?"

"Your personal life is so demanding, it's amazing you have any time for work."

*　*　*

At five o'clock I hunted down Smoky Joe, put him in his carrier, and made my way to the parking lot. The weather was warm and balmy. Too nice to head for home just yet, so I decided to run a few errands. I drove along the Green and found a parking spot a few doors down from Gourmet Delight. The previous night's unexpected guests had depleted my food supplies. Everything here was delicious, if rather expensive. My plan was to buy a few items and do some major supermarket shopping later on in the week when I had more time.

I selected a bunch of asparagus and a large box of strawberries, reached for a container of their tasty chickpea salad, and decided to take advantage of the sale on salmon steaks, which I'd marinate and bake for Dylan and me over the weekend. I added a can of their outrageous pâté to my wagon, then headed for the register with the shortest line.

Outside again, I was walking toward my car when someone called my name. I looked up, not sure where the caller was until he called my name again. I saw Charlie Stanton waving to me from one of the outdoor tables in front of the restaurant next door. I headed toward him, then paused when

I saw that he was sitting with two women. One of them was Serena Harris.

"Come on over, Carrie. Don't be shy!"

"I'm not shy," I mumbled, too low for him to hear. "I just don't want to sit with someone who tried to make my mother's husband look guilty." But I decided to go over there anyway. Maybe I could find out why Serena had thrown Tom under the bus.

"Sit down, sit down!" Charlie said, pulling out a chair for me. "We're bored and could do with some scintillating company."

I smiled, appreciating his friendliness. "I don't know about scintillating company, but I'd love to join you for a few minutes."

Charlie gestured to his companions. "Carrie, you remember Serena and Hattie, our makeup and hair expert. Carrie is Brianna's daughter. She works in the library."

"Of course. Hi." I smiled at the two women and sat down. Serena and Hattie smiled back.

Charlie gestured to the mug and crumb-filled plate that he'd pushed toward the middle of the table. "We've had our late-afternoon treat, and now we're taking a break."

"Sounds decadent," I joked.

"There's nothing for us to do but wait for news." Serena's one-shoulder shrug was dismissive. Clearly she was fed up.

"News on whether they'll finish filming the movie?" I asked.

"Yes." Hattie sniffed. "We wait and we wait."

"Dirk is meeting with the producers as we speak," Charlie explained. "They'll decide if we're going ahead with the actress Dirk wants to sign on to take Ilana's place. The thing is, she insists on knowing their decision by nine this evening because she's been offered another role. Then there's the problem of whether or not . . ." He looked at me, a sheepish expression on his face. For once, Charlie Stanton was at a loss for words.

"If Tom's going to be indicted for Ilana's murder," I finished for him. "That's understandable."

No one spoke.

"Well, he hasn't been charged," I said, "though he's been told to stay in Clover Ridge for the time being."

"We've all been asked to stay in Clover Ridge," Serena said. "Your police chief isn't done with any of us. I wonder who gets to sit in the hot seat tomorrow."

"Can you blame him?" I asked, incensed by her attitude. "A member of your group was murdered. The killer could be someone else from the movie."

"Are you forgetting? The night before, another young woman was murdered in your little town." Hattie pulled the edges of her cardigan over her generous bosom and shivered. "Maybe there's a serial killer on the loose."

"It's possible," I said. "Or perhaps someone had a reason to murder both Ilana and Daphne."

Three pairs of eyes studied me.

"Carrie, did you know Daphne Marriott?" Serena asked.

"Not well, though we were on our way to becoming friends. She gave a program at the library recently. On psychic phenomena."

"We heard she used to live here in Clover Ridge," Charlie said, "and that her father was murdered twenty years ago."

"So I've heard," I said, somewhat surprised at how well informed they were about Daphne's history.

"Two murders in one family!" Serena said, her beautiful violet eyes taking on the glow of a true gossipmonger. "We were told his murder was never solved. Maybe his daughter came back to find out who killed her father."

"After all these years? I don't think so," I said, following my instinct not to share any of my theories with them.

Charlie laughed. "You'd think the police would search for the killer among the people in town. But no—poor Dirk was grilled a few days ago because he used to come to Clover Ridge to visit relatives."

Their mocking attitude was getting under my skin. "The police have a few leads they're working on. They're waiting for the results of some tests."

"What kind of tests?" Hattie asked.

I shrugged. "I can't remember. Hairs or fibers they found at the murder scenes." To change the focus of our conversation, I turned to Serena. "Did you really see Tom talking to Daphne near her apartment the night she was murdered?"

Was it my imagination, or had her ears reddened? "As I told Lieutenant Mathers, I also saw him talking to her that Saturday afternoon on the Green."

"I'm sure Tom spoke to plenty of people that day," I said. "You all did. That was the purpose of the meet-and-greet."

"Then I saw them talking again the evening she was murdered," Serena said. "They were standing outside a drugstore. Turns out the drugstore is only a block from her apartment."

"How did you know that?" I asked.

Serena blinked. "I figured it out when I read her address in the newspaper. There was a photo of the building too, so I knew it was close to where I saw them talking."

"What were you doing there?" I asked.

Serena drew back, affronted. "What do you think? I was out walking. Getting in some much-needed exercise. Besides, it was only a few blocks from our hotel."

"Well, maybe Tom was out for the same reason and he happened to run into Daphne."

"Maybe he was. How would I know?" Serena very deliberately turned her back on me.

"Well, I'd better start for home," I said.

"Take care, Carrie," Charlie said, then raised his hand to catch the waiter's attention.

Chapter Twenty-One

"They seemed so—I don't know—*über*-sophisticated and *bored*," I said to Dylan that evening as we set out for our favorite burger place. "Talking about the murders with such relish, when one of the victims was someone they knew quite well." I snorted. "It was almost as though they were acting out parts in a play."

Dylan patted my leg. "Well, two of them are actors. And I'm sure they are bored, sitting around all day instead of working, not knowing if the powers that be will go ahead with the movie."

"They seemed very interested in Daphne and her father," I said.

"Did they say anything about Robby?" Dylan asked.

"No, and I didn't mention him, either. Why do you ask?"

"Just wondering how much they know about the Harper family," Dylan said.

"Their ears perked up when I said the police had a few leads and might be getting some test results very soon."

Dylan frowned. "I wish you hadn't done that."

"Why?"

"You obviously put them on their guard."

I reflected on how they'd reacted when I'd made that statement. "I suppose I was getting defensive because they were so dismissive of John's investigation. But you're right—one of them might be the murderer. Or might be defending the murderer."

"Did you happen to ask Serena why she said that Tom was talking to Daphne the night she died?" Dylan asked.

"I did, and she got all huffy. She said she saw them talking on the street near Daphne's apartment. She just happened to be walking by. I said that Tom could have been out walking too and simply ran into Daphne by chance." I gasped. "But if Serena is telling the truth—and it sounds like she is—then Tom lied about talking to Daphne that evening."

"Probably because he *was* guilty."

"Guilty? Tom didn't kill anyone!"

"He's guilty of falling for his old lover," Dylan said. "When a person feels guilty about something as serious as adultery, his or her sense of guilt could spill over onto other situations. And when the two situations are linked—well, things can get a little hairy."

I looked at Dylan. "Do you think John realized that was the case and that Tom wasn't his murderer after all?"

Dylan nodded. "I wouldn't be surprised. John's really good at interviewing suspects. I'm thinking he doesn't like Tom for the murders for now."

I scrunched up my nose as I thought. "But he's not getting anywhere, is he? First he focused on Dirk, then Tom. I wonder if Charlie's right—John should be interrogating men who live in Clover Ridge instead of the movie cast and crew."

"Except the murders occurred when the movie people were here." He shot me a wicked grin. "And why are we eliminating females from the suspect pool?"

I shrugged. "Why would a woman kill two young women? As for the movie cast and crew—I would hate to think that Charlie's the killer."

Dylan turned into the parking area of the strip of stores that included the hamburger restaurant. "I know you're fond of him, Carrie," he said, "but that's no reason to leave Charlie off the list of suspects. Murderers can be charming and handsome."

"Okay. Both Charlie and Dirk were involved with Ilana, at one time or another. But there's no evidence that links either of them to the crime."

Dylan let out an exasperated sigh. "There's no evidence, period! Who else is there?"

I thought. "I don't know the three or four actors with small parts or any of the crew members except Ronnie Rodriguez."

"Who is he?" Dylan asked.

"The head cameraman. A handsome Latino who's great at his work. My mother told me he's the only cameraman Dirk will work with."

"I'll check him out tomorrow when I'm in the office." Dylan parked and turned off the motor. "Now let's forget about the murders and enjoy our meal."

* * *

It was fun bingeing on cheeseburgers with three toppings and a slew of well-done sweet-potato fries. We finished off dinner with coffee and dessert—chocolate cake for me, apple pie for Dylan. The best part of the evening was having the cottage to ourselves. Dylan stayed over and we enjoyed a leisurely breakfast the next morning, since neither of us had to go to work until later.

My mother called, sounding calm and more composed than she'd been since she and Tom had arrived in Clover Ridge.

"Tom and I are talking a lot. We've agreed to take things one day at a time," she said.

"That's good. Have they made a decision about the movie yet?"

"Dirk called last night. They've decided to go ahead with the production. Marissa Varig will be joining the cast. She's arriving tomorrow. She's already started learning her lines. They'll start shooting by the weekend."

"That's good news," I said.

"The bad news is Tom isn't completely off the hook." My mother lowered her voice. "He finally admitted to your police chief that he'd run into the girl who was murdered when he was out for a walk."

"It's best that he came clean," I said.

"That's what I told Tom." After a moment, she said, "Carrie, thanks again for letting me stay with you when I had nowhere to go."

"You could have gone to a motel," I joked.

"Not the way I was feeling. I needed to be with someone who gives a damn about me." After a pause, she said, "I'm glad we got to spend time together."

"Me too, Mom."

I found myself smiling as I poured coffee refills for Dylan and me. It was a relief to finally have an ordinary mother-daughter conversation.

* * *

When we got to the library a few hours later, Smoky Joe dashed off to socialize with patrons and I headed to my office. Evelyn paid me a visit, and I gave her an update regarding Tom and my mother, along with the news that the movie producers had decided to go ahead with filming.

"I'm glad," she said. "Their decision is good for Clover Ridge's economy, especially when it comes to the influx of visitors we get in the warmer months."

"I suppose they've decided that neither Dirk nor Tom is a serious suspect, since neither has been charged, and that the murderer won't be found among their cast and crew."

"It's naïve of them to have such blind faith in anyone's innocence," Evelyn said dryly.

I released a sigh of exasperation. "Or else they're cynical enough to think the murders won't be solved anytime soon. And who can blame them? So far John's investigation has gotten nowhere. It seems the killer didn't leave one shred of evidence."

"Either he was very careful or very lucky. Or John didn't share his findings with you. Any way you look at it, having the movie cast and crew remain in Clover Ridge is good for the investigation," Evelyn said as she faded from sight.

I mentioned to Sally that I'd be attending the memorial ceremony for Daphne the following day.

"Are you planning to say a few words?"

"Gee, I hadn't thought of it," I said.

"It would be nice if you did. Now's the time to write something," Sally advised.

I found myself thinking about Daphne—not so much about what I would say at the memorial service, but about our budding friendship. Her murder was a personal loss to me as well as an outrage because an innocent person's life had been cut short. Because of my own family's problems, I hadn't done much in the way of finding out who had murdered her. I intended to change that, starting now.

First, I called Tom's cell phone. For all I knew, he'd been the last person to see Daphne alive.

"Hi, Carrie. Can't talk long. We just got a short recess from a meeting. Have to go back inside very soon."

"I'm glad you're no longer a serious suspect and they're going ahead with the movie."

"Not as glad as I am! Now to make things right with your mom."

"I wish you luck," I said. When I realized that might have come across as sarcastic, I quickly added, "I mean it. I think you're good for each other."

"Thanks."

"Tom, you may have been the last person to talk to Daphne the night she died. How did she seem to you?"

"Hard to say, since I hardly knew her except for our brief conversation that Saturday afternoon at the meet-and-greet event."

"Tom, this could be important. Who recognized whom? How long did you talk?"

"Let me think. Daphne was coming out of the drugstore, and I was about to go inside and pick up a few items. I think we recognized each other at the same time." He exhaled. "Your mother and I had been fighting, so I was in no hurry to go back to the house. I asked Daphne if she'd like to go for a cup of coffee."

"Uh-huh."

"Carrie, it wasn't like that! I wasn't making a move on her. I just could have used some company with someone, *anyone* not connected to the movie."

"Okay."

"I think Daphne got that," he said.

"She probably did," I agreed. "She was psychic."

"So I heard. Anyway, she looked disappointed and said she'd love to but she couldn't because she had to see something through."

My pulse quickened. "I wonder if whatever she had planned got her murdered."

"I have no idea," Tom said. "She did ask me something strange—she asked how well I knew the people I was working with."

Did she suspect one of them had murdered her father? "Did you tell this to Lieutenant Mathers?" I asked.

"He didn't ask me. Listen, Carrie, I gotta go. We'll talk soon, okay?"

"Of course, Tom. Give my love to my mom."

As I hung up, I shot my fists into the air. "Finally! Some insight into Daphne's mind the night she was murdered. She might have been planning to confront her father's killer."

Or not. Still, it was a place to start my own investigation.

Chapter
Twenty-Two

The Quaker meeting house was a small, square building, its wooden exterior painted white like most of the buildings around the Green. I pulled into the adjoining parking lot, surprised at the number of cars already there. I entered a square room with two rows of benches along all four walls facing into the center of the room.

I looked around, glad to see a few familiar faces. Cybil, the friendly receptionist at Parson's Gym, was sitting with Greg Tedesco, Robby's boss. With them were a man and two women who looked familiar. I was pretty sure I'd seen them at the gym.

Three women a few years older than me—Daphne's age— sat chatting in the back bench to my left. I wondered if they were old friends of Daphne's whom Robby had contacted. Behind the gym group, a man in his late seventies stared into the empty space in the center of the room as though waiting for the show to begin.

A tall, broad-shouldered man in his late forties/early fifties sat to the right of the door. It was Ronnie Rodriguez, the movie company's cameraman. Ronnie must have recognized me too, because he smiled at me. I was about to head in his direction when Robby suddenly appeared. I sat down in front of the three women.

The room fell silent.

Robby looked around, nodding to each of us in turn. "Thank you all for coming to pay your last respects to my sister Daphne and to celebrate her memory. Daphne was murdered in the town where she and I grew up. Now that she's gone to her rest, wherever that may be, I want to remember and honor her abbreviated life here on earth."

He drank from the water bottle he was holding and went on. "Daphne and I grew up in Clover Ridge. Our life here wasn't happy because our father was an abusive drunk. Someone murdered him, and I was charged and convicted for the crime. I did not kill my father. My case was reviewed and I was exonerated. Last year I decided to return to the area where I grew up to find the person who murdered my father. I'd changed my name to Robby Dowd and took a job at a local gym as a personal trainer.

"As of today, I'm going by my original name, Billy Harper, the name I was born with. I will do all I can to find my sister's murderer and hopefully my father's as well."

He flashed a smile at everyone present. "Enough about me. We're meeting today to celebrate Daphne's life. In true Quaker spirit, I would like each of you to tell us how Daphne impacted your life."

One of the trio of women stood. She was pretty, with long blonde hair. Robby—that is, Billy—asked her to approach the center of the room.

"Hello. My name is Tracy Halleran. I lived in the same apartment house as Daphne and Billy." She smiled at Billy. "Daphne and I were best friends for most of that time. She was the sweetest, nicest person. We all knew what a difficult time she was having—her father drinking and hitting them—and we wished we could do something to make her life better. I'm sorry she didn't contact me when she moved back here. I'm sorry someone murdered her."

We clapped, and Tracy sat down. To my surprise, the old man got up next.

"I'm Steve Dawson. I used to work with Chet Harper, Daphne's father. Yes, he was a mean drunk at times, but when he wasn't drinking, he was a decent man. And he loved his family, despite how he treated them. He didn't deserve to get knifed to death any more than his daughter deserved what happened to her."

Before we could react to Steve Dawson's contribution, the door opened and a man stepped inside, looking around as if he was lost.

Oh no! It was Bert Lutz! Billy strode over to his sister's ex-husband.

"This is a memorial service to honor my sister," Billy said.

"I know. I'm not here to make trouble," Bert said.

"Then sit down and remain quiet until it's your turn to speak."

Bert nodded and sat a few feet from me. I wrinkled my nose when a whiff of whiskey wafted my way.

Another old friend of Daphne's stood and said her piece; then Greg, Robby's—er, Billy's—boss, stood.

"I met Daphne once, when she came to the gym. It took no more than one meeting to know she was a kind, worthy person—just like her brother. I'm sorry her life ended so suddenly. I only hope the police find the person who killed her and her father, because my money says the person is one and the same."

"Thank you, Greg." Billy joined his boss in the center of the room and flung an arm around his shoulders. "And thanks for standing by me. Thank you all for coming here today. I can't put into words how grateful I am that though some of you didn't get to know my sister, you're here to give me support."

Applause broke out. I was touched and eager to offer my remembrance of Daphne, but Billy had something to add.

"I know it's premature, but I want to share some information with you."

Oh no! Don't do it!

But Billy was already grinning and pointing at me. "Thanks to Carrie Singleton and her partner Dylan Avery, I now know where my mother is living—not very far from here, it turns out. I intend to pay her a surprise visit in hopes of learning some vital information. Information that might very well expose the killer in our midst."

Cheers and whistles filled the meeting room. Bert Lutz stood and walked to the center of the room. Billy frowned but quickly decided that he had no choice but to let him speak.

"I was married to Daphne and probably knew her better than anyone here—except her brother, of course. Daphne was the best thing that ever happened to me, and I'm sorry I didn't treat her better." Bert looked at Billy. "Daphne never forgave herself for letting that policeman bamboozle her into saying she heard you fighting with your father the night he was killed when your argument with him happened a week earlier. She was determined to find you and beg your forgiveness. I'm glad she found you. I only hope you find the SOB that murdered her." He glanced upward. "Daphne, honey, rest in peace."

This time the applause was even louder than before. When it died down, I was moved to speak.

"I met Daphne when she came to the library wanting to give a talk about psychic phenomena. Her own recently acquired psychic ability had urged her to return to Clover Ridge. She wasn't sure why. I'm so happy that she got to reunite with Billy.

"Daphne and I spent time together and were on our way to becoming good friends when she was murdered. I hope the police will find her murderer very soon."

An older woman who turned out to have been a friend of Daphne and Billy's mother spoke, and the room fell silent. Billy addressed us one last time. He thanked us all for coming and for caring about his sister.

I timed my exit so that I'd fall into step with Ronnie Rodriguez. He acknowledged me with a grin.

"I have to hand it to the Quakers. They're informal and everyone gets to say his piece."

"Are you a Quaker?" I asked.

That inspired a deep belly laugh. "Me? I'm not anything, but my second wife was a Quaker."

"How did you happen to come to Daphne's memorial service?" I asked.

"I came for Robby—er, Billy. I'd heard what a great personal trainer he was, so I begged and begged until he agreed to squeeze me in for a few hours of training. The exercises he had me do eased the pain that was killing my shoulders for more than fifteen years."

"He's quite a person," I said.

Ronnie nodded. "I'm sorry as hell he had to spend all that time in prison for a crime he didn't commit."

"Me too." I thought a minute, then asked, "Does anyone else from the movie crew come to Parson's Gym?"

"Sure. Phil, the lighting guy, comes even more often than I do. He's into body building and won't give it a rest. Ilana and Serena came a few times. That's about it, I think. By the way, do you happen to know when Billy's planning to go see his mother?"

"No idea," I said.

"It's just that I hope he's not setting himself up for a big disappointment. Billy thinks his mother knows who murdered his father. My feeling is, if she really did, she would have told the police by now."

"I think Billy wants his mother to explain why she disappeared when the police focused in on him as their number-one suspect," I said. "No matter what she tells him, it can't be what he hopes to hear."

"Unfortunately, I agree," Ronnie said.

We were standing at the edge of the parking lot now.

"I hear you'll be resuming filming in a few days," I said.

"Righto! Marissa Varig's joining the cast, and we'll be back in business." Ronnie leaned toward me and lowered his voice. "I'm glad that Tom is no longer suspect number one."

"Me too. See you around, Ronnie."

He strode off, and I was heading to my car when someone grabbed my arm.

"Carrie!" Billy had been running to catch up with me. "I wanted to thank you for coming today."

"Of course," I said. "It was a lovely, down-to-earth service. Daphne would have liked it."

"And now we can move ahead and find out what my mother's been hiding all these years. Please let me know ASAP when you can make the trip with me."

"Of course." I hesitated, then added, "I only wish you hadn't announced your plans to go see your mother because you assume she knows who killed your father."

Billy laughed. "There's nothing to be afraid of. Everyone who came to the memorial service came for my sake or Daphne's."

"Still," I said, "when investigating unsolved homicides, it's best not to divulge your plans to too many people. Even if the murderer isn't present, he might get wind of what you intend to do."

"Yes, Miss Marple." Billy gave me a sharp salute. "From now on, I promise not to share our plans with anyone."

Chapter Twenty-Three

The days that followed Daphne's memorial service were warm and sunny. Flowers bloomed on lawns and in hanging baskets around town, proof that spring had arrived in its full glory. My mother and Tom seemed to be moving forward slowly. "A wary truce" was how my mother described it. But I was hopeful. At least they were living in the same house.

My father must have thought the same, because, after treating Dylan and me to a wonderful seafood dinner, he announced he was returning to Atlanta the following morning. Jim had been staying with me at the cottage since my mother moved out. That night we had a heart-to-heart talk till one in the morning. He told me he was dating someone and promised to bring her to Clover Ridge the next time he came to visit. I found myself crying the following morning when his taxi arrived to drive him to the airport.

"I'll miss you too," he said, hugging me fiercely before sauntering off with the charm that had never left him.

Despite the two unsolved homicides and the apparent standstill in finding their murderer, signs of panic and hysteria seemed to have abated as the mood surrounding Clover Ridge returned to the casual familiarity and security of small-town living. I wondered if this was because both murder victims had been outsiders and local residents had managed to convince themselves that these deaths had nothing to do with them. The attitude of business-as-usual was strengthened when the movie people resumed shooting *I Love You, I Do*. Surely, here was proof that the police thought it safe for everyday activities to continue while they continued to investigate.

Tuesday morning, I found myself part of a long line of cars creeping along at a snail's pace as Officer Danny Brower directed us away from the Green to a detour blocks out of my way. The inn, shops, and galleries facing the side of the Green adjacent to the library were the setting for that day's filming. Drivers craned their necks out of car windows trying to see the shoot—with little success, given the film company's vans blocking our view. I finally pulled into the library's parking lot, set Smoky Joe free, and found myself joining the staff and patrons gawking out the three long windows that faced the Green to catch whatever glimpse I could of the filming, which wasn't much.

Angela turned to me. "This is crazy. We can't see anything from here. And even if we could—so what?"

"I know," I said. "We're hardwired to watch when a movie's being made. Just as we drive slower so we can stare at an accident in the road."

"And gawk when we catch sight of the rich and famous. Well, I for one am going back to work." Angela started walking toward the circulation desk.

"Me too." I fell into step beside her. "I'm glad they found a replacement for Ilana and are planning to finish the movie."

"It kind of makes you feel that things are back to normal, even though they're not."

"They certainly aren't," I agreed.

"Two women have been murdered, and their killer seems to have gotten away with it."

I frowned. "So far it looks that way."

"What does John say?" Angela asked.

"I haven't spoken to him recently. Dylan talked to him over the weekend. He said John was in a foul mood because he had no new evidence to work with and no new suspects in sight."

"When are you going to Long Island with Billy Harper to talk to his mother?"

"On Friday." I sighed. "But I can't help but think that's a wild-goose chase. I mean, what can she possibly say that will help us?"

"Did you tell John you're going to see Mrs. Harper, or whatever she calls herself these days?"

I shook my head. "No. I'll let him know if she says anything worthwhile. I'm really doing this for Billy's sake. Though he's so angry at her, I'm afraid he'll start off accusing her of having been an awful mother for abandoning him and Daphne. I'm hoping he'll control himself and the trip doesn't turn out to be a bust."

Angela patted my shoulder. "That's why he asked you to go along. Billy clearly has the good sense to know when to bring a mediator to the table."

I settled down in my office and was scrolling through a slew of emails when someone knocked on my door.

"Come in," I called out, expecting it to be Sally dropping by. I looked up and was surprised to see Charlie Stanton sailing through the doorway. "Well, hello!"

He dropped a kiss on my cheek like we were old pals. "Hello yourself."

"Have a seat," I said, pointing to the chair at Trish and Susan's desk. "To what do I owe this pleasure?"

Charlie wheeled out the chair so we'd be facing each other and sank into it as though he was exhausted.

"We've just been filming for two hours. I finally got a break, so I came to seek respite here—away from the noise and the madding crowd."

"Well, sure," I said, wishing Angela were here to chat with her idol. "How's it going?"

"Frankly, better than I'd expected. Marissa arrived last night and is avidly studying her lines." Charlie sighed. "I just did a few scenes with Serena and needed to get out of the sun."

"Would you like to get something to drink at the library coffee shop?" I asked.

"I am thirsty, but I'd rather stay here, if you don't mind."

I understood. Charlie wanted a moment of peace and quiet without fans gushing over him. I felt flattered that he'd sought me out as his refuge. "I'll bring you back a coffee, if you like."

"Thanks, Carrie, but I'd prefer something cold to drink. Water. Anything." He grinned. "And whatever dessert they sell there."

He pulled a wad of cash from his pocket and peeled off a twenty.

"Please, no! My treat," I said.

"Mine," he insisted. "And get yourself something to nosh on. When you come back, there's something I'd like to discuss."

When I returned to my office with a cold drink and a brownie for Charlie and a cup of coffee for me, I found Sally sitting in my chair. The two of them were laughing and chatting like old friends.

"Carrie!" Sally said. She jumped to her feet, looking guilty, as if she'd been flirting with my boyfriend. I understood. Charlie had that mesmerizing effect on most females.

"Please sit," I said to her.

Charlie got up from his seat and offered it to Sally. Was she actually blushing as she sat down? He leaned against my assistants' desk. I handed him his drink and brownie. "And I have lots of change for you," I said, holding out the money.

He waved it away. "Please."

"Mr. Stanton—" Sally began.

"Charlie," he corrected.

"Charlie has just made the most wonderful proposal," Sally said, her face aglow.

"Really? What is it?" I asked.

She gestured to him. "I think you can describe it best."

I could hardly believe it. My boss was star-struck and, for once, too flustered to speak.

"Well," Charlie began, when he'd finished off the last bite of his brownie, "Serena, Tom, and I—and Marissa agreed when we presented the idea to her—would like to thank Clover Ridge for being such a wonderful host to us all, especially in view of the awful events of the past few weeks. The four of us would like to do a play reading at the library. No scenery. No props. Just us reading from a script."

"That's very kind of you," I said, "but the library's fully booked for the next two months with scheduled programs and events."

"However, nothing is scheduled on Saturday and Sunday nights," Sally said, grinning.

I looked at her. "No. The library's closed then."

"We've held special events on those evenings in the past," Sally said. "And we can do it again."

"That would be wonderful!" I said. "When were you thinking of doing this?"

"We were thinking two weeks from Saturday. We require nothing from your staff but a table and four chairs, a few mics—oh, and good lighting to read by."

"Unfortunately, our large meeting room only holds sixty people," I said. "So many of our patrons will be disappointed."

"Mr. Stanton—er, Charlie—had a wonderful idea!" Sally said. "He said the movie crew's sound engineer could rig up a system so people could hear the reading upstairs—in the reading room, the computer area, even the children's section—if we need more seats."

I smiled at him. "That *is* an ingenious idea. Since we have so much empty space on this level, we can rent chairs for the evening and accommodate a lot more patrons."

Charlie glanced at his watch and finished off the rest of his drink. "Then we're agreed. We'll give the reading the third Saturday night in May. If we start at eight o'clock, it will probably run until ten forty-five. Or, if you prefer, we can begin at seven thirty. Run it by the powers that be and get back to me, okay?"

Sally and I nodded.

Charlie beamed at each of us. "Terrific! I'll let the others know." He snapped his fingers as if he'd just remembered something. "Come to think of it, Carrie, I did want to ask you something . . ."

Sally took this as her cue to leave, and Charlie watched her close my office door behind her. "She didn't have to run off like that."

"What's on your mind?" I asked a bit tartly, because we both knew he wanted Sally gone.

"I was curious to know if you'd heard of any new developments regarding the investigation into Ilana's death—and the other poor girl's, of course. Naturally, the *I Love You* cast and crew are concerned. We've made inquiries, but your police chief tells us nothing."

"Why ask me?"

Charlie grinned. "I hear tell you have his ear. What about those tests you mentioned the other day? Hairs or fibers, you said."

"I have no idea, since I'm not privy to police matters."

"That's surprising. Didn't you help solve a few local murders?"

I shrugged. "I did, but this case is different. I don't have any leads to follow up."

"What about your upcoming visit to the mother of the first victim—Daphne Hyatt?"

"Marriott," I corrected him.

"Sorry. Don't you and Daphne's brother expect her to finally reveal the ID of her husband's killer?"

I stared at him. "Where did you hear that?"

"Let's see. Where *did* I hear it? Your mother mentioned it the other evening. And Ronnie Rodriguez said that Daphne's brother announced it at his sister's memorial service."

I gritted my teeth. *No wonder John and his ilk hate it when amateurs get involved in murder investigations.* "Billy and I plan to visit his mother in the near future, but honestly, I don't think she knows who killed her husband. She would have told the police years ago if she did."

"Interesting," Charlie said. "In that case, what does Billy expect to get out of this visit?"

"Some sort of closure. An explanation as to why his mother disappeared and ran out on him and his sister after the murder. I'm hoping they can repair their relationship."

"Does this woman have any idea that she's about to receive a visit from the son she hasn't seen in twenty years?"

I laughed. "Are you kidding? Give her a chance to avoid meeting Billy? I understand she sticks pretty close to home, so we're taking our chances."

"When did you say that you and Billy are making this trip?"

I grinned as I opened my office door. "I didn't. 'Bye, Charlie. It was good seeing you again."

Chapter Twenty-Four

For the rest of the day—between a long meeting with Sally to discuss some long-standing programs I wanted to drop and interviews with two possible presenters—I thought about Charlie. Was the play reading the real reason he had stopped by the library, or had he wanted to find out when Billy and I would be driving to Long Island to question Patricia Harper? As farfetched as it seemed, she was the only link to the person who had possibly killed her husband and then her daughter twenty years later. I had no clue how Ilana's murder fit into the picture—or if it was completely unrelated.

I began to worry about Patricia Harper's safety. Perhaps she'd fled Clover Ridge all those years ago because she'd feared her husband's killer. Today he still roamed free. Though she'd changed her name, it was safe to assume that if Dylan's secretary had managed to find her, then a murderer could as well. And would want to get to her before Billy. Which was why, when Charlie questioned me, I had decided not to tell him when we planned to drive to Long Island.

Why was he so interested in knowing, anyway? Was *he* Patricia Harper's secret lover? I shook my head, refusing to even consider the preposterous idea. Sure, Charlie was the right age, but age was the only factor that made the amiable Charlie Stanton a suspect in this infuriating case. As far as I knew, he'd never set foot in Clover Ridge before he'd arrived here to film *I Love You, I Do*.

That evening I called Billy at the gym. "Just checking that we're still on for Friday morning," I said.

"Absolutely. I'll pick you up at eight thirty."

"See you then. Call me if anything comes up."

"Will do," Billy said, "but nothing will come up between now and Friday."

* * *

Thursday afternoon Billy called me. He sounded awful. "I'm in the hospital."

A sense of dread spread over me. "What happened?"

"I'm hooked up to an IV and having my blood cleaned via hemodialysis. I'll be here a few days."

"Oh no! Is it food poisoning?"

"Poison is the operative word. They ran all kinds of tests—blood, urine, CT, EKG—to find out why I suddenly felt groggy and a few hours later nearly collapsed. Antifreeze poisoning, as they suspected."

"I'm so sorry."

"Lieutenant Mathers picked up the honeyed walnuts from my apartment and brought them to the crime lab." Billy snorted. "A bogus gift from a grateful client. Only my client, when the police called her, knew nothing about it."

I drew in a deep breath. Billy and I both knew why someone had sent him the poisoned nuts. The only thing we didn't know was who it was.

"This is creepy," I said. "How did he know where to send the nuts? How did he know what to send?"

"That's easy. The nuts were sent to the gym. He must have overheard my conversation with Stella Marks. How much I love honeyed walnuts. Loved," he said ruefully. "I'll never eat another walnut again."

"Will you be all right?"

"Looks that way. Good thing I wasn't hungry and only ate a handful."

"He doesn't want you talking to your mother," I said.

Billy let out a deep sigh. "You were right, Carrie. I should have kept my mouth shut about our plans to pay her a visit. I have no doubt this is the person who killed my father and Daphne. He knows my mother can identify him."

"Does John—Lieutenant Mathers—see it this way?"

"I don't think so," Billy said. "I heard him telling someone he wants to wait until all the test results are in before he starts involving people in other states."

"Meanwhile, the murderer got his wish." I shuddered. "And for all we know, he might go after your mother if and when he finds out where she lives."

"Carrie . . ."

"Yes?"

"I know it's a lot to ask, but you're the only one that can do this . . ."

"You want me to talk to your mother," I said.

"I do. You have to convince her to tell you who killed my father and Daphne and poisoned me."

I took a minute to think—about Billy, the murders, about Dylan and me.

"Billy, I've put my life in danger before tracking down murderers, and I promised Dylan and Lieutenant Mathers I wouldn't do it again. I need to talk to Dylan about going to see your mother. I'll do it if he agrees to go with me."

As soon as I ended the call, Evelyn appeared.

"Poor Billy!" she exclaimed. "Thank goodness he didn't become another victim."

"Either Billy was plain lucky or the murderer merely meant to stop him from going to see his mother." I frowned. "Though I have no idea how the murderer knew we were planning to go tomorrow."

"It could be he simply decided to put Billy out of commission ASAP."

"Maybe," I agreed.

Evelyn nodded as she thought. "What I don't understand is, why did the killer assume that Billy wouldn't communicate with his mother before going to visit her?"

"Billy made it clear at Daphne's memorial service that his mother had been out of touch all these years and he meant to surprise her with his visit."

"I see. Well then, I think we can conclude that Patricia holds the secret to the killer's identity."

"And if that's the case," I said, "then whoever killed Chet Harper, Daphne Harper, and Ilana Reingold and poisoned Billy yesterday is one and the same person. A man in his fifties or sixties who's terrified of being exposed."

"I agree with you," Evelyn said.

"I think John was wrong to focus on someone connected to the movie people," I said. "I think the killer is a Clover Ridge resident. Evelyn, you were around then. Is there anyone you can think of who was close to Patricia Harper?"

Evelyn crossed her legs, rested her chin on her fist, and thought. "I didn't know Pattie very well, but like most of the people in town, I was aware of her awful predicament. Her husband drank, and when he drank he was abusive to her and the kids. We all felt sorry for her. A few people tried to help her and she refused their help."

"Do you remember who tried to help her?" I asked.

"Sure. Your Great-Aunt Harriet, for one."

"Really?"

"Oh, yes! Harriet tried to talk to Pattie a few times, but each time she was told that everything was fine. Pattie insisted she had everything under control."

"I have to talk to Aunt Harriet," I said. "Was there anyone else?"

"Alvin Tripp felt sorry for her. I think he was smitten."

"The mayor?"

"He's the mayor of Clover Ridge now, but twenty years ago he was a lawyer with a soft spot for his neighbor who was being terrorized by her husband."

Having said her piece, Evelyn faded from view, leaving me deep in thought. Great-Aunt Harriet and Mayor Tripp had known Patricia Harper all those years ago. I had to speak to each of them, and soon.

* * *

That evening after Dylan and I had finished our simple dinner of omelets stuffed with cheese, sautéed onions, and mushrooms, accompanied by a baby-greens salad and fresh rye bread, we moved to the living room sofa, where I filled him in on the day's events. His expression changed from dismay to anger to disapproval as I related how Billy had ended up in South Conn Hospital and had asked me to visit his mother to convince her to give up the name of her long-ago lover.

"Carrie, I—"

"Before you say anything, I want you to know that I told Billy I would discuss it with you before giving him my answer."

"My answer is no."

I smiled. "That's quite a discussion we had."

Dylan shrugged. "What's to discuss? Now we pretty much know that, one, all three murders were most likely committed by the same person, and two, this person doesn't want Billy Harper to meet up with his mother. Talking to Patricia Harper is a matter for the police, though I can't see John rushing off to Long Island to interview her."

"I agree. He's much too busy here," I said. "My mother called before to tell me John has started questioning the movie people to find out who might have sent Billy the poisoned nuts. Several of them have been going to Parson's Gym. Some have even had sessions with Billy. I'm sure John is also questioning some local people—now that there's a strong tie between the poisoning and the three homicides."

"So there you have it," Dylan said. "When Billy's feeling better, there's nothing to stop him from going to see his mother."

"Still, I agree with Billy. It's important that I speak to her tomorrow as planned." I drew a deep breath. "I know it's short notice, but I'm hoping you'll go with me. I promised you and John that I wouldn't do anything dangerous. If you're there with me and there's a small chance the killer comes after us, well, I'll be protected."

Dylan stared at me, dumb struck. Clearly he was thinking I had some nerve making such a request. He started laughing, as though I'd just presented the most comical argument one could imagine. Laughing and pointing at me.

"Did you actually expect me to go with you tomorrow?" he said when he could speak.

"I was hoping, but I understand if you can't—"

"You're asking for my help in a potentially dangerous situation."

I nodded, starting to get annoyed. "Okay. You can simply say no."

Dylan wrapped me in his arms. "Sorry, babe. I'm not laughing at you."

I sniffed. "It sure looks that way."

"I'm just so blown away that you want me along for protection."

"I understand. Tomorrow's a workday. You have appointments. Investigative things to do."

"Did I say I couldn't go?"

I stared at Dylan. "No, but . . ."

"I'll call Rosalind now. Have her cancel my appointments. Tomorrow's a light day anyway, so it's no big deal."

"It's a big deal to me," I said, kissing him.

Chapter
Twenty-Five

I woke up early Friday morning and glanced at my clock. It wasn't quite six o'clock. I let Dylan sleep a while longer and got up to feed Smoky Joe. My heart thumped with excitement and anticipation. There had been so little evidence to follow up on regarding these murders. No clues to speak of. Of course, there was the chance that the forensic people would find fingerprints on Billy's poisoned walnuts. But even if they did, that still didn't link the poisoner to the three murders. Whatever Patricia Harper had to tell us could be important in solving all three homicides.

We'd decided to travel to Long Island by ferry. I was looking forward to the hour-and-a-quarter ride across Long Island Sound. I'd planned to sit outside and get a bit of a tan but had to give up that idea because it was drizzling, though sunny skies were in the afternoon's weather forecast.

The traffic wasn't too bad as we drove to catch the ferry in Bridgeport. Dylan kept the soft rock radio station on low so we could hear ourselves talk.

"Billy's feeling much better this morning," I said. "He thinks the doctor overseeing his case will let him go home later today or tomorrow morning."

"I'm glad he didn't end up being murder victim number four," Dylan said.

"The killer was clearly trying to stop Billy from visiting his mother as planned," I said.

"Let's hope no one knows we're on our way to see her now," Dylan said. "Unfortunately, too many people knew you were planning to accompany him."

"When my mother asked if I was going anyway, I said of course not. She would have passed that on to the movie people." I chuckled. "Gossip spreads like wildfire among that group."

"And if the murderer is one of Clover Ridge's fine citizens, we have to hope he'll assume you wouldn't be going without Billy."

That had me twisting my neck in every direction to see if a car was following us.

Dylan laughed and patted my leg. "No need to get nervous, babe. I've had my eyes peeled on the cars around us from the moment we left. Believe me, no one's tailing us."

Which reminded me. "Speaking of Clover Ridge's fine citizens, Evelyn told me something interesting yesterday regarding Patricia Harper."

Dylan glanced at me. "Your friend Evelyn the ghost?"

"Uh-huh."

A few months ago I'd told Dylan about my relationship with Evelyn. We'd been driving home from a restaurant and almost crashed into some bushes on the side of the road. While Dylan accepted the fact that Evelyn often hovered around the library in her ghostly state and sometimes gave me helpful information regarding homicide investigations, it didn't rest easily in his pragmatic, rational mind.

"If you'll remember, Evelyn lived in Clover Ridge most of her life and knew most of the people in town," I said.

"Go on."

"She said two people tried to help Patricia—Aunt Harriet and Alvin Tripp."

"Al Tripp, the mayor?"

"Uh-huh." I smiled, picturing Uncle Bosco's overweight friend who loved to make speeches. "Evelyn remembered that Al Tripp had a soft spot for Patricia."

Dylan frowned. "And she first told you this yesterday, when Daphne was murdered weeks ago?"

I let out a huff of exasperation. "That's Evelyn. I can't squeeze information from her like a tube of toothpaste. She tells me what she feels like telling me, when she feels like sharing."

Dylan made no comment, so I went on. "I suppose she didn't mention Aunt Harriet and Al before because she didn't think it was important. My great-aunt isn't a serial killer, and Al's too busy holding meetings to go around murdering people." I giggled, then quickly covered my mouth. "I know it's not a laughing matter, but can you see him tracking down women almost half his age? He'd be huffing and puffing."

"I suppose John is aware that Al Tripp had a thing for Patricia Harper since he was on the force when Chet Harper was murdered. You might mention it, but then you'd have to explain how you found it out." Dylan grinned. "That's the problem with getting information from a ghost."

I nodded. "I'll think of something."

We drove along in peaceful silence. I mused about Patricia Harper and how difficult it must have been to start over fresh with a new name and a new life.

"Tell me again about Patricia Harper's new persona," I said.

"She goes by the name of Sheila Rossetti. Sheila was her middle name. Rossetti is her husband Tony's last name. They've been married twelve years now. Tony has two grown sons from his first marriage. They moved to Long Island a few years ago to be close to one of his sons."

"I'll never understand how she could leave Billy and Daphne," I said. "Especially when she knew the police suspected Billy for his father's murder."

Dylan exhaled loudly. "I think she might have taken off before Mitch Flynn really got his claws into Billy. At any rate, I suspect she was too traumatized to be of any help to anyone."

I felt a pang of anxiety. "What if she's not home? Maybe they're away on vacation?" I said.

"Relax, Carrie. I called last night asking for a bogus name. A woman answered the phone. When I apologized for dialing the wrong number, she said not to worry, her husband Tony did it all the time. When Rosalind called this morning, Mrs. Rossetti sounded annoyed and commented on the sudden spurt of wrong numbers."

"I hope she doesn't suspect we're on her tail," I said. "Or have any plans to go somewhere today."

"Rosalind didn't get the impression she had a job, but I'm sure she has errands to run and the occasional lunch date with a friend." Dylan shrugged. "In which case, we'll wait. Pretend we're on a stakeout."

* * *

We drove onto the ferry and left the car to find seats on an upper level. There were more people on board than I'd expected, but then, ferries crossed the sound throughout the year. I gazed out at the water while Dylan spoke quietly on his cell to Rosalind about a few of his clients. When he was done, he reached for my hand and we sat quietly.

"Want some coffee?" he asked a few minutes later.

"No, but I wouldn't mind some French fries."

He laughed. "At eleven in the morning?"

"Why not? They smell delicious."

"So they do."

"Ask to make them well done," I called after him.

Dylan returned a few minutes later. He handed me my fries, which were yummy, and sat beside me sipping his coffee.

"Mmm, these are delicious," he said, sampling some of my fries.

"I'm a little nervous," I admitted as the ferry approached Port Jefferson. "I've never questioned anyone who ran off and took on a new identity."

"Go gently," Dylan advised. "I think Sheila Rossetti will want to know what you can tell her about her children."

"I wonder if she knows Daphne is dead," I said. "She must have read about it in the papers."

"You'll find out soon enough."

We returned to our car and waited our turn to drive off. I was impressed by how quickly and smoothly the ferry emptied out.

"Let's see," Dylan said as he put Sheila Rossetti's address in his GPS. "We should be there in twenty minutes."

Traffic was light and we found the Rossettis' house easily, a yellow, well-tended Cape Cod on a tree-lined street. The one-car driveway leading to the garage was empty.

"Shall we?" Dylan said, releasing his seat belt.

I stepped out of the car and accompanied him up the cement walkway. I pressed the bell. No one answered.

"She's not home," I said.

"Looks that way."

We got back in the car. "We have two choices," Dylan said. "We can get something to eat and come back in an hour, or sit here and wait."

I thought a minute. "Let's have lunch. Neighbors might find it suspicious if we stay here."

"My thinking exactly, though I don't see any neighbors out and about."

We drove back to Route 112 and soon came upon a Turkish restaurant in a strip mall that looked appealing. The waitress sat us at a table by the window. I ordered a cup of red lentil soup and a chicken kabob pita sandwich. Dylan ordered a small spanakopita and Mediterranean lamb burger. We ate with gusto and plenty of yogurt sauce.

"Mmm, this is delicious," I said, too full to eat more than half my sandwich.

Dylan finished everything on his plate. We ordered coffee, and I asked the waitress to wrap my sandwich.

"Bet you ten to one you eat that before we're back home," Dylan teased as we left the restaurant.

"You're probably right," I said. "We have to find a restaurant like this near us."

"And if we can't, we'll hop in the car and come back here," he said.

I squeezed his hand, appreciating the many days ahead that we'd be sharing. "I love you," I said.

"Love you back. Now, let's find out if Sheila-Patricia has returned from her outing."

I giggled. "Let's not get confused and call her Patricia Rossetti."

"Or Sheila Harper."

A few minutes later we were ringing the Rossettis' doorbell once again. No one answered. We returned to the car. I was disappointed. It was two o'clock. For all we knew, she wouldn't arrive home for another few hours.

"What should we do?" I asked Dylan.

"Well, if she went shopping, then met a friend for lunch, she could return in the next hour."

"Or she could have met a friend for lunch, then went running some errands," I said.

"That too."

Two mothers, each with a child under three in a stroller, came walking toward us. They continued on as they passed by, never giving us a glance or pausing in their conversation.

"At least we're not drawing attention," I said.

"We don't look very threatening," Dylan said.

"I should hope not."

"Would you like to get out and take a walk?" Dylan suggested.

"I would. We've been sitting all day."

It felt good to stretch my legs in the warmth of the sun as I admired the flowers that adorned many of the lawns. Hand in hand we circled the block. A woman retrieving the mail from her mailbox at the curb waved to us. A man walking his bulldog commented on the lovely weather. As we turned the corner, a school bus stopped close to our car. Several elementary-age children exited the bus. A few dashed to the other side of the street. A pretty, diminutive woman about my age emerged from the house next to the Rossettis' and reached for the hand of a blond boy. He shook his hand free, but continued to walk beside her up the front walk and into the house.

"I'm going to ask Sheila's neighbor if she knows where she is or when she might be coming home," I said.

"Good idea," Dylan said. "I'll wait in the car."

I rang the bell and the door swung open. I found myself facing the little boy who had just come home from school.

"Hello," I said.

"Oh," he said, sounding very disappointed.

"Jamie, I told you not to open the door."

"Well, I thought it was Brandon, but it isn't."

"Sorry to disturb you." I smiled at the woman who came to stand beside her son. "And I'm sorry that I'm not Brandon," I said to the boy, "but I was hoping you might be able to tell me if you have any idea when your neighbor—Sheila Rossetti—might be coming home. My boyfriend and I are from her hometown. We happened to be spending the day on Long Island, so we thought we'd stop by and say hello."

"That's sweet of you," the woman said.

"Mom, my snack," Jamie said.

"I thought you wanted to have it when Brandon comes."

"I'm hungry. I want some of it now."

"One minute, Jamie." I heard loud barking coming from the back of the house. "Please let Rudolf in. He's been missing you all day. And feed him, okay?"

Jamie disappeared, only to return a minute later followed by the largest black-and-white Harlequin Great Dane I'd ever seen.

"Wow! What a beauty!" I said.

"That's Rudolf. And I'm Jeannette. Rudy, get down!" Jeannette shouted as the dog jumped up and put his paws on her shoulders. "He's hungry, Jamie. Please feed him now."

Boy and dog disappeared in what I figured was the direction of the kitchen. Jeannette was shaking her head. "We've had several trainers come to the house, but we've yet to find one who can break him of the habit of jumping up on me." She sighed. "You'd think Rudy would know by now that I hate when he does it."

"Maybe it's his way of showing affection," I said.

Jeannette grimaced. "That's what my husband says. As for Sheila next door, I don't really know her very well. Her husband Tony's a friendly guy. He and my husband often chat over the fence—mostly sports and how to deal with the awful crabgrass we all have. But Sheila's kind of reserved. Was she like that—where did you say she comes from?"

I felt uncomfortable telling this woman anything about Billy's mother, but I had no choice. "A little town in Connecticut called Clover Ridge. I suppose we should have called before stopping by," I said. "Does she go to work? In which case we'll take off."

"I don't think so. I've always gotten the impression that Sheila spends a good deal of her time at home—fixing up their house, I imagine. It was in pretty bad shape when they bought it, but Tony's a carpenter and did some major repairs when they first moved in two years ago. I suppose Sheila's doing the decorating now, judging from the deliveries they get." She shot me a sideways glance. "Not that I've ever been invited inside their house. We had them over for coffee and cake when they first moved in. Sheila didn't say much. I got the feeling she couldn't wait to leave."

"She's shy," I said. "Do you think she might have gone out for lunch with someone?"

"I doubt it. I don't think she's made any friends. At least I haven't noticed anyone dropping by during the day. Though I have seen her and Tony in church a few Sunday mornings."

I sighed. "Well, maybe she went shopping."

Jeannette's face lit up. "She probably went to Bed Bath and Beyond. And to the library. I've seen her there a few times. I've noticed she's usually back home by three, three thirty. That time we had them over for coffee, Sheila told me she always likes to be home in plenty of time to make Tony a good dinner."

I thanked Jeannette and returned to the car. I told Dylan what she'd told me. He glanced at his watch. "Okay, it's two fifteen. I'll check the GPS, see if there's a mall around here. We can wander around till three ten and come back here."

"I can't see what else we can do," I said. "But what if she's not back by then?"

"Let's decide that when the time comes."

We found a nearby mall to explore while we waited.

"Great, they have an Apple store here," Dylan said, reading the directory. "I'll stop in, see if they can help me with a problem I'm having with my iPhone. Why don't you do some shopping?" He glanced at his watch. "Let's meet back here in forty-five minutes, then head back to Sheila's house."

Music to my ears! I breezed through Macy's, then checked out Banana Republic, one of my favorites, and bought a colorful top on sale. I had just enough time to scoot outside to Barnes and Noble and buy a paperback mystery. I hurried back through the mall and found Dylan waiting for me, a Macy's bag in his hand.

"The tech solved my problem, and I found a shirt on sale."

"I bought a few things too," I said.

Dylan put his arm around me, and we walked out to the car. "If she doesn't show up soon after we get there, we'll head for home. At least we had a nice day out."

"I suppose." I was disappointed. Talking to Billy's mother was the best and only chance we had of finding a possible suspect.

The traffic had built up, so it took a while longer for us to return to Sheila Rossetti's house. I rang the bell again. But still no one came to the door.

"On TV shows, the detective knocks on the front door of a suspect or a person of interest and he or she is always home," I groused.

"It's almost three thirty," Dylan said as we climbed back into the car. "We'll give it a few more minutes, then head back. We're bound to hit traffic on the drive to Port Jefferson. I hope we can make the four forty-five ferry. The one after that leaves at six thirty. Both will be crowded."

More people were around now, mostly mothers with young children and middle school kids riding bicycles in the street. Jeannette drove her car out of the garage and passed us. I waved, but she pretended not to see me.

"She probably thinks it's weird that we're back here, waiting for Sheila," I said.

A few minutes later I was proven right. A police car pulled behind our car and an officer stepped out to talk to us.

Chapter
Twenty-Six

"Do you mind telling me what you folks are doing here? A neighbor called to say you've spent a good part of the day waiting for the homeowner to come home."

The cop appeared to be about thirty-five; he had a burly build and a ruddy complexion.

"Good afternoon, Officer," Dylan said, not at all perturbed. "My name is Dylan Avery. I'm a private investigator. Miss Singleton and I drove from Connecticut this morning to speak to the woman who lives here."

"Can I see some identification?"

"Of course. And your name is?"

The cop's complexion turned a shade brighter. "It's Pete Reynolds."

"Thank you."

I gave Dylan my driver's license. He removed his PI and driver's licenses from his wallet and handed all three to Officer Pete, who glanced at them before bringing them to his cruiser, no doubt to check them out on his computer.

"These seem to be in order," he said a few minutes later as he returned our licenses to Dylan. "Is this a case you're working on, Mr. Avery?"

"In a manner of speaking," Dylan said. "Anyway, we don't plan to wait here much longer. We hope to speak to Mrs. Rossetti briefly, then return home on the four forty-five Port Jefferson ferry."

Hearing that we didn't intend to hang around for any length of time must have pleased Officer Pete, because he smiled. "You'll be cutting it close, given the buildup of traffic in the next hour."

Dylan grimaced. "Don't I know it."

"Safe trip home," Officer Pete said. A minute later he pulled around us and drove off.

"I'm glad to know the Suffolk County police are checking out anyone who parks in front of someone else's house."

"He was only doing his job," Dylan said. "Wouldn't you be suspicious if two people sat in a car in front of your neighbor's house, waiting for her to come home?"

"I suppose," I said.

My cell phone rang. It was Billy. "Hi, Carrie. I was hoping to hear from you. What's happened?"

"Sorry, I should have called. We've been waiting for hours for your mother to come home. In fact, a neighbor called the cops to check us out."

Billy laughed. It wasn't a happy sound. "Maybe she's on the run again."

"Let's not go down that road," I told him. "We plan to stay here a little while longer. Maybe she'll come home by then."

Dylan started up the car.

"Just a minute." I covered the phone. "Why are we leaving?" I asked Dylan.

"We're not. A car's approaching at a slow rate of speed. I have a feeling it might be Sheila. Finding an occupied car in front of her house will make her nervous."

"Billy, I think your mother is finally coming home. I'll call you tonight when I'm back and tell you everything she says."

I felt a growing excitement as we slowly circled the block. In the side mirror I spotted a navy SUV turning into the driveway of Sheila Rossetti's house.

"It is her!" I said. "Finally!"

"Good," Dylan said calmly. "We'll give her a few minutes to unwind, then ring the doorbell."

It suddenly hit home that this was the first time Dylan and I were going to interview a potentially important witness together. I wondered if I was up to the job. In past investigations, I'd always depended on my intuition when it came to the questions I asked, and for the most part I'd been successful. But Dylan was a trained investigator. A *professional* investigator.

I turned to him as we approached the Rossettis' house again. "I think you should be the one to question Sheila."

"Why?" Dylan asked.

"Interviewing persons of interest is what you do for a living. I could say the wrong thing and screw it all up."

"We're here because Billy asked you to come in his place. I'm your wingman, babe. You'll do just fine."

I reached over to hug him as best I could, given my seat belt. "Thanks, Dylan."

"I'll be right beside you," he said as he brought the car to a stop and turned off the motor.

Minutes seemed to pass as we waited for Sheila Rossetti to answer the door. She opened it a few inches and peered at us anxiously. She was a slight woman in her early sixties, pretty, with delicate, even features. I could imagine the beauty she must have been when she was younger. She wore her dark-brown hair shoulder length and greeted us with a wary expression.

"Yes? What is it?"

Thank goodness this was a safe neighborhood and she'd been willing to open the door to strangers. Now to say the right thing so she didn't slam it in our faces.

"Mrs. Rossetti, my name is Carrie Singleton. This is my partner, Dylan Avery. We want very much to talk to you."

Singleton. Avery. Her eyes widened with apprehension as she recognized two surnames well known in Clover Ridge. Though younger than she, we were intruders from her past, bringing trouble.

The door started to close. Dylan stepped forward so she could meet his gaze as he prevented the door from shutting. "May we come in, Mrs. Rossetti?" He spoke calmly, his voice filled with concern. "There are things you should know, and we're hoping you might be able to help us too."

She viewed us with sad, mournful eyes. "How did you find me?"

"With great difficulty," Dylan said.

Her expression grew more fearful.

"We have no intention of disrupting your life," he said.

Sheila Rossetti released a deep sigh of resignation. "You may as well come in and tell me why you're here."

She led us into a small formal living room. A sofa covered in a shiny blue fabric was separated from two blue-and-white-striped chairs by a wooden coffee table. On the wall behind the chairs were three eight-by-ten photos set in the most beautiful picture frames I'd ever seen.

"How stunning!" I moved closer to better observe them, the purpose of our visit temporarily forgotten. They appeared to be made of rope or yarn intertwined with beads of various colors and sizes in the most artful arrangements. Each frame was unique. The one holding a photo that appeared to have been taken on Sheila and Tony Rossetti's wedding day was of gray-and-white rope with purple and lavender stones. The one featuring a young couple and three children was done in various shades of blue and aqua. The third, framing a different young couple, a toddler, and a dog, was beige, apricot, and brown. Three different color schemes that somehow worked well together.

"Lovely photos," I said belatedly.

Was that a chuckle I'd heard? "Thank you. My husband and his sons' families are quite good-looking. But I think you were admiring the frames."

"I was," I admitted. "I've never seen anything like it. They're beautiful!"

"I thank you again, since I made them."

"You did?"

Dylan cleared his throat. "I'm sure Mrs. Rossetti would like to hear why we're here."

"Sorry," I said, and moved to sit beside him on the sofa.

Sheila perched on the edge of a chair, the frightened expression back on her face. I found my voice and began telling her what I knew. "Your daughter Daphne moved back to Clover Ridge a few months ago. I met her when she came to the library where I'm head of programs and events, and told me she wanted to give a talk on psychic ability."

"Really? Daphne doesn't have psychic ability."

I controlled my shudder as best I could. Sheila had no idea that her daughter was dead. Of course! If she happened to have read about the murder in the newspaper, the name Daphne Marriott would mean nothing to her. The police were keeping Daphne's connection to Chet Harper under wraps.

"It seems Daphne acquired her abilities later in life. She presented her program and we became friends." I swallowed, dreading to have to break the news of her daughter's murder.

Sheila smiled. "How is Daphne? I've missed her and Billy so very much all these years."

"Then why did you leave them?" I hadn't meant to ask, but the question had acquired a force of its own and demanded an answer.

Sheila Rossetti clutched her chest and shrank into herself, making herself as small as she probably felt. A position she had no doubt assumed when Chet Harper started beating on her.

I crossed the room to where she sat and placed my hand on her back. She flinched, then leaned against me. Dylan headed into the kitchen. I heard water running. He returned with a glass of water and handed it to Sheila. She sipped, then placed the glass on the table.

"It was a terrible thing I did—abandoning my children— but I had to get away. I couldn't breathe. I felt like I was suffocating. I thought I would die if I didn't escape from Clover Ridge. Away from Chet's murder. The memories."

PTSD. Post-traumatic stress disorder or something like it.

"Where did you go?"

"To Oregon. It was the farthest I could travel on the money I'd saved and still have something to live on until I found a job."

"But your husband was dead," I said. "He couldn't hurt you any longer."

Sheila Rossetti put her hands to her head. "Living with Chet was difficult. When he drank, he turned nasty. He took his anger out on me and my son. Daphne was spared the worst of it." She closed her eyes. "His murder set me over the edge."

"Did you see it happen?" I asked.

"No, but . . ."

"But you know who killed him."

"I don't want to talk about it."

I looked at Dylan.

"Mrs. Rossetti, we think you know who murdered your husband," he said.

She remained still as a statue.

"Please tell us if you do," I said, "because we're afraid he's murdered again."

No response.

"Two women." I drew a deep breath. "One of them was Daphne, your daughter."

"No!" Her shriek rang through the house. The dreadful cry of a mortally wounded animal. It seemed to go on forever.

"I'm so sorry." Feeble words I doubted she heard through the noisy sobs that followed. When they subsided, I said, "Your son Billy is living outside Clover Ridge. He's working as a personal trainer. Since he couldn't be here today, he asked me to come and talk to you."

Sheila Rossetti's tears spilled down her cheeks. "Billy, I am so sorry I abandoned you. Leaving you to face prison for something you didn't do. But I was too frightened to tell that bent police chief what he didn't want to hear. Too frightened to do anything but run."

"Billy wants to see you," I said softly.

She shook her head. "No. He hates me. How can he not hate me? A mother doesn't desert her children. But I did. I did."

"He was planning to come see you today."

Sheila stared at me. "Really?"

"Yes."

"He's not here today because he was poisoned," Dylan said. "We think by the same person who killed your husband and your daughter."

She reached across the table and clutched Dylan's arm. "But he'll be all right?"

"Yes," Dylan and I said at the same time.

"Daphne and Chet dead. Billy poisoned. Because of me," Sheila said softly.

"Not because of you," I said.

"But you can help the police solve this case by telling them what you know," Dylan said.

Sheila Rossetti shook her head. "I couldn't. I simply couldn't. That Lieutenant Flynn. He knew how to twist your words around. Make you say things you didn't mean. He got Daphne to say Billy must have killed Chet when Daphne knew nothing of the sort. I couldn't bear for him to find out . . ."

"Find out what?" I demanded, sounding more exasperated than I'd meant to. After all these years, this woman was still afraid to say what she knew.

"Would you please give me Billy's phone number so I can call him," Sheila said.

When I hesitated, she said, "You said he wanted to see me."

"Of course."

I waited while she went into the kitchen for a piece of paper, on which I wrote Billy's cell phone number. "He'll be happy to hear from you," I said.

* * *

Dylan and I left shortly after that. I leaned back into the leathery comfort of the BMW's passenger seat as we started our journey home.

"So that's that. A waste of an interview after all that waiting."

Dylan turned to smile at me. "I wouldn't be so dismissive. We investigators have to be grateful for every small piece of evidence we gather."

"Like what? Sheila knows who killed her husband, but she still won't tell us his identity, even after learning he must have killed her daughter."

"Which tells us she's either afraid to reveal his name—or ashamed, for some reason."

"Sure, he must have been her lover all those years ago, but committing adultery is small stuff compared to murder and poisoning."

"Could be she's still afraid of this person," Dylan said.

"Uh-huh." I nodded as I thought. "If this man killed Chet, it was on her behalf. Which means he cared a great deal about

Sheila, I mean Patricia. But if he cared so much about her, why didn't they end up together?"

"We don't know that they didn't—at least at first. She may have been protecting him."

"But she didn't marry him," I said.

"No," Dylan agreed.

I sighed. "So, in a sense we're back to square one."

"Not exactly. She asked for Billy's phone number."

"True, but will she actually call him?"

Dylan patted my leg. "That's her move to make. We did what we could today. Now we have to sit back and wait."

*   *   *

The traffic moved slowly as we wended our way north on Route 112. We reached the harbor just as the ferry was loading its last car, and they waved us on. Minutes later we were climbing the stairs to the passenger cabin as the vessel began its trek across the Sound.

"Hungry?" Dylan asked.

I shook my head. "Are you kidding? I'm still full from lunch."

We found seats on the outside deck and gazed out at the water. The peaceful setting and the sound of the motor soothed my overactive mind, and I stopped mulling over our visit to Billy and Daphne's mother. I stopped wondering if she intended to call Billy and reveal the identity of her secret lover. For the time being, I was content to sit quietly beside the man I loved.

Dylan must have felt the same. After calling Rosalind to find out what was happening in his office, he stretched out his legs and promptly fell asleep. When we were back in the car and leaving Bridgeport, Dylan said, "Carrie, please remind Billy that he can't tell anyone—and I mean *anyone*—about our visit to his mother today."

"After ending up in the hospital, I'm sure he's gotten the message."

He shot me a sidelong glance. "That goes for you too. Don't mention it to your mother. She'll blab it to the movie crew."

"And considering Ilana's murder, there's a chance that the killer is one of them."

Dylan nodded. "We have no idea who he is, but we're sure he didn't want Billy visiting his mother. Which means he'll come after us if he knows we spoke to her."

I shuddered.

"Babe, until this is over, we keep this on a need-to-know basis. And never let up our guard."

Chapter
Twenty-Seven

That night I called Billy and repeated what his mother had said as best I could remember. When I finished, he released a mournful sigh.

"So, she still refuses to give up the name of her lover."

"Right. I don't know if she's afraid of this person or wants to protect him."

"Still? After all these years?" Billy's voice cracked. "And she couldn't offer one good reason why she ran off, leaving Daphne and me?"

I pressed my lips together. Of course I'd told Billy what she had said about her emotional state at the time, but people only heard what they wanted to hear. "I think she was traumatized with a serious case of PTSD. She didn't say she saw this person stab your father, but she must have seen something that left her in no doubt that her lover had killed him."

After a minute, Billy said, "And she asked for my phone number?"

"Yes. I gave it to her, though I can't promise that she'll call you."

Billy made a scoffing sound. "And I have no intention of waiting around, hoping she'll call—not after all these years."

"Please let me know if she contacts you."

"Of course, Carrie. I can't thank you and Dylan enough for taking a day off to drive all the way to Long Island to see her."

"We wanted to hear what she had to say—for your sake and hopefully to get a lead on the person who killed Daphne and Ilana. Billy, please don't tell anyone that we visited your mother. If the killer finds out, he'll assume she gave him up and come after Dylan and me."

Billy's laugh was anything but humorous. "You don't have to remind me to keep my mouth shut. I'm still recovering from that stupid announcement I made at Daphne's service."

* * *

My life resumed its usual pattern over the next few days. Angela's bridal shower was at the end of the month and I had a few things to attend to, including phone calls to a few of her female relatives who hadn't bothered to RSVP.

Every so often I felt a pang of guilt for not telling John that Dylan and I had paid a visit to Patricia Harper aka Sheila Rossetti. Then I'd think, why risk getting bawled out for what he'd see as interfering in his case when in fact we hadn't learned anything new? Besides, she had been cleared of all charges regarding her husband's death. As for her lover, she'd refused to tell us his name, and there was no reason to believe John would be more successful in getting her to talk. Sheila lived in another state, so I doubted he could force her to come in to be interviewed. Still, I felt bad for not letting him know that we'd seen her.

I ran into Danny Brower outside the post office. When I asked if the police had any new leads regarding the investigation, he sighed and said they were still waiting for some fiber and hair results to come back but otherwise they had zip.

I talked to Evelyn about our visit to Long Island, and she had a few things to say on the subject.

"I'm disappointed in Pattie Harper. You'd think catching her daughter's killer would be her priority, even if it was her long-ago lover."

"I'm wondering if the man has some sort of hold over her," I said.

"A good point," Evelyn said. "But why is she so afraid, after all these years?"

I thought a bit. "What if she tells John the name of the person who killed her husband. Then he, in turn, points a finger and claims he only did it because she asked him to?"

Evelyn's head bobbed up and down in agreement. "That would explain why she skipped town so quickly after she was cleared of Chet's murder."

"Daphne and Ilana were killed here in Clover Ridge," I said. "That means the killer might still live here . . ."

"Or?"

"Or he's a member of the movie crew." I groaned in frustration.

Evelyn frowned. "For her children's sake, Pattie should tell the police what she knows."

"I'm hoping she'll contact Billy," I said.

"Given her track record, I'm not holding my breath."

* * *

I found myself checking in with my mother every day. I'd helped her through a rough time and felt our relationship had taken a turn for the better. But now that her life was back on track, she'd reverted to her old ways. Though she always sounded happy to hear from me, her mind was on Tom and his glorious future.

"Carrie dear, I can't talk!" she said when I called her the morning after our excursion to Long Island. "They're filming all day today down by the water. Would you like to come and watch?"

"Sorry, Mom. I have to work. But I'm glad they're moving right along."

"Absolutely! Marissa Varig is such a sweetie. Not like that bitch Ilana."

"How's Tom?" I asked.

"Fine. I watched him and Marissa run through a few scenes. They are *perfectly* cast and bring out the best in each other." She giggled. "I wouldn't be surprised if this role wins him an Oscar nomination."

An Oscar? The woman's delusional. "I'm glad Tom's doing well. And the two of you are good?"

Another giggle. "Better than ever. He's still apologizing for falling for Ilana's tricks. We'll be fine. Have to go now. They're about to shoot one of Tom's big scenes. He likes to know I'm close by."

My mother and Tom would be all right, I decided when I disconnected. They were back in tandem. Once again on the same page. He was her husband and she was back to showering him with all the attention she'd never given Jordan and me. I sighed as I realized that my mother loved me in her own way, though it wasn't the way I would have wanted.

* * *

"You knew Pattie Harper, didn't you Aunt Harriet?" I asked during dinner at my aunt and uncle's house a few days later.

Aunt Harriet put down her fork and sighed. "I suppose her daughter coming back to town and getting murdered has people talking about Pattie Harper all over again."

"What was she like twenty years ago?"

"A pretty woman, worn out from working two jobs and being the punching bag for that brute of a husband. I didn't know her well, just enough to smile and say good-morning when we saw each other shopping or running errands. I knew about Chet and his drinking, of course. So did everyone in town."

"You can say that again," my uncle chimed in. "Al Tripp had a thing for Pattie. He kept after Mitch Flynn—he was the police chief before John—to throw the SOB in jail for abusing his family, but Mitch claimed he couldn't unless one of his victims filed a complaint. Of course Pattie and the kids were too frightened to do anything of the sort."

Aunt Harriet smiled. "Yes, Al was half in love with her. Offered to represent her for free if she filed for divorce."

"Look who's talking," Uncle Bosco said to Aunt Harriet. "You tried to take her under your wing. Even offered to let her stay with us awhile, though she and I had never exchanged two words."

"It was the only decent thing to do, Bosco!" My aunt turned to me. "One Saturday morning I was shopping early—we were having people over that evening. I ran into Pattie in the supermarket. She'd been crying. And there was a large bruise on her cheek. No one was around, so I pulled her to one side and offered to help her. At first she pretended not to know what I was talking about. Then she said I wasn't to worry. She had a friend who was helping her and things would be better very soon."

Uncle Bosco raised his hand. "That happened two days before her husband was murdered."

My heart began to pound. Maybe Dylan and I had gotten it all wrong. Maybe Patricia Harper *had* planned with this mysterious person to kill Chet.

"Do you have any idea who she was talking about?" I asked.

"None whatsoever," Aunt Harriet said. "For a while Lester Brown was under suspicion because he'd made no secret that he thought the world of Pattie. She only had to say the word and he would have taken her in."

I cleared my throat. "What about Al Tripp? Could he have killed Chet?"

My uncle burst out laughing. "Are you kidding? Our esteemed mayor?"

I shrugged. These days our mayor's driving passions were his family and the welfare of Clover Ridge, but we were talking about twenty years ago.

"You said he had the hots for Patricia Harper."

"So I did," Uncle Bosco said. "Al was grilled along with Lester Brown, and he provided a solid alibi. As a young lawyer, he worked crazy hours and was able to prove he'd been in his office with a client till close to midnight the night Chet Harper was killed."

"Pattie was at work, so she couldn't have done it," Aunt Harriet said. "And so Mitch, who always took the easiest path, turned to their son Billy. He'd heard that Billy had argued with his father a week or two earlier, so he put the screws to poor Daphne and voilà! He managed to find himself a murderer and tie up the homicide with a ribbon."

"She should have stayed to give Billy moral support," Uncle Bosco said, "but she was gone by the time he was charged."

"And if she knew that her friend or lover had murdered her husband, she should have said so," I said.

Aunt Harriet reached over to pat my shoulder. "If that person really existed. No one ever saw Pattie's so-called lover. I agree, she should have stood by her children, but we'll never find out why she didn't, since we'll most likely never see her again."

I remained silent, hating not being able to tell them we'd seen Sheila-Patricia.

My aunt got to her feet. "Carrie dear, let's clear the table and make room for some homemade apple cake and coffee."

* * *

Days passed. On a beautiful May afternoon, I left the library at five, dropped Smoky Joe off at the cottage, and drove to the gym. I was puffing away on the elliptical when Billy walked over, a broad grin on his face.

"My mother's coming to visit," he said softly so no one could hear us.

I stopped the machine and stared at him. "What made her change her mind about coming back here? From spending time with her, I got the impression she was terrified of the person she believes killed your father and Daphne."

Robby nodded. "Don't I know it. A complete turnaround. I think it took my sister's death sinking in to make her think how it could have been prevented if only she'd spoken up years ago. She said she's tired of being afraid and will tell the police everything she knows."

I hugged him. "I'm so glad. When is she coming?"

"Next Tuesday. I'm taking a few days off so we can spend time together," Billy said. "Do you have any suggestions where we might go? From what she's told me, she and her husband rarely go out."

"She might enjoy the event at the library Saturday night. Four of the movie actors will be reading Gurney's *The Cocktail Hour*. The seats in the meeting room are all taken, but the movie company's sound engineer is setting up a system so patrons can sit upstairs and hear the play being read. I'll reserve two seats if you like."

Billy laughed. "Just like the radio. Thanks, Carrie. I think she'd like that."

"I'm glad you'll have this chance to spend time with your mother."

"Me too."

* * *

The following day, as Angela and I walked over to the Cozy Corner Café, I told her that Billy's mother was coming to pay him a visit.

"I hope this isn't a mistake," Angela said.

I shot her a look of surprise. "Why do you say that?"

"Because Billy must be furious that she abandoned him and his sister. I bet they get into an argument first thing."

"Hopefully, she'll tell him why she left," I said. "Not that it excuses what she did, but it will explain why she acted that way."

"Ha! And never contacted him or Daphne in twenty years," Angela said.

I prodded her. "What's really bothering you?"

Angela exhaled a deep sigh. "My brother. I keep wishing he wasn't coming to the wedding."

"Angela!"

"I told you Tommy did really mean things to me when I was growing up. And the one time I told my mother, she downplayed it. Well, the last time he was in town, I brought it up. At first he denied it. Then he began laughing in that stupid way of his—the way he laughs when he knows he's done something bad. I yelled at him before he could spew out one of his usual excuses. He yelled back. And so it went until my father came into the den to ask what was going on. Tommy ran out of my parents' house. He came back late that night and flew back to Hollywood the next morning, earlier than he'd planned. That was two years ago."

"I'm so sorry." I stopped walking and put my arm around her.

Angela shrugged. "Anyway, my mother insists he's changed. He has a new girlfriend he's bringing to the wedding, and he's working on a movie that he claims has great promise. Ha! I keep worrying he'll do something stupid on the most special day of my life and ruin everything."

I hugged her close. "Guys grow up. My cousin Randy used to tease me mercilessly. He turned into a really good guy. And Tommy will only be here a few days, right?"

Angela nodded. "I know. It's crazy. Lately, I keep thinking of things that might go wrong."

"Nothing will go wrong at your wedding," I said. "I promise."

We started walking again. "Getting back to Billy and his mother," Angela said. "She's had plenty of time to think about everything you and Dylan told her. I suppose part of the reason she's coming to visit Billy is so she can tell John Mathers what she knows or suspects."

"Let's hope she doesn't chicken out."

* * *

That afternoon I received a phone call from Charlie Stanton.

"Hi, Carrie. Any chance your library's meeting room is free tonight or tomorrow evening? We'd like to do a run-through of the reading in the library, if possible."

I glanced at my schedule. "You're in luck. A program that was scheduled for tomorrow evening was canceled. You can have the room from seven till nine."

"Awesome!" he boomed over the phone. "We start filming extra early tomorrow morning and should be finished by three the latest. That gives everyone some time to relax before coming over. Thanks."

"You're most welcome," I told him. "Everyone's looking forward to this event. I've ordered forty folding chairs for the patrons who will be sitting upstairs."

"Ralph, our sound engineer, will be coming along to set up the sound system that will transmit the reading to the upstairs area. By the way, you can tell your patrons they're welcome to watch our rehearsal if they like. As long as they realize it's a rehearsal and we'll stop occasionally for various reasons. Some people find that pretty damn annoying."

"I'll be sure to mention it," I said.

I posted about the rehearsal on the library's Facebook page, then went to tell Sally. She was delighted, as I'd known she would be. Any program or event that drew patrons to the library gave her joy.

At five o'clock, I put Smoky Joe in his carrier and headed out to my car. I drove to my favorite drugstore, which was a few blocks off the Green. "I won't be long," I promised Smoky Joe as I locked the door behind me.

I was trying to decide between two brands of sunscreen when I heard someone chuckle. "Well, well, look who's here."

I glanced up at John Mathers. "Hi, John. What are you doing here?"

"What do you think? Shopping. Same as you. Sylvia asked me to pick up her prescription, and I wandered down this aisle."

"I need some sunscreen. That is, I don't really need it. I still have some from two years ago, but I'm afraid it's no longer effective."

Why am I babbling about sunscreen? More to the point, why am I feeling so uncomfortable?

I reached for the brand I'd been favoring and drew a deep breath. "Anything new on the murder investigation?"

John shrugged. "You know how it is. We check out every lead, then recheck."

That's about as vague as you can get. Clearly, he's not planning on telling me a thing. "I'm sure you do. Thank God there haven't been any more murders."

John winked at me. "We haven't talked in a while. Is there anything you've learned recently that might have bearing on the homicides?"

My ears grew warm. I knew they must be blazing red. "Recently? Let's see. I've heard that Alvin Tripp had taken an interest in Patricia Harper around the time her husband was murdered. Do you think he was her secret lover?"

"The secret lover who supposedly murdered her husband and more recently her daughter and Ilana Reingold?" John burst out laughing. "Come on, Carrie. You can do better than that. If you heard that Al Tripp was once interested in Pattie Harper, you must also know he had a foolproof alibi the night Chet Harper was murdered."

"So I've heard," I admitted.

"I was thinking about more recent developments. Like Pattie Harper's upcoming visit to Clover Ridge."

"Oh. You know about that."

"Why am I not surprised that you know it too?" John put on an expression of fake innocence. "But then, you've already met the mysterious lady."

I sighed. "Okay, you got me. Dylan and I went to see her last week."

John shook his head. "You should have told me, Carrie. You should have told me."

"I'm sorry," I said softly. But he was halfway to the register and didn't hear.

Chapter
Twenty-Eight

My mother called that evening just as I'd finished cleaning up after dinner.

"Carrie dear, how are you? I hope to see you tomorrow evening when Tom and the others come to the library for their rehearsal."

"I'll be there, Mom."

"I'm so glad. It feels like ages since we've gotten together."

"How are things?" I asked. "How's Tom?"

"Couldn't be better. Dirk couldn't stop raving about the two scenes they shot today with Tom and Marissa." She lowered her voice. "If you ask me—I hate to speak ill of the dead—but Marissa is a much better actress than Ilana. Tom simply *glows* when they're on camera together."

A glowing Tom. He sounds radioactive. I stifled a giggle.

"This movie is turning out to be such a godsend," my mother went on. "Tom's agent called to let us know that two directors want him to read for parts. Not leads, but very *substantial* roles."

"That's wonderful," I said, meaning it.

"And how are you and Dylan doing?"

"We're good," I said. "He might be able to come to the rehearsal tomorrow."

"I'd love to see him. We really should make a dinner date. Before you know it, they'll be finished filming and we'll be heading back to California."

"When do you think that will be?" I asked.

"Dirk refuses to say, except that it's sooner than he'd thought. After Ilana was killed, there was talk of scuttling the movie, but Charlie, Serena, and Tom were all for soldiering on. And with Marissa being such a professional, they were able to get back to work and shoot scenes more quickly than expected."

"I'm glad, especially for you and Tom."

My mother sighed. "Tom's happy that people are beginning to recognize his talent. But he and all the others are upset that there hasn't been any progress in the investigation into Ilana's murder."

"I can understand that," I said.

"Carrie dear, have you heard of any new developments? Are the police interviewing any new suspects?"

Ah, so that's why you called! "Sorry, Mom. Nothing I know of."

"You're good friends with Lieutenant Mathers. He didn't happen to bring you up to date on the investigation?"

"Nope."

"And you haven't found out anything that points to a guilty party?"

"Sorry, Mom. I haven't."

Was that a tsk *I heard?* "I've told everyone in the cast and crew how you virtually solved the last few homicide cases here in Clover Ridge single-handedly. I showed them the articles I printed out of all those online stories about you!"

"Thanks, Mom. I wish you hadn't."

"Why? What are you ashamed of? You should be proud that you're so clever. I'm very proud of you."

I let out a humph of exasperation. "Did it ever occur to you that if someone in the movie crew murdered Daphne and Ilana, he'd be angry if he found out I was trying to track him down and might come after me?"

After a pause, my mother said, "I think you're being very unreasonable, Carrie. I doubt very strongly that anyone involved in the movie is the murderer. First your police chief suspected Dirk, then he suspected Tom. He couldn't hold either of them because they're innocent."

When I remained silent, my mother went on. "I'd think you'd want to find this murderer. Especially since your friend Daphne was his first victim."

And you're hoping I'll tell you everything I learn so you can impress the movie people. That's not going to happen. "I have no clues to chase down," I said. "I'm leaving this investigation to Lieutenant Mathers."

"Well, let me know if you happen to find out anything, okay?"

"Of course. See you tomorrow night."

* * *

The following day, I left the library at five o'clock sharp. As soon as I got home, I fed Smoky Joe his dinner, then ate a tuna salad sandwich and made one for Dylan, which he ate on our drive back to the library for the read-through of *The Cocktail Hour.*

We hadn't had a chance to talk for any length of time during the past two days, so I filled him in on my conversations with my mother and John on the way to the library.

"John's pissed at me for not telling him we went to see Sheila."

Dylan laughed. "Which means he's pissed at me as well."

I grinned. "I'm glad I have company."

"He'll get over it. Next topic. Why are you annoyed with your mother?"

I exhaled loudly. "Because she only called to pick my brain about the murders."

"So? What's unusual about that?"

I stared at him. "She's my mother. She should be interested in me, her daughter. Not using me so she can impress the movie people."

Dylan snorted. "This is Brianna—er, Linda—we're talking about. Have you forgotten what she's like?"

"No, but I was hoping that after staying with me, she had changed."

"Uh-huh. A woman in her midfifties makes a startling behavioral change after staying with her daughter for—how many days was it? Two? Three?"

I stared at Dylan, then burst out laughing. "Okay. Point taken. She didn't change. She won't change. She—she's the same as she's always been."

Dylan patted my hand. "Now you're learning."

"I hope so. For some reason, though, I keep expecting her to relate differently to me," I grumbled.

"Carrie, your mother loves you, but her number-one concern in life is her husband, Tom."

I nodded. "I know."

"And once you truly understand and accept that, it won't hurt as much as it does now."

We drove on in silence as I thought that over. We must have traveled a few miles when Dylan said, "Of course, there's no telling how things will shift once she becomes a grandmother."

My mouth fell open. When I managed to speak, I said, "Now where did *that* come from?"

Dylan chuckled instead of answering.

The library parking lot was full, what with all the regular patrons as well as those planning to attend tonight's rehearsal, so we parked on the street.

"It's only six thirty," I said. "I didn't expect this many people to turn up for a read-through."

"I'm not surprised," Dylan said. "The public views actors as icons, even when they're not big names like Brad Pitt and Nicole Kidman. I imagine the people coming here tonight want to hear what Tom and Charlie and the others say to one another when they're not reading their lines."

"I suppose you're right."

The back door was locked, which was very unusual, so we walked around to the front of the library. Inside, Sally was counting heads as people entered. "Thank God you're here! Marion and Harvey are holding back the horde. They have instructions to let those people to whom I've given numbers go downstairs at a quarter to seven. There are fire laws and we have limited seating."

She eyed Dylan. "Dylan, would you and Carrie be so kind as to go down to the meeting room and—once they're allowed downstairs—urge the audience to take seats ASAP?"

"Glad to be of service," he said, smiling.

I returned waves and greetings as we made our way through the crowd gathered at the top of the staircase. Marion, the children's librarian, and Harvey, the head of our computer department, looked harried as they stood guard.

"Lucky you," Harvey said as Dylan and I walked past him.

I looked forward to the fall when work would begin on the library expansion, which would include a stadium-seating auditorium with a capacity four times the number of seats we had now.

"Yoo-hoo, Carrie!"

As I entered the meeting room, Charlie Stanton waved to me from his seat behind the long table he was sharing with Tom, Serena, and a beautiful young woman with long blonde hair who I assumed was Marissa Varig. Tom was listening to something Marissa was saying, while Serena was deep in conversation with Hattie Fein, who stood at her side.

Always the hair and makeup artist, I thought as Hattie smoothed a strand of Serena's hair in place. A man wearing earphones—no doubt Ralph, the sound engineer—was snaking a wire across the floor behind the table so the reading could be heard upstairs the evening of the actual performance.

My mother broke off chatting with Liane Walters and turned to Dylan and me. "I'm so glad to see you, Carrie. And Dylan, of course!" She hugged us as though she were welcoming us to the event.

Now that her marital relationship had dramatically improved, my mother had reverted to true form. My boyfriend quickly faded from the scene like the investigator par excellence he was, leaving me to deal with my mother.

"I was just suggesting to Liane the idea of inviting the local TV station here to do a feature on the reading," she said. "It would show the library in a good light and provide great publicity for the movie."

"Doesn't Firestone Productions have its own publicist?" I asked.

My mother dismissed that with a wave of her hand. "They sent a reporter here when the filming began, but nothing's been in the papers or on TV since then."

I refrained from mentioning that Ilana's murder had received plenty of publicity in the news.

Like Dylan, Liane had found the opportunity to escape my mother's attentions. I was about to move on too when she grabbed my arm as though she knew what I was planning.

"Carrie dear. I'd like you to meet Marissa Varig. Such a lovely young woman." *Not like Ilana, you mean.*

"Mom, I really have to—" I began, to no avail. She practically dragged me over to the table, which caught the attention of the others.

"Marissa, I'd like you to meet my daughter, Carrie. She's responsible for every program and event the library presents. Carrie, Marissa is an up-and-coming movie star." My mother winked. "I expect her to be nominated for an Oscar one of these days."

Marissa held out a slim hand. "It's a pleasure to meet you, Carrie."

"Likewise," I said.

Marissa tilted her head as she smiled. Every movement was fluid. Graceful. "Tom and your mother have been telling me that you're also a detective. In fact, they said you've helped the police catch murderers."

"A few." I felt my ears grow warm with embarrassment.

Marissa scoffed. "A few murderers are more than I've ever caught."

"We're hoping Carrie will find poor Ilana's killer," Charlie chimed in.

"Yes, indeed," Serena agreed. "Especially since the official investigation has come to a dead standstill. Pardon the pun."

Marissa shivered. "I almost didn't take this job because I'd heard of the two murders in town, but Dirk convinced me I'd be safe."

Charlie grinned. "What he did was offer you enough greenbacks to overcome your fears."

That earned him a roar of laughter from everyone present, including Marissa. I shot Charlie a look of admiration. He had the rare ability to say what was on everyone's mind without rubbing people the wrong way.

"Carrie, have there been any new developments in the case?" Tom asked.

I didn't answer. Hattie had just turned her head, and I was too busy staring at the barrette holding back her curly black hair. It appeared to be made of braided silver rope and was decorated with an array of purple, copper, and gold-colored beads.

"Carrie?" Tom prodded.

"Sorry. There's nothing new that I'm aware of. But John Mathers is a good man. I'm sure he's chasing down every lead and every tie-in between the two homicides."

"I heard there also might be a connection to a murder that took place twenty years ago," Marissa said.

"The police are looking into it," I said, craning my neck to catch another glimpse of Hattie's barrette. "I wouldn't be surprised if there's a break in the case very soon."

"I certainly hope so," Hattie said with a toss of her head.

"Hattie, your barrette is absolutely gorgeous! I've never seen anything like it."

Hattie smiled. "Why thank you, Carrie. I'm quite fond of it myself."

"Where did you get it?" I asked.

She cocked her head as she thought. "You know, I really can't remember." She waved to her friends. "And now I must bid you all adieu and let you do your thing."

I watched her walk to the rear of the room.

"Carrie, love, what break are you referring to?" Charlie asked, his tone teasing. "Come on! Don't hold back. Tell us what you know."

My mother took this as her cue to chime in. "Carrie runs rings around the police when it comes to finding clues and solving murders."

I felt a pang of guilt, remembering the times I'd gone sleuthing and didn't let John in on what I'd learned.

"Tell us what you know, Carrie. It's only fair," Tom urged.

Fair or not, I thought of Patricia Harper aka Sheila Rossetti's upcoming visit. "All I can say, is maybe something or someone will turn up soon. We'll have to wait and see."

Why did I refer to a person? I bit my tongue, but it was too late. At any rate, no one seemed to notice.

"Anything would be better than what's been happening up till now," Serena said. "If you ask me, that lieutenant doesn't know his ass from his elbow. He's questioned suspect after suspect and has yet to charge anyone with the crime."

I felt myself growing angry in John's defense. "Lieutenant Mathers is a wonderful detective. He's working the case and is sure to find Ilana's killer very soon!"

Serena cocked her head. "Really? And you're privy to this? Do tell."

Chapter
Twenty-Nine

B efore I could comment, the back door opened and the mob that had been waiting poured into the meeting room. I caught Dylan's eye, and he headed over to make sure people didn't trample one another in their eagerness to get what they considered the best seats in the house.

Soon every chair was occupied. A few patrons remained standing in the back of the room. I nodded to Dylan, and we took up positions against the side wall. Sally walked to the front of the room to address the audience.

"Good evening. The Clover Ridge Library is happy to welcome the four stars in Firestone Production's *I Love You, I Do*—Serena Harris, Charlie Stanton, Tom Farrell, and Marissa Varig. As you know, next Saturday evening they will be presenting a reading of A. R. Gurney's *The Cocktail Hour*. Tonight is a run-through of their reading. They will be stopping occasionally to discuss whatever they choose to discuss, so if this isn't to your liking, you're welcome to leave and come back Saturday night—if you have a ticket."

Sally paused. No one stirred.

"Though this is an informal rehearsal, I ask that you not talk among yourselves."

Much as I wanted to, I couldn't get absorbed in the play—about a playwright and his family—because every few minutes one of the actors stopped to make a comment or raise a question off-mic. The remarks were often humorous, judging by the laughter from the viewers in the first few rows. When Charlie called for a fifteen-minute recess, Dylan signaled to me that he'd like to leave, which was fine with me. We were coming on the following Saturday night to see the play in its entirety. I waved good-bye to my mother and headed for the door.

We weren't the only ones who had decided to call it a night. As we started up the stairs, I realized I was right behind Al Tripp, Clover Ridge's mayor and Uncle Bosco's good friend. He was with one of his teenage daughters. Al huffed and puffed so loudly, I feared for his heart. He paused when he reached the top of the stairs.

"Are you all right?" I asked.

"I will be, soon as I catch my breath."

"We do have an elevator," I said.

He continued to huff and puff. His red face had a sheen of perspiration. I exchanged worried looks with Dylan. "Al, I think you should sit down a minute."

He looked around. "Lindsay won't know where I am."

I spotted his daughter chatting with one of her friends.

"I'll tell her where you are," Dylan said.

I shot him a smile of appreciation and led Al to a seat in the reading room. Then I walked over to the coffee shop and asked Katie Rollins for a glass of water.

Al gulped down most of the water, then sat back and sighed. "Don't tell Dolores," he said.

"I wouldn't dream of it."

"She's after me to start a diet and an exercise regime. And I will—one of these days when I don't have a luncheon to attend. Or a dinner or late meeting." He exhaled heavily. "All of which involve food and drink."

"I know, but you have to consider your health."

He looked up at me. "Would you mind getting me some more water?"

"Of course not." I got him a refill, which he sipped slowly.

I sat down in the chair next to Al. "You're making a good start," I joked. "Drinking water's good for you."

Al rested his head against the back of the chair and closed his eyes. "You're doing a terrific job here at the library, Carrie. From what I hear, more Clover Ridge people are using its services than ever before. And that Haven House you got your uncle to run for the homeless is a godsend."

"I didn't start Haven House," I protested.

The mayor shot me a perceptive glance. "Maybe not, but you sure put it into the right hands."

I shrugged.

"Your Uncle Bosco is so very proud of you."

"That's the nicest thing I've heard all day," I said, smiling.

"You're an asset to this town, Carrie." He grinned. "Maybe one of these days you'll run for town council."

I burst out laughing. "I doubt that very much. I have enough going on in my life without being on the town council."

"I suppose that's the case right now, especially since you've been instrumental in solving several homicides," Al said.

"Not the latest cases, I'm afraid."

Al shook his head in dismay. "Terrible that two beautiful young women were murdered. John's working hard, trying to find their killer, but so far he's come up with zilch."

"This one hit close to me. Daphne and I were getting to be friends," I said. "And her brother Billy works at the gym Dylan and I belong to."

He nodded as he gazed down at the floor. Not going to speak? In that case, I was going to prod.

"Aunt Harriet told me you were friendly with Daphne and Billy's mother."

The tips of his ears turned red. "Sure, I knew Pattie. I knew her husband Chet. The town was smaller twenty years ago. We all knew one another and everyone's business."

I grinned. "I heard that Patricia Harper was quite the beauty and you had something of a crush on her."

"Come on, Carrie. She was a married woman. A harried, married woman and a mother who worked two jobs."

"And attracted the attention of several men. I heard Lester Brown thought highly of Patricia too."

Al exhaled a gallon of hot air. "Les did. I did too. Part of it was, we felt sorry for the woman."

"Was that all it was?" I asked, my tone teasing.

"All right. I was smitten. Beautiful, unattainable woman in need of a man to whisk her away from her awful abusive husband. At the time, I was so busy working that I hadn't had a date in months. Too thick to see how trite the premise was. The draw of a damsel in distress. Nothing more than a fantasy."

I stared at Alvin Tripp, impressed by his insight. "That's looking at it in hindsight. What did you and Patricia Harper talk about?"

"Various things. Her children. Her jobs. The hopes she'd had when she was young. I told her I'd get her a divorce pro bono. She simply smiled in her Mona Lisa way and said a divorce was impossible. Chet would kill her before any papers were signed."

"She seemed resigned to her fate?" I asked.

"Not resigned so much as certain that while I couldn't help her via the usual channels, someone else was going to."

"And she never said who this person was?"

Al shook his head. "I got the feeling it might have been someone she worked with, but to this day I've no idea who it was."

Chapter Thirty

"I can't stop thinking about that barrette," I said. "It's so similar to the craftwork on Sheila Rossetti's picture frames."

"So you've told me three times tonight." Dylan caressed my cheek with the back of his hand. "And for the third time, I'm saying I believe you. But that doesn't mean there's a connection between the two women. Give it a rest, babe. Lean back and enjoy our post-Precipice glow."

"You're right."

It was Saturday night and we were driving home from eating an outstanding meal at the Precipice, a spectacular ultramodern restaurant built on a rise high above a lake. But ever since I'd spotted Hattie Fein's barrette, my mind had refused to stop thinking about its similarity to Sheila Rossetti's picture frames. Tenuous though it might be, this was the only link I knew of that connected Sheila's husband's murder twenty years ago and Ilana's. And I wanted Dylan to agree with me.

"Sure, thousands of people make crafts and there's always a possibility that two or more craftspeople will create similar items, but what are the odds of this so-called coincidence occurring between interested parties close to a murder investigation?"

Dylan released a humph of exasperation. "Don't you think it's a bit of a stretch—considering Hattie Fein a serial killer? Who knows where she got the barrette? She could have bought it at a craft show years ago. It could have been a gift."

"I think she was lying about not remembering where she got the barrette," I said. "That in itself is suspicious."

"So what do you suggest? Tell John what you're thinking so he can bring Hattie in for questioning?"

"Bad idea. She'll close up like a clam."

Dylan exhaled loudly. "So? Any ideas?"

I shot him a smile of pure innocence. "A few, but I have no intention of sharing them with a doubting Thomas."

* * *

It was time to do some research, research I should have done weeks ago. I waited until Dylan was gently snoring, then headed to my office and turned on my computer. There were several Hattie Feins listed, but I quickly found the hair and makeup artist I knew listed in IMDb—the Internet Movie Database. The basics were there, but I needed more. I struck gold when I found an article about Hattie in one of the movie industry magazines.

Hattie Greenfield Fein had grown up in a small Michigan town outside Detroit. Her parents divorced when she was four and her sister was seven. Her mother, Pamela, decided to follow her dream of becoming an actress and moved the girls to Hollywood. Pamela managed to get a few small roles in movies and commercials.

Hattie, who often hung around the set when her mother was working, was drawn to the hair and makeup side of the industry. Since she was amiable and eager to learn, the crew allowed her to help out when there was a time crunch. A well-known makeup artist noticed her talents and took Hattie under her wing. All this stopped when Hattie married Jerry Fein, a lighting technician, at eighteen. They had a child who died in an accident at age three. Hattie and Jerry divorced shortly after.

Hattie resumed her career in the movie and TV industries as a hair and makeup artist. She worked on the sets of some prominent movies. Five years ago she'd suffered a heart attack. These past few years she had worked for indie movie companies, mostly Firestone Productions.

I closed the computer and stretched my arms overhead. All very interesting, but I didn't feel I knew Hattie any better than I had before reading about her. No recent spouses or lovers. No indication that she might have spent time in or near Clover Ridge years ago, or that she'd ever crossed paths with Patricia Harper aka Sheila Rossetti.

I wanted to research the others involved in the movie: Charlie, Ronnie Rodriguez, Ralph the sound engineer. Even Tom, my mother's husband. But I was too tired. Yawning, I padded back to bed and fell asleep almost immediately.

* * *

Monday morning Billy called me at the library to say he was picking up his mother the following afternoon at the train station. "She said she'd love to see you and Dylan while she's in town. Any chance of the four of us getting together?"

"She really wants to get together with Dylan and me?"

I must have sounded surprised, because Billy felt the need to explain. "She feels she wasn't as hospitable as she should have been when you guys drove all that way for my sake."

"Please tell her not to be concerned in the least. I understand how difficult it must have been, dealing with two strangers connected to her past. But since she's so inclined, I'd love to have you both come to dinner while she's here." I quickly ran through my schedule for the week. "How does Wednesday night sound?"

"That should be fine," Billy said. "The only set plan we have so far is the reading at the library on Saturday night."

"Your mom knew my Aunt Harriet. I'll invite her and Uncle Bosco to join us. And ask Dylan to try not to work late that night."

"That's very kind of you," Billy said. "My mother will be delighted."

"Don't tell her Aunt Harriet's coming. Let it be a surprise."

"All right."

"Are you aware of anything she can't or won't eat?" I asked.

"No, but I'll ask to make sure and let you know if there is."

"And of course you have an ulterior motive regarding this dinner," Evelyn said a moment later. She'd materialized as I ended my call.

I exhaled a lungful of air. "I give Sheila credit for gathering the courage to return to Clover Ridge, where both her husband and daughter were murdered. Not to mention facing the son she abandoned to trumped-up charges that landed him in prison. But finally telling the police what she's been hiding all these years might prove more difficult than she realizes. Since Sheila already knows me, I figure she might be more comfortable first talking to me about whatever it is that traumatized her."

Evelyn shot me a look of admiration. "Carrie, that's very thoughtful of you."

I smiled. "And I thought I'd mention Hattie's barrette."

She grimaced. "That again. You can ask Pattie if she knew Hattie Fein all those years ago, but I doubt there's a connection. The similarities between the picture frames and that woman's barrette could simply be a coincidence."

"I don't believe in coincidences," I said, as Evelyn faded from view.

* * *

I called Dylan. He promised to be home in plenty of time to make dinner at six thirty Wednesday evening. And Aunt Harriet was thrilled when I invited her and Uncle Bosco to join us.

"I'm so glad Pattie has remarried and that she's coming here to see her son."

"Billy told John she's coming. I'm hoping that means she's finally willing to give him an official statement of what she's been holding back all these years. I have a feeling she knows who killed Daphne and Ilana as well as her husband all those years ago."

"Carrie, I hope you're not setting too much store on that poor woman's secrets," my aunt chided me. "Even if she comes up with a name, that doesn't mean John can charge that person with three counts of murder."

"Yes, Aunt Harriet," I said meekly, secretly marveling at how savvy she'd gotten regarding homicides and the law this past year.

"I'll bring two desserts, so don't you go fussing with that," she said before she hung up.

I was so busy the rest of the day, I didn't even have time to go out for lunch with Angela. Instead, I asked her to bring me back a sandwich. Between phone calls and making sure all programs were running smoothly, Trish and I worked on the August-September newsletter. At three thirty I stretched my arms overhead and headed for the library's coffee shop for a much-needed break.

I treated myself to a cappuccino. The coffee shop was empty for a change, and I was content to sit quietly in a place that wasn't my office. I sipped my drink and mentally ran through the upcoming events that required my attention. Dinner for six on Wednesday night was no biggie. I'd buy a few barbecued chickens and make a salad and veggies. I could stop at the supermarket after work today. Dylan would supply the wine and Aunt Harriet the desserts. Saturday night was the reading of *The Cocktail Hour*. I'd introduce the actors, then sit back and enjoy the show along with the others.

The following Saturday would be our Adopt-a-Pet fair—to be held outside in front of the library if the weather was good. Inside if it rained. Angela's shower, for which I was largely responsible, was the weekend after that. I sighed. I loved running all these activities, but each required time and attention. When was I going to have a few hours to myself, maybe take a yoga class at the gym?

Smoky Joe accompanied me as I walked back to my office. Thinking about the gym got me thinking about Billy, which reminded me of my intention to Google the other movie people when I had a free moment. I found Susan drawing at her desk. I glanced over her shoulder to see what she was working on.

"Fantastic!" I said. She'd turned the Green with the buildings surrounding it into a summer playground—a small sandy area where people sunbathed, a playground with a seesaw and swings, and a picnic area with people barbecuing and eating on blankets. "This is much too nice for the newsletter."

Susan beamed. "Thanks, Carrie. I told Martha what I was drawing, and she said to make a large version of it in oils and she'd put it in the gallery's window."

"That should bring in some big bucks," I said.

Susan's smile grew wider. "So we're hoping. Ron and Martha want to have a show of my work six months from now."

"How wonderful, Susan!" I hugged her. "I'm so proud of you."

She looked pensive. "Martha wants me to do at least four more big pieces and several smaller ones. I might have to take time off from work to get everything done."

"Don't you worry about it," I said. "Starting in September, Trish's kids will all be going to school full-time, so maybe she can work more hours. Or I'll hire someone."

"Temporarily, please," Susan said vehemently. "I don't want to give up this job. I love working here—with you."

"Thank you, Susan. I feel the same way." I hugged her again, then went over to my desk. "What's this?" I asked, lifting the manila envelope beside my computer.

"I found it lying outside the door when I arrived," she said. "It says it's for you."

"So I see."

My name was printed in the center of the envelope. A tremor ran down my spine as I opened the metal fastener and pulled out the sheet of drawing paper. I stared at the message. Susan must have sensed my anxiety, because she came to stand beside me.

"*Stop prying or you're next*," she read aloud. "Carrie, this is awful."

"Did you see anyone leaving when you came into the library?" I asked.

She thought a bit. "A woman—can't think of her name, but she often comes in with her mother. Oh, and the mayor. He was talking to Sally."

My racing heart pumped even faster. "Really? The mayor? He rarely comes to the library."

Susan's eyes widened. "Carrie! You can't think Mayor Tripp sent you this."

"I don't know what to think, but I'm calling Lieutenant Mathers."

Chapter Thirty-One

" S o where is this threatening note?" John asked. Though Susan and I had both offered him our chairs, he remained standing.

"Here it is." I waited while John slipped on a pair of gloves, then handed him the envelope.

"*Stop prying or you're next,*" he read aloud. "Where did you find this?"

"Susan found it on the floor outside the office when she arrived."

John turned to Susan and asked her a barrage of questions: What time had she entered the library? Did anyone rush by her in the parking lot? As she entered the library? Did she notice anyone near the office? Finally satisfied that she couldn't identify the person who had delivered the note, he told her he'd like to speak to me privately.

"Of course," Susan said, and left the office.

"So," John said, settling into the chair she'd just vacated. "A warning from the possible murderer. I'll have this checked for fingerprints."

I gave him a half smile. "You have my prints on record. I'll tell Susan to stop by the precinct to have hers taken."

"Thanks, Carrie." He drew a deep breath. "A similar warning was left for Billy Harper at the gym this morning."

"What did his note say?" I asked.

"*Remind your mother that silence is golden.*"

"Oh."

He fixed his gaze on me. "You told no one she was coming to stay with him?"

"Absolutely not." When John continued to stare at me, I added, "Well, I mentioned it to Angela, but I know she didn't say a word to anyone. And when Billy called this morning to say his mother would like to see Dylan and me, I invited them to dinner, then called Dylan and Aunt Harriet about dinner Wednesday night."

John snorted. "Anyone else you care to add to the list?"

I thought a moment before shaking my head. "No one. Though I happened to say I thought there might be a break in the case real soon, which might have left some people with the impression that I knew something." I gave him a guilty smile. "And I might have said that maybe something or someone would turn up soon. Sorry."

John leaned across the desk to glare at me. "Which people exactly might have gotten the impression that you know more than you told them?"

I frowned. "Believe me, I had no intention of talking to the movie people about the homicides, but they brought up the subject, and my mother just had to brag about her daughter, the detective. She told them I was most likely working the case, no matter how much I denied it."

"Which movie people specifically?"

"Let's see—Charlie Stanton, Tom, Marissa Varig, Serena Harris, and Hattie Fein, the hair and makeup artist. Oh, and Ralph, the sound engineer, was crawling around on the floor, though I don't know if he heard."

John whipped out a small notepad and made a note of what I'd just told him. When he finished writing, I said, "I suppose that means one of them is the killer and sent out the warnings."

"Not necessarily. Any one of them could have mentioned what you said to other people in Firestone Productions. Like the director and the cameraman." He pursed his lips, a sign that he was angry. "Unfortunately, word leaked out that Patricia Harper aka Sheila Rossetti is coming to the area to visit her son. The person responsible will never make a mistake like that again."

Did Danny Brower accidentally spill the beans? "I have one more person to add to the list," I said. "Al Tripp, our mayor, was here in the library at the time this note was delivered," I said.

John raised his eyebrows. A smile tugged at his lips. I felt myself growing angry.

"Come on, John. You can't just shrug him off because he's the mayor. Remember, Alvin Tripp was smitten with Patricia Harper around the time her husband was knifed. And, I might add, except for the rehearsal play reading, I've never seen him in the library before. So there!"

To give John credit, he didn't smile. He didn't snort. He didn't frown. "And you'll remember," he answered calmly, "he had an airtight alibi for the night Chet Harper was killed. But

I'll talk to Al, along with everyone else you mentioned, and ask him what he was doing in the library."

Mollified, I nodded. "Since you're here, I want to run something by you." I proceeded to tell him my theory regarding Hattie Fein's barrette and the picture frames in Sheila Rossetti's living room. "The work is so similar, John. I know it might be no more than a coincidence, but it might be a link."

"I'll check it out, Carrie. Now, getting back to this warning. I don't have to remind you not to do anything that might encourage the killer to take action against you. No sleuthing. Got it?"

"Of course. But as I told you, I invited Billy and his mother to dinner Wednesday night. And Aunt Harriet and Uncle Bosco, since Aunt Harriet tried to help her all those years ago."

"That's fine. Nothing wrong with all of you getting together."

I suddenly had an idea. "John, you're planning to have Sheila—we have to start thinking of her as Sheila—come down to the precinct, right?"

"Of course I want to interview her, since her husband's murder was never solved, but I can't order her to come in. And I understand she's—shall we say—rather delicate."

"She is nervous and easily upset," I agreed. "It must have been very difficult for her to decide to come back here."

"Billy read the threatening note to his mother over the phone. She refused to cancel her visit. She said it was high time she took a stand for Daphne's sake and his."

"I suppose that means she'll head over to the station to tell you what she knows as soon as she arrives."

John exhaled noisily. "Not necessarily. She's already taking a big step by returning to Clover Ridge. Giving up this person is something else. Sheila Rossetti will decide when and where to talk to me."

"John, what if you and Sylvia came to dinner Wednesday night too? I needn't introduce you as the police chief—at least, not at first. Or do you think Sheila will be overwhelmed by so many of us?"

"Run it by Billy, and I'll ask Sylvia what she thinks. She's better at situations like this than I am."

I called Billy's cell phone and got his voice mail, so I left a message. When I disconnected, Evelyn reappeared.

"Twice in one day," I said. "To what do I owe this honor?"

"I happened to overhear your conversation with John Mathers," she said.

"Happened to?" I grinned.

She sent me a frosty look. "Carrie dear, you did ask me to stay informed about ongoing cases we're investigating."

Were we *investigating these homicides?* I smiled, not wanting to get into an argument with my friendly ghost. "So I did. I'm happy to see you, Evelyn."

"I think inviting John and Sylvia to your dinner with Billy and his mother is an excellent idea. It might be easier for her to talk to the police chief about what's been terrifying her till now in a friendly environment rather than down at the station."

"I was thinking the same thing. I'm so glad today's warning didn't scare her off."

"Don't forget for one minute that you've received your own warning," Evelyn said firmly.

"Don't worry. I'm not planning to raise suspicions by questioning anyone, but I did start to research the movie people online—something I should have done right after Ilana was murdered." I let out a sigh of frustration. "Though I don't expect to uncover anything in their bios and press releases that will reveal murderous tendencies. I've already checked out Hattie Fein and learned nothing worthwhile."

"Why don't we do that right now, unless you have some library work to take care of this afternoon?" Evelyn said.

"I have to call two presenters regarding upcoming programs; then I'm all yours."

"Great! This way we can discuss anything that sets off warning bells. After all, two heads are better than one."

Ten minutes later, I turned to my computer and typed in *Dirk Franklin*. "So many listings," I mumbled. I felt a chill as Evelyn glanced over my shoulder. "I'll read them out to you," I said quickly.

"Oh, sorry," she apologized as she stepped back. "When I visit the library, I sometimes forget I'm no longer in my earthly form."

I read parts of Dirk's bio aloud—the schools he attended, several plays he acted in and directed. He'd been married twice. "How sad. His first child, a boy, was afflicted with a rare disease. He died at age ten."

Evelyn *tsk-tsk*ed her sympathy.

I checked out a few articles about Dirk. "There's nothing here that's helpful regarding the murders. We know Dirk visited Clover Ridge when he was younger, and he was here around the time Chet Harper was murdered."

"And he's here now," Evelyn said, "when the two recent murders were committed."

"John questioned him and never charged him," I said.

"That doesn't mean he's innocent," Evelyn pointed out. "Just that there's no evidence linking him to the crimes."

"I believe John's still waiting for some tests to come back, but the internet's no help where Dirk is concerned."

"Don't be discouraged. On to the next," Evelyn said.

"Charlie Stanton," I said, clicking away on the keys.

I read to myself about Charlie's early years growing up in Montana, where his parents owned a ranch. His entry into movies and TV. His bout with alcoholism and two failed marriages.

"Anything of interest?" Evelyn asked.

"A list of his movies and TV shows and guest appearances," I said. "He was drinking heavily in his early forties. Oh my God!"

"What is it?"

For a moment I couldn't speak because I was hyperventilating. "Charlie was driving drunk when he struck a woman and her child. They both survived with injuries. Charles Stanton was fined fifty thousand dollars and spent four months in jail. He swore never to touch another drop of liquor as long as he lived."

"He's lucky he didn't kill them," Evelyn said.

I read further. "Charlie Stanton has contributed part of every film he's made since then to MADD—Mothers Against Drunk Driving."

"As he should," Evelyn declared.

I looked at her. "I had no idea that Dirk had lost a child and Charlie is a reformed drunk."

"Why should you?" Evelyn replied. "You hardly know them. They aren't your friends. What about Tom, your mother's husband?"

"Tom? What could he have done that was out of the ordinary except marry my mother?"

I looked up Thomas Randall Farrell, which was Tom's full name. I read a bit, then said, "He did well in school and was a success in finance until he moved on to acting. Oh!"

"What is it?" Evelyn asked.

I released a deep sigh. "Tom's father killed his wife when Tom was three years old. He was tried and sent to prison."

"How awful!" Evelyn said.

We stared at each other.

"Poor Tom," I said. "My mother never told me anything about Tom's life or his family."

"I wonder if his father is still in prison. I wonder if he's still alive," Evelyn said.

"I have no idea." I thought a moment. "That means Tom was brought up by a relative."

"Or he was adopted," Evelyn said. "Or raised in foster homes."

I looked at Evelyn, knowing my face bore an expression as sad as hers. "Poor Tom. I suppose it explains why my mother is so protective of him."

"Everyone is walloped by some trauma or tragedy when they least expect it. The way we cope helps form the people we become," Evelyn said.

"I suppose you're right."

"Take you, for example, Miss Carrie Singleton. You had plenty of rough patches in your life, with your father a thief, your parents' divorce, and poor Jordan's early demise. But you rallied, and you're leading a well-rounded, productive life."

"Well, thank you, Mrs. Havers." My face grew warm as I blushed from her praise. "I'll look up Ronnie Rodriguez and hope I don't find anything too awful that happened to him."

A few minutes later I read aloud, "*Ronaldo Rodriguez immigrated to the United States with his family from Mexico*. Okay, this article mentions a few of the movies he worked on. Two of them Charlie was in."

"So they know each other from previous jobs," Evelyn said.

"And I remember Charlie saying he and Serena had been in a few indie movies together and that he had parts in two or three of Dirk's earlier movies."

"Interesting."

Her tone had me perking up my ears. "Why interesting?" I asked.

"Making movies involves long hours of people working together in close quarters. A breeding ground for strong friendships, affairs, animosities, and romance."

"Isn't that the truth? Look how quickly Ilana and Tom rekindled their relationship."

"But even if someone in the cast or crew had it in for Ilana, it doesn't account for Daphne's murder or the killer's fear that Pattie Harper will reveal his identity."

"I know," I said. "We're back to square one. I can't see a connection between Ilana's murder and Chet Harper's twenty years ago."

"Hopefully, his widow will provide some information or insight into the case," Evelyn said, and promptly disappeared.

* * *

Billy called a few minutes later. When I asked him if he thought his mother would mind having the police chief at dinner Wednesday night, he offered to phone her ASAP to find out. Fifteen minutes later he called back with good news.

"Mom says that will be fine, since she was planning to talk to Lieutenant Mathers and thinks it will be easier to talk to him in your home."

"Of course! They can talk privately for as long as they like."

I called Dylan to give him an update on everything I'd learned since I'd arrived at the library that morning.

"Wow!" he exclaimed when I'd finished. "Lots has been happening. I'm glad Sheila Rossetti is okay with John and Sylvia coming to dinner. It should make for an interesting evening."

He'd no sooner hung up than the phone rang. I smiled when I heard Sylvia Mathers's voice. She was warm and forthright. We shared a special bond because she'd known Aunt Harriet since she was a little girl.

"Hello, Carrie. I understand we'll be coming to dinner Wednesday evening—if your guest of honor approves."

"She's already given her okay, so if you and John are free, I'd love to have you join us. Aunt Harriet and Uncle Bosco will be coming too."

"I'm looking forward to it! It's been too long since we've seen them. That goes for you and Dylan as well. How is your handsome boyfriend?"

"Busy in his new office."

"I know you're at work, so I won't keep you," Sylvia said. "How about I bring a cheese-and-veggie dish? I just bought some asparagus and zucchini and make a mean casserole."

"I'd love it! I'm serving barbecued chickens, and your casserole will be a great addition. Of course Aunt Harriet is bringing a dessert or two."

"Of course she is," Sylvia said. And we both laughed.

"See you Wednesday night," I said, still smiling as I disconnected.

Chapter Thirty-Two

E xcitement coursed through me as I set the dining room table for eight. Finally! We were about to learn the identity of the man who'd been Sheila Rossetti's lover all those years ago. The person who had probably killed her husband and possibly murdered Daphne and Ilana.

There were so many questions I wanted to ask her.

Had she actually witnessed the murder?

If she had, why didn't she tell Lieutenant Flynn at the time?

Of course, no one knew for sure if Sheila had been having an affair. But if that wasn't the case, what hold did this person have over her that had driven her to the West Coast and kept her from talking until now?

Dylan, John, and Aunt Harriet all took it upon themselves to remind me not to bring up the subject of the murders. As if I would. I knew how high-strung Sheila was, and the last thing I wanted to do was upset her. My role was to be a good hostess and make her comfortable—as comfortable as a person could feel in this situation. If she wanted to discuss it, that was her prerogative. And if she didn't bring up the subject, I was certain John would invite her to "talk about things" in his office. Eventually we would find out what had taken place the night Chet Harper was stabbed to death. I had to be patient, though patience wasn't one of my virtues.

Dylan arrived at ten after six as I was heating up some of the appetizers and placing others on platters. Since there were so many of us, I'd decided to serve mini quiches and stuffed mushrooms along with cheese and crackers and hummus and guacamole while we gathered in the living room.

"Hi, babe." He kissed me quickly, then put a few bottles of wine in the fridge. "Excited about tonight?" he asked.

"I am. I hope we're not disappointed."

"Just don't push," he said, stuffing his mouth with a hummus-laden cracker.

I frowned. "I wouldn't dream of it, especially after the many warnings I've received."

"Mmm, this is good." He cut off a piece of cheese and gobbled it up.

"Leave some for the company," I said.

The doorbell rang, and I rushed to the front door. My aunt and uncle were carrying so many bags, I couldn't even hug them.

"What have you brought?" I asked as I followed them into the kitchen.

"When you told me we were now eight, I decided to make cookies and two fruit pies. And we stopped for some ice cream on the way here."

"And?" I asked, pointing at Uncle Bosco's bag.

"You can always use another bottle of wine," he said, "and some fresh fruit for after dinner."

After they set down their bags of food and drink on the counter, I hugged my aunt and uncle. They were my compass, the family I'd never had growing up, and I loved them dearly.

"Mmm, guacamole," Uncle Bosco said, dipping a cracker into the green spread.

"Bosco, can't you wait?" Aunt Harriet asked. She was putting the ice cream in the freezer.

"No, I can't. I'm hungry."

"What can I do?" my aunt asked me.

"I'll bring out the hot appetizers as soon as everyone's here, but I still have to dress the salad."

"In that case, I'll get out the serving platters," she said, and opened the drawer where she knew I kept them.

"I'm heating up the chickens and veggies on a low temp," I said. "I figure we'll have the main course half an hour from now."

Dylan and my uncle stood at the kitchen table, chatting as they opened bottles of red and white wine. Dylan removed wineglasses from the cabinet above the sink, poured some Chardonnay into a glass, and handed me my drink.

"Thanks, hon," I said, and sipped.

The doorbell rang again. My heart rate went into overdrive when I saw Billy and his mother standing at the front door.

"Come in, come in!" I said, perhaps a bit too heartily.

Billy kissed my cheek. Sheila offered me a smile. I hesitated, wondering what to do when she moved closer to embrace me.

"It's so nice to see you again, Carrie," she said.

Dylan appeared at my side and kissed Sheila's cheek. "We're glad you're here with us tonight."

"Thank you both for having me. And for coming to see me on Long Island. I'm sorry I was less than welcoming."

I waved away her apology. "There's someone here who's been waiting to see you."

Sheila blinked at the sight of my aunt as if she couldn't believe her eyes. "Harriet Singleton, is that you? Oh, my dear! What a pleasant surprise."

My aunt, who was considerably larger than Sheila in both height and girth, all but crushed her in her arms.

"Harriet, dear, let the poor woman breathe."

Aunt Harriet pursed her lips at Uncle Bosco, then turned back to Sheila. "Pattie—I mean, Sheila—this is my husband, Bosco. I don't think you two have ever met."

"Pleased to meet you," Uncle Bosco said with a bow. "May I offer you a glass of wine?"

"Yes, please."

"Red or white?"

"I think red."

I signaled to Dylan to lead our guests into the living room, then motioned to Aunt Harriet to follow me into the kitchen, where I removed the warming hors d'oeuvres just in time to prevent them from burning. We set them on platters, which Aunt Harriet carried out to the living room. I followed a few minutes later with trays of cold appetizers, crackers, and cheese.

I was pleased to see that Sheila had not retreated into her shell but seemed to be enjoying the company of the three males present. Of course, Billy was her son and she'd met Dylan before. And Uncle Bosco could charm anyone age nine to ninety. Sheila sat on my sofa, munching on a mini quiche as my uncle regaled them with a story I'd heard at least four times before. When Sheila smiled, I saw what a beautiful woman she must have been twenty years ago.

The doorbell rang, and the room fell silent.

"That must be Sylvia and John," Dylan said. "I'll get the door."

Sheila gazed down at her lap, suddenly shy because Clover Ridge's police chief was about to join us. Aunt Harriet, who was sitting beside her, put an arm around her. "You'll see, John is really very sweet."

But he can also be intimidating. I remembered John's cold, unbending demeanor when I'd first met him and asked questions about an ongoing homicide and related cold-case investigation I'd helped solve. He hadn't welcomed my involvement, but over time we'd become friends, even though he occasionally got exasperated with what he considered my interference in his cases. Still, I knew John had grown as fond of me as I had of him, and not just because of his close relationship with Uncle Bosco and his deepening friendship with Dylan.

Now he and Sylvia entered the hall—a handsome couple in their midfifties: John, tall and spare, looking every bit the lawman; Sylvia's red hair and grin reflecting her friendly, open personality. I embraced them both and relieved John of the casserole he was carrying.

"I'll pop this in the oven," I said. "Go say hello to everyone and have a drink."

I heard Dylan introduce them to Sheila. When I returned to the living room, Sylvia had joined Sheila and Aunt Harriet on the sofa, while the four men stood near the bay window facing the river, talking and laughing as they sipped their drinks.

*　*　*

Fifteen minutes later we were gathered around the dining table spooning portions of salad, chicken, veggies, and Sylvia's casserole onto our plates. I'd placed Sheila between Billy and John and across from me. Dylan sat to my right, at the head of the table. Aunt Harriet sat next to me, Sylvia sat beside her, and Uncle Bosco sat across from Dylan. Not exactly girl, boy, girl, boy, but it suited me, as I needed to get up a few times to serve, and I figured Aunt Harriet and Sylvia would want to be able to reach the kitchen easily too if I needed assistance.

At first the only conversation was about the food. As soon as everyone was busy eating and imbibing, I said, "Sheila, have you noticed many changes in Clover Ridge since you left?"

Sheila looked up from the chicken she'd been cutting and paused to think. "Billy drove me round the village and the neighborhood where we used to live. The shops and buildings around the Green look pretty much the same, but there are so many new condos and stores in the area. And a new town hall."

"We try to keep up with the times," Uncle Bosco said, "while preserving the old buildings that have landmark status."

"I'd say the population has almost doubled in the past twenty years," John said.

"We have two new schools," Sylvia said. "The high school is old and sure could use a facelift."

"I don't see that happening anytime soon," said Aunt Harriet darkly.

"The library's being expanded in the fall," I said. "I'm looking forward to holding events in our new stadium-seating auditorium, though I dread the construction period."

"Billy said you have a movie crew making a movie here in town," Sheila said. "That sounds exciting."

"It is," I agreed. "Especially since my mother's husband has a feature role in the movie. The actors have kindly offered to do a play reading Saturday night."

Sheila smiled. "Thank you for inviting us."

From her comments, I realized Billy hadn't told her that one of the cast members had been murdered a day after Daphne. Which reminded me of the artwork on Hattie Fein's barrette.

"Sheila, where did you work when you lived in Clover Ridge?"

Silence reigned as Sheila took a bite of her chicken and chewed. Just when I thought she wasn't going to answer, she said, "I had a few jobs over the years in Clover Ridge and nearby towns. For a while I worked in an insurance office, then in a clothing shop, and in a bank."

"Oh," I said, disappointed by her answers but determined to learn if there was a link. "Where did you learn to do the artwork decorating the frames in your living room? It's so unique."

I knew I was taking a chance—giving her the opening to tell an outright lie—but Sheila opted to tell the truth.

"The most interesting job I held when I lived in Clover Ridge was in a craft workshop a few miles outside of town. It didn't pay much, so I couldn't give it many hours, but working there I learned the rudiments of certain craft techniques." She smiled. "Including the rope and beadwork you admired. It sure was helpful when I moved to Oregon. I found a sales job in an arts-and-crafts store and took a few courses in making jewelry. Soon I was making earrings, pendants, and bracelets. I was thrilled when a nearby gallery took a few pieces on consignment and sold all of them in a month."

"How fascinating!" Sylvia exclaimed. "I often thought of doing something crafty but couldn't decide on what I'd be good at. I can't draw to save myself. And my knitting is awful." She turned to Aunt Harriet. "Remember the time you tried to teach me to knit?"

Aunt Harriet laughed. "I don't know how you did it, but the yarn tangled up into knots."

The conversation was drifting away from where I wanted it to go.

"But who taught you to do the rope and beadwork when you were still living here in Clover Ridge?" I asked Sheila.

"Why does it matter, Carrie? What difference does it make?"

"I'm simply curious," I said. "A woman in the movie crew was wearing a barrette with the exact same type of work."

Sheila shrugged. "I'm sure many crafts people make similar pieces."

"Her name is Hattie Fein," I said.

"Please, Carrie. I don't know anyone named Hattie Fein!"

"What was the name of the woman who taught you how to do that kind of work all those years ago?"

Frantically, Sheila turned to Billy. He glared at me. "Stop torturing her, Carrie."

"No, I want to tell her." Sheila looked at John. "I want you to know. Then perhaps you can stop the murders, once and for all."

John patted her arm. "We can do this privately, if you like."

She shook her head. "No, it's time the whole world knows, regardless of the consequences. The woman's name is Helen. Helen Stravos. And I wish to God I'd never met her!"

Dylan and I exchanged glances.

Who the hell is Helen Stravos?

Chapter Thirty-Three

"I met Helen the day I started working at Crawley's Crafts. Bob, the manager, was in a hurry when he showed me around the shop. He pointed to different drawers, saying where the various supplies were kept: beads, hooks, dried flowers, yarns, craft-making tools. There were hundreds of items. Thousands! 'Everything's labeled, along with their prices,' Bob told me as he slid open drawers and cabinets. 'When a customer comes in, give her what she wants.'

"He looked at me fiercely. 'Under no circumstance are you to let them touch these drawers or what's inside them. Got it?' I said I did. 'Good!' He led me to the cash register, made sure I knew how to handle charges, figure out tax. Then he said he had to run out for a few minutes.

"Well, Bob was gone for more like half an hour. A customer came in wanting some rope and beads for a macramé project. She pointed to the cabinet where they were kept. I brought out several samples of beads, and she picked out what she wanted. So that was easy. But the next customer was a different situation entirely." Sheila paused to finish off her wine.

I sat back, marveling how she'd remembered every detail of that day. A glance around the table told me everyone had stopped eating and was waiting for her to continue.

"This customer was a large woman at least ten years older than I was. She wanted to start a new jewelry project but wasn't quite sure what. First, she asked to see some chains. I brought out a tray of them. She examined each in turn, but nothing was just what she wanted. She asked to see more. Soon she had chains scattered all over the counter. I suggested putting some of them away. Instead, she told me to bring out trays of blue and green beads. She felt certain that finding the right beads would give her a sense of what her next project should be.

"I was beginning to panic. There was something off-putting about this woman. Actually, she frightened me. What if she started grabbing whatever she liked and ran out of the store? I'd lose my job or worse."

"How awful!" Aunt Harriet exclaimed. "What did you do?"

"The customer started walking toward the drawers," Sheila said. "'You're wasting my time,' she said. 'This will go faster if I search for what I want.' I chased after her. 'No! You can't do that! Customers can't rummage through the inventory.' She drew back and told me she wasn't rummaging. She didn't rummage.

"'What's going on here?' We both spun around to stare at the newcomer we hadn't heard enter the shop. She was tall and statuesque, with long auburn hair. And beautiful. For some reason she reminded me of Wonder Woman.

"'I'm trying to choose supplies for a new project and this saleswoman isn't very helpful. Not that it's any of your business, miss.'

"'I'm Helen Stravos, and it happens to be my business because I work here too.' Her glance took in the array of chains and beads spread over the counter. 'From what I can see, you were shown a variety of items, many more than our manager allows to be shown at one time.' And with that, she started putting the inventory back in their respective trays and packed them away."

Sheila smiled. "The woman huffed with indignation. 'Well, I never! You can tell your manager he's lost a good customer.' She made a quick getaway, slamming the door behind her.

"I was terrified. I'd been working there less than an hour, and I'd already chased away a customer. But when I turned to Helen, I saw she was laughing. Soon I was laughing, too. When I could speak again, Helen told me that Bob often took off for hours at a time and that she'd meant to come in earlier, knowing someone new was starting."

Sheila glanced around the table at each of us. "And that was how my relationship with Helen Stravos began."

In the silence that followed, I considered what Sheila was really telling us. The person she'd been romantically involved with twenty years ago was a woman! A woman named Helen Stravos. A woman none of us had ever heard of before today. My mind was churning with questions. Before I could open my mouth to ask Sheila if she'd seen Helen Stravos kill her husband, Aunt Harriet stood. In her warm but practical way, she said, "As curious as we are to hear the rest of her story, I'm sure Sheila could use a well-deserved recess. Carrie and I will clear the table, bring out the desserts, and get the coffee and tea started. How many for coffee?"

Everyone but Sylvia and Sheila raised their hands.

"Tea, Sheila and Sylvia?"

They both nodded as Sylvia and I helped my aunt gather up plates and cutlery. In the kitchen, Aunt Harriet drew me aside. "I hope you aren't angry at me for taking over like that, but the poor woman needed a break."

I hugged her. "Don't think that for a minute. Sheila's been through hell. And reporting it to all of us has to be very difficult."

I filled the twelve-cup coffeemaker, knowing some people would want refills. Sylvia boiled water for tea, then got out the desserts, while Aunt Harriet covered the platters of uneaten food and put them in the refrigerator. By the time we brought out the dessert plates, cups, spoons, and forks, the mood in the dining room had changed. Sheila, along with the others, was listening avidly as Dylan recounted the story of one of his stolen art recoveries. I was filled with love and admiration for the people I'd chosen to invite here tonight to spend the evening with Sheila Rossetti.

When we were all seated once again, filling our mouths with sweets, John turned to Sheila. "Do you feel up to answering a few questions?"

Sheila suddenly looked nervous. Billy put his arm around her shoulders. "Only if you want to, Mom."

"I know," she answered softly. "I do want to. I've wanted to all these years, but I was afraid. I still am."

"Afraid of what exactly?" John asked softly.

Sheila looked at him. "Everything. Of discovering I was falling in love with a woman. Of Chet finding out. Of *anyone* finding out. I was so ashamed, but I couldn't help myself. Helen made me laugh. She listened to me. She cared." She drew a deep breath. "At least, it felt like she cared about me."

"You don't think her feelings for you were genuine?" John asked.

I stared at him, marveling at his questions. They were much—*kinder* was the best word I could think of—than I'd expected. John Mathers was proving to be more sensitive than I'd ever imagined.

"I thought so at the time. Helen must have been ten years younger than I was then, but she took me under her wing. She saw to it that I knew my way around the craft store and could deal with customers if I was ever left on my own. I discovered she was a talented craftswoman herself, and sold her work to various galleries. Her specialty was beautiful macramé wall hangings."

Sheila glanced at me. "Helen also made items using cord and small beads, like the picture frames you saw hanging in my living room. When she caught me admiring them, she sat me down one day and taught me how to make them." She laughed. "But mine never turned out as good as Helen's."

"Did you tell her how Chet was treating you and the children?" John asked.

Sheila frowned. "She saw a bruise on my arm and asked me how I got it. At first I wouldn't say, but Helen was persistent. I never talked about my family situation, but somehow people in Clover Ridge knew. In fact, a lawyer in town had been offering to help me get a divorce." She shuddered. "But whenever I thought about Chet finding out, I imagined he'd try to kill me."

"How did Helen react when you told her Chet was beating you?"

"She got angry. She said I didn't have to put up with that crap. From the way she spoke, I got the feeling she'd had to deal with an abusive husband herself." Sheila drew a deep breath. "As things between us got more involved, she tried to convince me to leave Chet and move in with her. I told her I couldn't leave Daphne and Billy. Helen said they were old enough to fend for themselves. That really upset me."

"Did you ever consider ending it with Helen?" John asked.

Sheila nodded. "Often. My life was a total mess. I hated myself for all the bad choices I'd made—marrying Chet when I knew he had a drinking problem, turning to the first person who showed me warmth and kindness." A small bitter laugh escaped. "Not that there weren't plenty of men in town who had been willing to do the same. At least I'd been smart enough to avoid them. Only to end up with someone as controlling as Chet. I was numb. Too frightened to end things with Helen. Too frightened not to."

"Did Helen notice the change in you?"

"Yes, but she had no idea that she was starting to frighten me—almost as much as Chet. She thought I was afraid to tell Chet and the children. She threatened to talk to Chet herself. I begged her not to, but she wouldn't listen to me. Each conversation we had got worse and worse. Finally . . ."

We waited.

"I came home late one night from working at the craft shop and ran into Helen on the stairs. I asked her what she was doing there, but she only put her finger to her lips and rushed past me. When I walked through the open door, I saw Chet lying on the floor with a knife sticking out of his chest."

"What did you do?" John asked.

"I ran through the apartment, looking for Daphne and Billy, but neither of them was there. Then I called the police and told them I'd come home from working at the craft store and found Chet stabbed to death."

"And never mentioned Helen," John said.

Sheila shook her head. "I couldn't. I knew she'd done it for me. For my sake, so we could be together."

"But you didn't remain in a relationship with Helen."

"Of course not. The police questioned me that evening, and Daphne and Billy when they came home. We couldn't even stay in the apartment but had to spend the night with neighbors, where I finally fell asleep close to dawn. The following day, I went to Helen's apartment and confronted her for killing Chet.

"'That's what you wanted, wasn't it?' she said. 'Of course not!' I said. 'I never told you to come to my apartment and stab my husband.'

"'I didn't go there intending to kill Chet,' she said, 'but he went crazy when I told him we were in love and came after me. I wasn't going to let him knock me around like he did you and the kids, so I jabbed him a few times. It was self-defense.'

"'Where did you get the knife?' I asked. Helen said she always carried one for protection." Sheila bit her lip. "When she saw how horrified I was instead of showing my *gratitude* for taking care of our problem, she turned ugly.

"I'd seen her like this once before, but never directed at me. This time she went on the attack. She said if I ever told the police or anyone that she'd killed Chet, she'd say she did it because I'd begged her to finish him off once and for all. Then I'd go to prison, same as her."

Sheila lowered her gaze. "I couldn't bear the thought of standing trial, of spending years behind bars, and so I flew out of her apartment, ran home, and gathered up some clothes and my money and left. Not very admirable, I know."

The sound of shattering glass startled us. I raced to the living room and gaped at the smashed window that faced the river. I started for the door, but two pairs of strong arms held me back.

"Are you crazy?" Dylan asked. "Whoever it is could still be out there."

John released his grip on me and ran outside as a car took off at top speed. When Smoky Joe entered the room to investigate the commotion, Sylvia swept him up and shut him inside my bedroom.

Dylan peered out the front door. Outside, John stood staring at the road when his cell phone rang. He said a few "Uh-huhs," then disconnected.

"That was Danny Brower," he told us. "He was parked halfway between here and Dylan's house when a vehicle drove up. Not five minutes passed before it came speeding like a bat out of hell from this direction. He gave chase but lost whoever did this."

My mouth fell open. "You had Danny watching the cottage because Sheila was coming to dinner?"

"I did."

I noticed that neither Dylan nor Billy seemed surprised by his news.

"They knew!" I said.

"Uh-huh. A lot of good it did."

"Did Danny get the number of the plate?" Dylan asked.

"He's running it as we speak."

Sheila huddled into herself. "Even now I'm bringing trouble to everyone."

"No, you're not!" Aunt Harriet said.

"She's still here! I never should have come back to Clover Ridge," Sheila said.

"You came back because you're courageous and want to do what's right," John said. "The fact is she's frightened and trying to drive you away." He exchanged glances with Billy. "I think it would be best if you and your mother spent the night at a hotel."

He turned to Sheila. "I'd like you to come down to the precinct tomorrow morning and go over everything you told us tonight. Meanwhile, I'll start searching through data files. There has to be a clue somewhere that leads us to this Helen Stravos."

John looked at each of us in turn. "And I'm ordering you not to discuss what Sheila has told us with any living soul. I'll get to the bottom of these homicides if it's the last thing I do."

We all nodded solemnly. The evening was over. John got into his car and followed Billy and Sheila to Billy's apartment; they would pick up a few overnight items, then drive to a local motel. While Aunt Harriet, Sylvia, and I cleared the table, Dylan called Jack Norris, the property's handyman, and arranged for him to remove the broken glass and call a glazier first thing in the morning.

Uncle Bosco and Aunt Harriet left to drive Sylvia home. I gathered up some clothes, cat food, and Smoky Joe's litter box, slipped the unwilling cat inside the carrier, and went to spend the night at Dylan's manor, as I privately called his large house.

"That was some story Sheila told us," I said as Dylan and I were getting ready to go to sleep. "I only hope she doesn't decide it's too dangerous to remain in Clover Ridge and takes the first ferry back to Long Island."

"Now that she's told us about her involvement with this woman, I'm pretty sure Sheila will do all that she can to help John track down Helen Stravos through various criminal databases."

"But what if she doesn't have a record?" I asked.

Dylan stared at me. "Are you kidding? A woman tough enough to carry a knife for protection? I can't imagine that Chet Harper was her only victim."

I shrugged. "Just sayin'. She wasn't a thief. At least, she was working in the craft store when Sheila knew her. And selling to various galleries."

"She's volatile and she wasn't afraid of confronting a known abuser." Dylan kissed my cheek. "John's getting closer, babe. This Helen's running scared."

"And I'm scared that she's on the loose."

Chapter
Thirty-Four

News of last night's incident had already reached the library by the time I arrived at work on Thursday morning.

"I heard someone threw a rock through your living room window," Angela said, looking worried. "Weren't Billy and his mom there for dinner?"

"As were my aunt and uncle and John and Sylvia. Thank goodness no one got hurt. The glazier was heading for the cottage to replace the window as I left for work," I said. "How did you find out so quickly?"

"Danny's mother called Mom while we were having breakfast."

I laughed. "I should have figured."

"What did Billy's mother have to say?" Angela asked.

"John's sworn us to secrecy, but I'll fill you in as soon as I can."

Angela's eyes lit up. "I can hardly wait."

I had no sooner unlocked the door to my office than Evelyn appeared. Since John had told us not to breathe a word of last night's revelations to any living soul, I felt free to share Sheila's story with her.

"Poor Pattie, or whatever she's calling herself these days," she said when I'd finished. "Are you thinking that Hattie Fein is Helen Stravos?"

"Difficult to say. Hattie has black hair and Helen's hair was auburn. But people dye their hair all the time. Hattie's in her fifties, which Helen would be now. And she was here in Clover Ridge when both women were murdered. Not to mention the barrette that's the same kind of crafty work Helen Stravos did all those years ago."

"I'm sure John is checking out this Helen Stravos every which way he can," Evelyn said. "I think he's getting closer to resolving these homicides."

"So do I," I said. "The stone thrower's license plate number might be the best lead we have."

John called me just before I was about to leave for the Cozy Corner Café with Angela. "I figured you'd appreciate an update after last night's revelation."

"I sure would."

John exhaled a deep sigh. "Unfortunately, there's not much to report. Billy brought Sheila in early this morning. I went over her story, checking for details. I tracked down Bob, who used to manage the craft shop. He's now retired in Arizona. He remembers both women. Remembered Helen Stravos better, since she worked part-time at the craft shop for almost two years. Said she was beautiful and talented and had one hot temper. She disappeared the same time Pattie Harper's husband was found dead and Pattie took off."

"And there's nothing about her anywhere?" I asked.

"Zip."

"Maybe she changed her name," I said.

John laughed. "To Hattie Fein?"

"It's possible," I said defensively. He had no business mocking me. "Hattie's a tall woman. A bit heavier, twenty years later. Remember, she was wearing a barrette very similar to the macramé work that Helen Stravos taught Sheila to do." I thought a minute, then added, "I did read her bio online, but she could have made that up."

"I'll look into it," he said.

"What about the license plate number Danny was checking?"

John exhaled loudly. "A dead end. A rented car. Whoever rented it used a disposable cell phone for the transaction and picked it up when the place was closed. The car was found abandoned behind a supermarket."

* * *

Sheila called after lunch. "Carrie, I want to thank you for dinner last night. It was so thoughtful of you to have us over."

"It was my pleasure. I'm sorry the evening ended so abruptly."

"Me too. Especially since whoever threw the rock had me in mind."

"I'm glad it didn't send you packing on the first ferry back to Long Island."

"Believe me, I considered it, but John—Lieutenant Mathers—told me that the person's intent was to frighten me and stop me from talking about Helen."

"Does John think it was Helen who threw the rock?"

"He thinks there's a good chance she threw it. He also thinks she had no idea that he was there at your house, since he and Sylvia drove to your cottage in Sylvia's car."

Interesting. "What else did John say?" I couldn't resist asking.

"I happened to be in his office when he received a report on some fibers and hairs found at the murdered actress's home. The dark hairs were from a woman, it turns out, but there's no proof that they came from the killer."

How interesting he shared this with you and not me.

"Carrie?" Sheila's tone was hesitant.

"Yes?"

"I hope you weren't, er, put off by what I said last night—about my relationship with Helen."

"Not at all, Sheila. I'm only sorry she turned out to be such an awful person. You met her when you were vulnerable and at a low point in your life."

"I keep going over those last few days—when Helen and I were arguing constantly and I thought things couldn't get worse. But they did, didn't they? Helen murdered Chet, and I ran, terrified of being charged as a coconspirator. At the time I thought Mitch Flynn was simply questioning Billy as he had me and Daph. I had no idea he'd make it look like Billy had stabbed his father. My poor son! And now Daphne's gone. I should have prevented all that from happening."

She began to sob.

"Sheila, you were very brave to come back here and tell John what you know about this woman. I feel certain that he'll track her down before she does any more harm to anyone."

"If only—"

I cut her off before she could heap more blame on herself. "Sheila, it doesn't help to dwell on what's already happened. You need to be strong for your husband's sake and your own. And now you have Billy back in your life."

"I have you to thank for that," Sheila said, sounding stronger. "I can't believe he doesn't hate me for abandoning him."

"He loves you and he needs you," I said.

"I know, and I thank God for that every day."

"I have to get back to work," I said. "Dylan and I will see you at the play reading Saturday night?"

"Certainly," Sheila said. "Billy has a few outings planned before then. I'm heading home on Sunday." She gave a little laugh. "My husband's missing me, and I just got some good news. Recently I've started working on a few craft projects again. My husband encouraged me to bring samples to two local galleries. This morning one of the galleries called to say they're interested in carrying my work. Can you believe it? Starting over again at my age."

"I can believe it, since I've seen your handiwork." I was pleased that, despite the tragedies she'd experienced, Sheila was finding fulfillment in her life.

* * *

The next few days passed without any incident. My mother called, upset after hearing about the rock-throwing incident. I let her believe it was a random act of vandalism and didn't mention that I'd had dinner guests that evening.

"Dirk's been riding the cast like a taskmaster," she said. "Working them from early morning to late in the evening to finish shooting on schedule."

"How's Tom taking it?"

"He hates the pressure, though he's giving the performance of his life. The upside is, if there are no more snags, the movie will be in the can a week from Saturday," my mother said. "Earlier than Dirk thought. We'll fly home that Sunday. I hope we can meet for dinner one night before then."

"Of course!" I said, more heartily than I felt. "You and Tom will come for dinner one night next week."

"We'd be delighted," my mother said.

Charlie called me a few times to make sure everything was in order for Saturday night's performance. After the third call on Friday, I exploded.

"Charlie, our custodians are conscientious workers. They carry out our instructions in a responsible manner. Everything here will be set up as you requested."

"I'm glad to hear that!" he boomed. "By the way, Ralph will stop by this afternoon to make sure the sound system is in working order."

"I'm impressed by your attention to every aspect of the performance," I said.

"Of course! We don't want any unpleasant surprises tomorrow night."

"We sure don't," I answered. I'd had enough surprises to last me a lifetime.

Chapter
Thirty-Five

S aturday evening, Dylan and I left his car in front of the new Thai restaurant where we'd enjoyed a delicious dinner before walking the few blocks to the library. With so many people attending the play reading, I knew we'd never find a parking space in the library lot. It was a balmy night, and the streets around the Green were filled with pedestrians enjoying the fine weather along with residents lucky to have gotten tickets to the play reading.

We greeted Sally, who stood outside the library's main entrance checking tickets. Since this was a community event, as Sally put it, I was relieved of guard duty. Whatever the reason, I was glad Dylan and I had seats in the meeting room downstairs. Still, I had every intention of strolling about the main level early on in the performance to make sure the audience sitting there could hear every word. Though Ralph had assured me the temporary system he'd installed was working properly and I hadn't arranged this particular event, I still considered it my job to see to it that all was running smoothly.

"Happy?" Dylan asked as he squeezed my hand.

"Very," I answered, and leaned over to give him a quick kiss.

"Me too," he said.

Downstairs, Marion and Norman Tobin, our new reference librarian, were checking patrons' names at the door to make sure only those with tickets entered the meeting room. Dylan and I stopped to chat with friends and acquaintances. I was surprised at how many people he knew, though I shouldn't have been. Dylan had grown up in Clover Ridge.

My mother came over to talk to us, all excited about the upcoming event. And she had good news. Tom had auditioned for a new movie, and they'd just received word that he'd gotten the part. We found seats near John and Sylvia and made plans to go out for coffee after the performance.

A few minutes after eight o'clock, the four actors took their seats at the long table in front of us. Charlie, who was acting as emcee, introduced the other actors and himself, said a few words about the playwright, A. R. Gurney, and the reading began.

Though I'd watched a few of the movie scenes being filmed, I wasn't prepared for the amazing presence that each of the four actors brought to the reading. Even without scenery and props, their portrayals of a WASP family having cocktails were so powerful, I found myself totally absorbed in the family dynamics. There was a mother, father, brother, and sister. Just like my family, except that these characters weren't like my family at all. John, the son, had written a play called *The Cocktail Hour*, and big surprise! It was all about his family—the four people having cocktails together. John wanted his father's permission to put on the play in New York, but things weren't going quite as he had hoped.

I was so entranced that several minutes had passed before I remembered my intention to check on the acoustics on the upper level.

"Be right back," I whispered to Dylan as I slipped out of my seat and left the room.

Upstairs, I walked around the dimly lit reading room and alcoves where patrons were listening to the reading of *The Cocktail Hour*. The sound system was working beautifully. The voices of the four actors came through clear and resonant. Everyone appeared to be listening with rapt attention.

Satisfied, I headed for the staircase in anticipation of enjoying the rest of the reading in my seat downstairs. As I passed Billy and his mother, Sheila reached out and grabbed my wrist. It was the grip of someone in great distress. I had no choice but to kneel before her.

"It's her!" she said.

"Who?" I had no idea what she was talking about.

"It's Helen. Helen Stravos!"

"Shh," someone close by said. Another scowled at her.

Sheila lowered her tone to a whisper. "I know that voice! It's Helen. You have to call Lieutenant Mathers."

For a moment, I thought she'd gone crazy. Then, as I listened to the reading, it all came together. The way a jigsaw puzzle does when the last piece is put in its place. Of course! Serena Harris was Helen Stravos.

She'd changed her name. The color of her hair. Her profession.

Hattie's barrette was a gift from Serena. They were friends. No, they were lovers.

Poor Daphne must have recognized Serena or intuited she was her mother's friend all those years ago and said she wanted to talk to her. Or Helen/Serena had recognized Daphne because she looked like her mother and decided to tie up loose ends.

But where did Ilana come into the picture?

"Please, Carrie. Call him now!"

I nodded to Sheila, then to Billy, who, I gathered by his expression, understood what his mother wanted me to do.

I realized I'd left my pocketbook with my cell phone on my seat. I asked Billy for his phone, then dashed to the ladies' room and dialed John's cell number.

It rang three times. Finally he answered. "Who's this?" he asked in a gruff whisper.

"John, it's me. I'm calling from Billy Harper's phone."

"Where are you?" John asked. I got the impression he was walking. No doubt exiting the meeting room as fast as he could.

"Upstairs. Sheila identified Helen Stravos. She recognized her voice."

"She's in the library?"

"On the stage," I said. "She's Serena Harris."

John muttered a string of curses, so I figured he was in the hall where no one but me could hear him. "Is she sure? I mean, she hasn't talked to this woman in twenty years."

"Oh yes, and she's terribly upset," I said. "It all makes sense, John. Did you ever check Serena's history?"

"I did, and I noticed that her early history was sketchy. It didn't set off any alarms. Damn it, it should have. I should have looked at her bio more closely."

"At least you have the hairs found in Ilana's hotel room."

"There's that," he said glumly. "Is an intermission coming up anytime soon?

"At the end of act one, about fifteen minutes from now."

"I'm calling Danny and ordering him to get some backup. Meanwhile, return to your seat ASAP. Act cool."

"Right," I mumbled.

"Don't worry, Carrie. Everything will turn out fine."

Somehow I wasn't reassured. Serena was nobody's fool. She'd seen John leave his seat when I called him. If he'd as much as glanced at her, Serena would have realized something was in the wind.

Would she stop in the middle of the reading and try to make a run for it? John wasn't prepared to take down a suspect fleeing past a roomful of people. I hoped Danny showed up very soon, along with a few carloads of state troopers.

I returned to my seat. Dylan wanted to know what had taken me so long.

"Don't look surprised," I whispered in his ear, "but the killer is right in front of you. Serena Harris."

God bless my boyfriend. He absorbed what I'd told him with a smile and leaned over to kiss me.

I tried to concentrate on the performance taking place before me and not stare in horror at Serena Harris aka Helen Stravos. Who would have thought that this beautiful, personable woman had murdered three people and tried to poison a fourth? Reflecting back on our conversations, I realized what a consummate actress she was—both on and off the stage. Twenty years ago she'd murdered Chet Harper for her lover's sake, or so she'd claimed. He had been a violent man. It might even have been a case of self-defense. But why did she have to kill Daphne and Ilana twenty years later?

Minutes passed. The play reading went on. I began to wonder if Serena knew the game was up as she continued to perform her role as the mother with humor and warmth. I got my answer the moment the lighting on the four actors dimmed. Serena leaped to her feet, sprinted up the aisle farthest from John's seat, and made a beeline for the door at the back of the room. John raced up his aisle. People turned to watch the two runners. A few stood. Dylan and I scooted out of our row and chased after Serena. We burst up the stairs in time to see Danny Brower snapping handcuffs on her and reading her her rights.

I turned to Dylan. "It's over."

He raised an eyebrow. "You sound disappointed."

"I admired Serena. I was hoping it wasn't her or anyone involved in the movie."

Dylan laughed. "We can't pick our murderers, now, can we?"

Chapter
Thirty-Six

S erena was arraigned and charged on three counts of homicide, one count of attempted murder, and one charge of vandalism and destruction of property. Luckily, all but one of her scenes in *I Love You, I Do* had been filmed, so Dirk had the screenwriter revise the ending to one where Charlie was alone, reflecting on life and love.

There were heated discussions about whether or not the movie would be released, but when movie theaters expressed enthusiasm in showing the movie because the notoriety of the murders had stirred up curiosity rather than repugnance among moviegoers, the powers that be decided *I Love You, I Do* would be released a few months later than previously planned. This would give the publicity department plenty of time to capitalize on the murders. There was even talk of making a documentary about the real-life events going on while the movie was being filmed.

I decided to host a farewell dinner for my mother and Tom the following Friday evening. The cast and crew were having their own party Saturday night, and most of them were heading for home, a vacation, or their next job the following day.

Who to invite? I texted invitations to Charlie and Dirk, the two movie people I knew best. I would have included Hattie Fein, but I figured she probably resented me for helping the police arrest her lover. Aunt Harriet and Uncle Bosco, of course, John and Sylvia Mathers, and Angela and Steve. Angela would be over the moon, knowing she'd have a great opportunity to chat with her idol, Charlie Stanton. And Billy. Sheila was back on Long Island with promises to visit her son very soon, this time accompanied by her husband.

By Tuesday morning I'd heard back from everyone I'd invited. Not a refusal in the bunch.

"Maybe I should have invited more people," I said to Evelyn, who had appeared at my side. "Like Sally and Trish and their husbands and Susan. Maybe Ronnie Rodriguez, and Ralph. Oh, and the lovely Marissa."

Evelyn pursed her lips. "I believe you're getting carried away, my dear. The way I see it, thirteen people for a dinner party is quite a large number. Is your dining room table long enough to seat thirteen people?"

I released a sigh. "Just about. To make things easier, I'll serve buffet style. I'll put the platters of food on the kitchen table and let my guests select what they like."

"What are you planning to serve?" Evelyn asked.

"Dylan suggested that I cater the dinner. Then Angela told me her mom was sending along a tray of eggplant parmigiana. Aunt Harriet insists on making a roast, and Sylvia decided to make a huge array of grilled veggies and quinoa. Angela's bringing desserts, Charlie's bringing a caseload of wine, and"—I laughed—"I've decided to make a huge everything salad and my double-chocolate brownies. I'll buy an assortment of hot hors d'oeuvres, and that should do it."

"Sounds lovely. I wish I could be there," Evelyn said wistfully.

I smiled at her. "I wish you could too."

* * *

Friday turned out to be a beautiful sunny early May day. I sang as I drove home from the library. It must have irritated Smoky Joe, because he began to howl, something he'd never done before.

"Okay, pal," I told him. "No more singing."

The howling stopped.

When I arrived home, I set Smoky Joe free and fed him his dinner. That done, I unwrapped a package of large sturdy paper plates and set them on the kitchen table, along with paper bowls for salads and plastic cutlery. This was going to be an easy dinner to prepare, serve, and clean up.

I took a quick shower and had just slipped into a new colorful tunic and leggings when the doorbell rang. I hurried to see who was arriving at six thirty when the invitation had said seven. The local florist's delivery truck was driving off. I bent down to pick up the long box and carried it into the cottage. I let out a gasp when I saw the lovely array of pink and purple tulips just beginning to open. The card read:

Carrie dear,

    Thank you so much for hosting a dinner for us as we prepare to leave Clover Ridge. It was wonderful spending time with you, and we hope to have you visit us very soon. You are important to us both.

Love, Mom and Tom

I smiled as I trimmed the stems, filled a vase with water along with the packet of powdered stuff that was supposed to prolong the life of the flowers, then arranged the tulips in the vase. It was a warm and touching note. I was glad my relationship with my mother had improved, but we were light-years away from a close mother-daughter bond. I didn't think we'd ever have that. Still, Tom and my mother were family. I intended to take them up on their offer and visit them in California—but not in the immediate future.

I placed trays of hors d'oeuvres in the oven and set the temperature low. Dylan arrived a few minutes later with another array of flowers—red roses. I held him close for a minute or two.

"I'm so glad I have you," I said.

"The feeling is mutual," he said, then headed for the kitchen to put the flowers in a vase.

"Ah! And which admirer gave you these lovely tulips?"

"Tom and my mom," I said. "I'm glad you were able to get out of work early."

He made a face. "Don't think it was easy. Rosalind said someone with what sounded like a big case called and wanted to see me at six. When I begged off, the client pushed for an early-morning meeting tomorrow."

"What time?" I asked.

"Eight o'clock. I told Rosalind to see if the client would agree to a breakfast meet at the diner across the street from my office. He said yes."

"Hmmm. Sounds intriguing," I said.

"I hope it's worth my while, because this means I have to be up at six thirty tomorrow to make it in time."

My guests started showing up in small groups. My mother, Tom, Charlie, and Dirk arrived in one car. I thanked my mother and Tom for their lovely flowers, and they each embraced me in a bear hug.

"Thanks for finding Ilana's killer," Tom whispered in my ear.

"I didn't—" I began, but then my mother was hugging me tight.

"I'm so lucky that you're my daughter," she said. "Now that I have you, I won't let you go. Promise me you'll come visit us."

"I will," I said. I surprised myself by adding, "I really will."

Then Charlie had his arms around me. "You are one special lady, Miss Carrie Singleton! Smart and beautiful. If I were twenty years younger, your boyfriend would have a run for his money."

"Did you forget you're a married man?" I reminded him. Still, I was flattered.

He grinned. "Actually, I did—for the moment." His expression sobered. "I'm still reeling from the fact that Serena killed Ilana and that other young woman. I never would have guessed it. She seemed so—normal."

"How is Hattie taking it?"

Charlie grimaced. "She's walking around in a fog."

"Do you think she knew Serena was a murderer?"

"Hard to tell," Charlie said. "I would imagine Serena kept that side of herself from Hattie. Though they'd known each for years, they'd only gotten together a few weeks ago."

"John will find out," I said darkly.

"I understand he'll be here tonight," Charlie said.

"He and Sylvia are coming later. He's kind of tied up with the case."

And then Billy was handing me two bottles of wine and a cake box. As soon as I put them down, he swung me around.

"Carrie, thanks so much for inviting me tonight," he said when my feet were back on the ground.

"Of course."

"And thanks for getting my life in order. That woman is being charged with killing Daphne and my father, and my mother and I are back in touch."

I nodded. "You've had to deal with so much heartbreak. I hope you can move forward now."

"I intend to, though I'll never stop wishing that Daphne had been spared."

"Me too," I said. "We were on the way to becoming close friends."

As Billy headed to join the others, I couldn't help but think what a good-looking, *single* man he was. Now who could I fix him up with? I chuckled as an acquaintance who had a habit of getting involved with bad-news men came to mind. It was time she met a nice, responsible guy. Someone capable of treating her right.

Soon everyone but Sylvia and John Mathers was gathered in the living room. Angela, Aunt Harriet, and I served platters of mini quiches, pigs-in-blankets, coconut shrimp, and mini eggrolls. The conversation was animated. I was happy to see Angela chatting with Charlie, her idol, while Steve talked to Billy.

The Matherses arrived as the others were forming a line in the kitchen to fill their plates with food.

"It's still hot," Sylvia said as she handed me a huge platter of grilled veggies and quinoa covered with tinfoil.

I placed it on the kitchen table and turned to John. "Everything in order regarding Serena/Helen?"

"It sure is," he said, grinning. "Once she realized we had her, there was no stopping her from telling all. Her lawyer tried once or twice and got shot down for her efforts."

Minutes later, when all thirteen of us were eating, it was Charlie who broke the silence by raising the first question.

"Lieutenant Mathers, is there anything you can tell us about the case against Serena Harris?"

John finished chewing what was in his mouth. "Yes, I can. Serena Harris aka Helen Stravos and a few other aliases is being charged with three counts of homicide, an attempted homicide, and a few other lesser charges."

"Why did she murder Ilana?" Tom asked. He looked so earnest, I wondered if he was truly over his ex-fiancée. Perhaps, as much as he loved my mother, he never would be.

"According to Ms. Harris, Ms. Reingold followed her the night she murdered Daphne Marriott and then tried to blackmail her."

I found myself nodding. It made sense. Ilana had needed money desperately.

"And why did that woman kill my sister?" Billy asked.

John's expression turned to one of compassion. "Daphne was in the crowd the day the movie crew was being introduced to everyone on the Green. She went up to Serena, gave her real name, and told Serena she looked like someone her mother used to know. Serena had no idea if Daphne had seen her the day she'd killed her father, but she wasn't taking any chances. I'm sorry, Billy."

Billy muttered under his breath. "Why didn't she do a better job of murdering me?" he asked.

"It's true—those poisoned nuts wouldn't have killed you," John said. "I got the sense that Serena had had her fill of murder and simply hoped to stop you from contacting your mother, at least until the movie crew had left town. Your mother was the key to everything, but until recently she'd been too terrified to talk about your father's murder."

"I think that's enough questions for John," my mother said. "This is an active murder case. Besides, we should let the poor man eat his meal in peace."

I stared at her. *Such unexpected consideration and tact.*

"Great suggestion, Linda," Charlie said. "But Lieutenant, on behalf of the cast and crew, I want to thank you for solving this case and doing so before we all leave Clover Ridge."

John grinned. "My pleasure." He winked at me and smiled at Billy. "I sure appreciated the help I got from these two. And from Sheila Rossetti."

"Formerly known as Pattie Harper," my aunt added. "All these people changing their names." She sighed. "So confusing."

For some reason, my guests took it in their heads to applaud, and then conversation resumed. A few minutes later, Aunt Harriet, Angie, and I were clearing the table and preparing to serve dessert.

Too soon, the evening was over. I discovered I had tears in my eyes as I bid my mother and Tom good-night. Dylan was the last to leave.

"Wonderful dinner, babe," he said, holding me tight. "Only you could put a bunch of people with little in common together and make it a social success."

I laughed. "You think? I'd never given a dinner party before I came to Clover Ridge."

"Now look at you! All your talents are unfolding one by one."

We kissed.

"I'm a lucky guy," Dylan said.

"And I'm a lucky girl," I answered.

Acknowledgments

I am grateful to my dear agent Dawn Dowdle, who always takes the time to answer my questions; to my wonderful editor Faith Black Ross and the terrific people at Crooked Lane who make each book a success. A special shout out to my copy editor Rachel Keith, who took the time to explain the complicated intricacies of the past perfect tense.